right kind of wrong

fabiola francisco

Copyright © 2021 by Fabiola Francisco
Publication Date: March 24, 2021
The Right Kind of Wrong
All rights reserved

This book is a work of fiction. The names, characters, places, and incidents are products of the writer's imagination or have been used fictitiously and are not to be construed as real. Any resemblance to persons, living or dead, actual events, locales, or organizations is entirely coincidental.

The author acknowledges the trademarked status and trademark owners of various products referenced in this work of fiction. Any trademarks, service marks, product names or names featured are assumed to be the property of their respective owners and are used only for reference. There is no implied endorsement.

This book is licensed for your personal enjoyment only and contains material protected under the International and Federal Copyright Laws and Treaties. Any unauthorized reprint or use of the material is prohibited. No part of this book may be reproduced, stored in a retrieval system, or transmitted in any form, or by any means, electronic, mechanical, photocopying, recording or otherwise, without prior permission of the author. This book may not be re-sold or given away to other people. If you would like to share this book with another person, please purchase an additional copy for each recipient. Thank you for respecting the hard work of this author.

Cover design by Amy Queau, Q Designs
Cover photo by Deposit Photo
Interior design by Cary Hart
Editing by Rebecca Kettner, Editing Ninja

Dedication

Joy and Ally ~
For your friendship despite the distance and time change. Our conversations inspired a lot of this story. And for making me love surprise pregnancies *almost* as much as you do.

Chapter 1

Allyson

"Hmmm… That was one of the best lays I've ever had."

My eyes snap open when I hear the gruff voice next to me, and my heart slams against my ribs. A wave of nausea hits me as my memory returns, knocking my stupid sense out of the way so I can regain my wits.

I shriek, "Oh. My. God. Camden! I can't believe I just had sex with you!" I jump off the bed, covering myself with one hand as I try to rip the sheets from the bed, although it's pointless. He's seen me naked already, more naked than a lot of people have. *Fuck! Fuck! Fuck!*

I squeeze my eyes shut, hoping that the spinning of the room is to blame for me being here as if that would mean I were in some kind of alternate universe and any minute I'd wake up in real life, *not having been sexed up by my brother's best friend.*

"We didn't *just* have sex. It's been…" He reaches for his watch. "About six hours. If you want to do it again, I'm ready." He lies back, placing his hands behind his head as the sheets leave his broad chest exposed. I eye his torso longingly and stop where the sheet barely covers his length, one that I now know is big and thick—in case the pitched tent he's sporting wasn't obvious enough.

I shake my head out of the fantasy, unable to believe I actually thought about having sex with him again.

"I need to go." I grab my dress from last night, throwing it on, not bothering to look at myself in the mirror. There's no point in adding insult to injury. I'm sure I look like shit.

When I slip out of his room, I see Averly, the owner of the bed and breakfast where I'm staying and one of Faith's—my new sister-in-law—best friends standing in the hallway. She lifts her eyebrows in silence.

"Please don't say anything," I plead with wide eyes. My voice sounds desperate even to my own ears.

She lifts her hands. "Secret's safe with me." She smiles, clearly biting back her amusement.

"Ugh," I drop my head back against the wooden door, and I yelp when it opens suddenly, a half-dressed Camden looking at me with raised eyebrows and a cocky smirk.

"Couldn't get…" He sees Averly. "Oh, hey, nice place you run here. I was just checking to see if the paper was outside my door."

Averly sputters as she tries to hold in her laughter. I glare at Camden. "She already saw me walk out of here, dumbass."

"We've already got pet names for each other," he tells Averly. I roll my eyes and walk away, ignoring him. When I step into my own room across the hall from Camden's, I lean against the door and take a deep breath. What the hell did I do last night?

I jump in the shower and scrub my body on auto-pilot, as if that would wash away the remnants of memories of feeling Camden's body over mine. My sore muscles remind me of the night before. Sweaty, tangled limbs. Breathless moans. Purposeful thrusts.

the Right kind of Wrong

What possessed me to sleep with my brother's best friend on the night my brother, Easton, got married? Scratch that, on *any night*. Camden is... Not the guy for me, whatsoever. Not even a little bit. Not even if it was—using his words—one of the best lays I've ever had. Once I return to Spain, this will all become a distant memory.

I blame this on my current life situation. Having moved to a country I knew nothing about to help start an international branch for my company, feeling as if my personal life is on hold because of my career, and not having any intimacy since before I moved. It all adds to this terrible decision.

Rinsing the conditioner from my hair, I wring out the excess water and sigh, turning off the shower. I pray to God that no one saw me leave with Camden last night. My brother would kill me... Or Camden. Or both of us. I cringe and grab the towel from the hook next to the shower and wrap it around my body, water droplets from my hair soaking my shoulders and back.

Okay, Allyson, get it together.

Last night was...emotional. Watching Easton get married to his high school sweetheart after being apart for years was great. Having attended his wedding as a single gal was not. That's probably why I leaned on Camden. It was easy to do so.

Yeah, that's totally why. I nod my head, looking at myself in the mirror and gripping the edge of the gray and white granite that covers the top of the vanity. No one has to know about this. It was a mistake. A one-night stand. Scratching an itch.

And he sure as hell scratched it, with precise perfection.

I jolt when my phone pings with a message and step out of the bathroom to check who it is, hoping it isn't someone asking me about my night with Camden.

Speaking of my mistake, the text is from him. Opening my messages, I groan when I see a picture of my panties on the screen with a message below.

Camden: You left these here... Unless they're my souvenir

I roll my eyes and hold in my scream. I hope to all that's mighty that I don't regret this one mistake.

Getting dressed, I grab my purse and phone, lock my room, and rush to Camden's, hurriedly knocking as I look around the narrow hallway.

"Yes?" He opens the door with a crooked smirk, his hand gripping the side of the door as he stands shirtless before me, smattering of hair on his chest.

I do my damnedest to keep my eyes on his face, not even thinking about looking at his chiseled abs or defined arms. Okay, clearly, I'm thinking about it, but I won't do it.

"You know why I'm here," I bite out, keeping my voice low.

"Already back for seconds?" His smile grows, cocky and confident.

Jesus, Mary, and Joseph, I swear he's out to torture me.

"No," I hiss. Then, I turn my head to both sides and lean forward. "My underwear?" I whisper.

"Oh." Camden pouts. "You mean, they *weren't* a souvenir?" His eyebrows furrow and a pout claims his full lips in mock disappointment.

I take a deep breath and clench my jaw, counting to five before responding. "No, Camden, not every woman you fuck

the Right kind of Wrong

wants you to have a keepsake of your night together." I surprise myself by the calm in my voice, the almost monotone way I reply.

Camden's eyes briefly narrow before he's back to his smiling self. "Well, I guess I'll give them back to you." He pulls my underwear from his jeans pocket and dangles them in front of me. My eyes widen, and I yank them from his hand, shoving them in my purse before someone walks down the hall and sees our exchange.

"Don't tell anyone what happened," I plead.

"Trust me, I'm the first person who wants to keep this a secret." His tone switches from the lighthearted joking to a tight bite.

Taken aback by his words, I nod once and turn around to walk away. I need coffee, stat. Of course, Camden doesn't want anyone to know. I'm not the type of woman he tends to associate with, and I bet he wants to keep it that way. Better for me, too.

Walking down to the main room of the bed and breakfast, I wave at Averly and head outside, inhaling the crisp morning air despite it being summer. It has been years since I've been back to my hometown of Everton. My family and I moved to Virginia when I was an early teen, and Virginia has always felt more like home. Not for my brother, though. Easton always loved Everton, and I knew he'd return here one day.

I walk down the road that wraps around the bed and breakfast, following the GPS on my phone to get to the local coffee shop, Cup-O-Joe. I look around my surroundings, taking in the mountains looming nearby and peaceful quiet. I finally begin to relax for the first time since I woke up in Camden's bed, his warm body enveloping mine.

fabiola francisco

I can't believe I had sex with him. I've known Camden since he was assigned as my brother's roommate in college over ten years ago. Never in my wildest dreams did I think I'd be waking up in bed with him. Not after a few drinks, and definitely not stone-cold sober. Not that I was totally sober last night—there was an open bar at the wedding after all—but I knew what I was doing. I was aware of the choices I made. Yet, I have no idea what part of going to his room made sense in my muddled mind. Thankfully, I did not share a room with my mom, or it would've been totally awkward and obvious that I did not sleep in my bed last night.

I sigh when I see the center of town come into view, and I turn off my navigation, strolling toward the store-lined street where the coffee shop is located. Coffee will help. It always does. Then, I can go back to pretending that Camden is nothing more than an acquaintance. Definitely not one of the few people I've slept with. And definitely not the only one-night-stand I've ever had.

The town is busy. Groups of people walk around, greeting each other and laughing. The camaraderie between the townspeople is felt all around. I remember being a part of this community, even if only for the first thirteen years of my life.

I greedily inhale the bitter scent of roasted coffee beans as I make my way to the line to order. The sweetness from pastries blends perfectly in the air, creating an aroma that makes my mouth water.

Once I order and grab my cup, adding a splash of creamer from the bar, I take a seat at an empty table and lean back, closing my eyes for a second. When I blink my eyes open, I look around, catching the smiles from a few people in here. I

the Right kind of Wrong

don't remember most of the people in this town, but they all remember me.

It became obvious when I first arrived, and I got asked a ton of questions and a few comments praising my dad and his memory. I just wish he were still here with us to have witnessed Easton getting married. There's not a day that goes by that I don't miss him.

Inhaling a stabilizing breath, I blink back tears and take a sip of my warm drink. This is damn good coffee. I take another drink, closing my eyes again, but they snap open right away. Flashes of my night with Camden fill my mind, and I shake them out. It's pointless to even entertain the idea of Camden. Tomorrow, I'll be getting on a plane back to Spain. To my life, my job, my apartment.

When my company offered to extend my contract for five years in the new branch office in Spain, I took it, knowing it's an amazing opportunity to say I helped start an international office from the ground up. Human resources isn't always fun, but when my boss asked me if I wanted to embark on this new journey, I eagerly agreed.

It's been almost two years since I packed my stuff and moved to Madrid with the hopes of adventure and possibly finding Mr. Right among the stone streets, old buildings, and rich history. I've found adventure. Not so much luck in the love department, which is probably why I was feeling vulnerable last night and landed in bed with Camden. A girl can only deal with so many unanswered wishes upon a star.

"Rough night?" I lift my gaze to the person standing before me and groan when I see smiling, brown eyes. "Hey, now, you wound me." Camden places his hand over his chest.

"Mind if I sit?" He points to the empty chair across from me. I shrug noncommittally.

"Come on, any other time, it would've been perfectly normal for me to sit and have a cup of coffee with you." He places his hands in his pockets and rocks back on his heels, a small, hopeful smile marking his face.

"Fine," I relent, sitting up tall from my slouching position.

As soon as Camden orders his coffee, he takes a seat across from me in silence, the same easy smile on his face, as if all is right in the world, and he didn't just have sex with his best friend's younger sister the night before.

Chapter 2

Camden

I don't know what the fuck possessed me to sleep with Allyson. Internally, I'm freaking the fuck out, but I'm playing it as cool as I can in front of her, pretending it's no big deal. That way, Easton won't realize something's up and kick my ass. Actually, I'm pretty sure he'd clip my balls, cut off my dick, and feed it to that horse of his. Or better yet, give it to his dog as a chew toy to remind me of what it feels like to be dick-less.

Fuck my life. *FML,* as the kids say nowadays. This is messy as hell right now, and the only thing I can think to do is act indifferently. As if Allyson Locke, my best friend's little sister, didn't rock my world a few hours ago.

I take a deep breath, looking around the coffee shop to ignore her curious gaze and will my dick to ignore the memories of her soft body beneath mine, her desperate pleas, and her moans.

"Anyway…" I slap the top of the table harder than I meant to, startling her. *Smooth, Camden.* "Lunch at your brother's house today before they leave for their honeymoon, huh?"

"Mhmm…" Allyson presses her lips together, avoiding my eyes.

"Should be fun. A few of his friends are going, too, right?" I try to make small talk.

Allyson's eyes snap up to mine, wide like a deer in headlights. "You won't say anything, right? About last night…" Her voice lowers as she leans in. "You promised."

"I'd like to keep my dick intact. I don't need to lose my best friend and my masculinity because of a one-night-stand," I grit out. Allyson flinches and leans back on her seat. She's dead-set on no one knowing she slept with me as if she were ashamed. I'll make damn sure no one ever finds out about this. It's not like I come around for seconds anyway.

"You don't have to be so crass. A simple yes would've sufficed." She pushes back her chair, the legs scraping against the tile floor, and she stands to leave.

Crap. I take a deep breath and follow her out of the coffee shop. "Wait." I reach for her arm, but she turns around before I can wrap my hand around her.

"I didn't mean it like that," I begin to apologize, running a hand down my face. I've never been in a situation like this before.

"It's fine," Allyson shrugs me off, but I know better.

"No, it's not. Clearly, this is an uncomfortable situation for both of us, but I promise not to say anything. I won't even tease you about the way you yelled—" I bite down hard when she shoots daggers at me.

A slow grin tilts my lips up. "Okay, I won't tease anymore…starting now." I lift my hands in surrender. She visibly relaxes, her shoulders sagging as she nods.

"Come on, Ally, it's me." I wrap my arm around her shoulder, and she tenses again.

the Right kind of Wrong

"Maybe we should just keep our distance for a little while," she suggests, her cheeks turning pink.

"Understood." I remove my hands from her shoulder and nod once. "So, how's life in Madrid?"

She side-eyes me. "Hey, I'm just trying to act normal here." I shrug.

"As if you didn't see me in my birthday suit a few hours ago?" she adds, and I hear underlying humor in her tone.

"I did more than that," I waggle my eyebrows, and her cheeks flush deep red.

"Uh… I'm gonna… Yeah, I'm gonna go… That way." Allyson looks around the town, desperate for an escape route. When she points to the closed pharmacy, I chuckle, but let her get away with her stuttering and frightful expression. I'll cut her some slack. It'd probably be best if I keep my distance as well since all I can think about is how she'd look riding my dick.

I find myself sitting out on Easton's patio after we've finished eating lunch, talking to two of his friends, Knox and Harris. It's fascinating to hear how the music business works. Knox Bentley is a big country musician, and he and Harris have their own music label.

Easton has made a home for himself here, after living away from his hometown for years. The way he'd talk about it when we were in college, and how he'd bring up Faith after a couple of beers, I knew he'd end up here one day. It was only a matter of time, which works for me since I can travel and visit.

"Hey," Easton says, as he sits next to me.

"How's it feel to be married?" I ask with a grin.

"Fucking fantastic." He leans back, stretching his legs beneath the table, and smiles.

Knox and Harris agree, and that's when I realize all of these people are married, some with kids.

I haven't thought about marrying a girl since… Well, never, actually. I've never had that one girl who's made me want to settle down, have a white picket fence, and grow old on rocking chairs.

I look around his backyard, and I catch Allyson talking to her mom, Charlene, and Faith. She giggles and slaps the top of the table, a snort coming from the back of her throat. Damn, she is beautiful. How had I never noticed her before?

"Camden." Someone calls my name, and I turn my attention back to our table. Easton is looking at me with raised eyebrows.

That's right, he's the reason I've never noticed Allyson as anything more than a friend or a kid—although she's definitely a woman. It's easier to pretend she's still that annoying teenager I met when Easton and I were in college.

"What did you say?" I lean back with a tight smile.

"What time do you leave tomorrow?"

"Oh, I think at four. I have to double-check."

"You're not flying to Richmond? My mom leaves at noon." Easton tilts his head, tipping his beer bottle back and forth on the tabletop.

"Nope, I'm going to New York. I've got to meet with the people from Hotline Hookup about the dating app they needed help with." Working as a computer engineer is great

the Right kind of Wrong

when I freelance since I get to travel to a lot of places, but it's also a lot more work than being with one stable company.

A new dating app is starting up, and Logan, a buddy from college, called me up a few weeks ago saying they need help with a glitch they hit while working on the app. Since Logan and I worked together with a few other people on another dating app a year or so ago, he called in an SOS. I guess the owner also wants to make sure he's getting what his competition has or better. Works for me—a job is a job, and if it pays well, even better.

"How long will you be in New York? We're headed that way next week for some shows," Knox says.

"Really? Let's meet up if you have time. I'll be there until the end of the month."

Knox nods, and we swap numbers so we can have dinner one night when he and Harris are out that way.

"How about you?" I look at Easton. "Honeymoon starts when?"

"We leave for Greece in the morning. Ready for some R&R with my girl," he smiles, rubbing his hands together. Happy for him, I slap his shoulder and shake my head. This guy's been destined to marry Faith since before I knew him, and it's great to see him finally living that life.

What he says next definitely gets my attention, though, and I'm not sure if it's in a good or bad way, but it's definitely taunting. "I think Ally flies to New York, too, on her way back to Madrid. Maybe you guys are on the same flight.."

I swallow thickly and offer a tight smile, tipping my head back as I drink my beer. "Maybe." I nod. Fuck, as if I needed another reason to think about her, now we may be on an airplane together for hours.

I'm doomed if I thought I could sleep with her one wild night and forget it ever happened. All day I've been trying to erase the memory of her touch and her cries. All day I've been fighting against sneaking away with her and stealing one more kiss. All fucking day I've been averting my gaze and reminding myself that it'd ruin my friendship with Easton. He's like family, more of a brother than a friend, which should make me consider Allyson like a sister, not someone I am fantasizing about. No woman is worth tearing this apart. Not even his own flesh and blood.

Chapter 3

Allyson

I rush into the airport, freaking out that I'll miss my flight. Instead of getting a ride with my family and waiting hours for my afternoon flight, I decided to wait around town. Unfortunately, the taxi took forever to pick me up at The Farm House Bed and Breakfast, making me arrive with forty-five minutes to spare. If the check-in line is long, I'm screwed.

As I race to the counter, I find it empty and almost chastise myself. I should've known there'd be no line. This airport is tiny, servicing the few towns in the area, and it's definitely not the hustle and bustle you find in Madrid or even Richmond.

Releasing a sigh of relief, I make my way to security and pass through in no time. Checking the gate, I make my way over and freeze when I see disheveled brown hair looking down at a phone that has earbuds attached. This is not happening.

Pretending I don't see Camden, I roll my bag toward the line starting to form for boarding. Except my traitorous eyes glance his way as I pass by him, and he must sense it because he looks up with raised eyebrows and a slow smile that I'm sure is the same one he gave me when I agreed to sleep with him. A shiver runs through me, and Camden's smile grows, misreading my reaction.

"Your brother mentioned you might be on this flight." He leans back, placing his hands behind his head in an attempt to be cool, except he accidentally knocks the back of the head of the person behind him, who turns with a glare. His grimace is almost comical as he drops his hands on his lap.

"Are you going to New York?" I scrunch up my nose in confusion.

"Yup, for work." Camden sits taller, patting the seat next to him. "You're welcome to sit."

"Uh, I'm actually going to go stand in line... See when they're boarding." My voice does nothing to conceal my discomfort, and it all has to do with the reason that I can't stop thinking about him. Camden probably reads right through me, but he nods without another word and lets me walk away.

He probably doesn't want to deal with a woman who is clingy. Not that I'm clingy. I'd rather hide in a bathroom than seem clingy to a guy, which might be why my status is #singleAF. But Camden is one guy I don't want to think I'm expecting more from him. I'm not. Whatsoever. Not even a repeat of my fuzzy memory to catalog for a lonely night.

I've got steamy romance novels for that.

I take a gulp of air as I stand in line, reading the time on the board over the counter. Fifteen minutes until we board. Surely, Camden and I will be seated rows apart.

the Right kind of Wrong

As I stow my bag in the overhead compartment, a flight attendant informs me that my seat has been changed.

"Excuse me?" I arch an eyebrow, double-checking the seat on my boarding pass.

"Right this way." She turns and guides me back toward the front of the plane, signaling to an empty aisle seat in business class.

"Uh, this must be—"

"No mistake, Ally." My eyes dart toward Camden in the window seat. "Figured the least I could do is offer you a nicer seat."

"Least you could do, my ass," I mumble. I'll never erase the memory of him if he's this close to me, doing nice things.

"Stop grumbling under your breath and sit." Camden rolls his eyes.

"Thanks," I squeak and drop on my seat after stowing away my bag. "You didn't have to," I add as I buckle my seatbelt.

"The seat was empty, and it was no big deal. I fly enough that I've got miles saved for any upgrade."

I nod, grabbing my e-reader from my purse and switching it to airplane mode before opening my current book.

"What are you reading?" Camden leans over to look at the screen. "Is that a naked guy?" His voice fills with humor.

"He's not naked," I argue. He's just shirtless. I don't have to defend my reading preferences to anyone.

"What's it about?" He shifts to look at me.

With raised eyebrows, I assess him, waiting for the punchline. Instead, he genuinely waits to hear what I have to say.

"It's about friends-with-benefits that have had a rough upbringing and are afraid of commitment."

"Cool," he says casually. "I'm more of a non-fiction reader."

"Okay," I say awkwardly, looking back at my e-reader and finding my spot.

As the airplane begins to move, I lean my head back on the headrest and close my eyes, taking deep, even breaths. I say a quick prayer, my heart beating fiercely in my chest.

"Are you afraid of flying?" Camden's breath tickles my ear.

"No," I respond through clenched teeth, keeping my eyes shut.

"You could've fooled me," he chuckles, and I open one eye, glaring at him.

"Just the takeoff," I add as a way of explanation. "Freaks me out." I let the e-reader rest on my lap and hold the armrests as the plane rolls through the runway. Once I feel the tires lift from the ground, my hands grip the armrests until my skin stretches and the rubber from it marks my skin.

"It's okay, Ally." Camden's soft voice sounds in my ear. I nod tightly, taking a deep breath. Blinking my eyes open, I peek out the window to see a ton of clouds passing through. Or the plane passing through the clouds. Whichever it is.

A jolt makes me forget about clouds and planes, and my hands are back on the armrests as if holding on with all my might would prevent me from falling if this thing goes down.

"Breathe," Camden whispers, placing his hand over mine. The soft touch is a contrast to his teasing these last two days, comforting me instead of making fun of what happened between us.

the Right kind of Wrong

"It's just a little turbulence on the way up," he says softly, and I nod, unclenching my jaw.

"Yeah." My voice comes out hoarse as my body bounces along with the plane. "Damn it," I murmur.

"There… You see." Camden says after a few minutes, once the plane has righted itself and we're soaring above the clouds. "No harm done. Well, except for the armrest you had a chokehold on." His teasing words make me laugh as my body relaxes.

"I hate takeoff."

"No shit. I never would've guessed," he teases me, and I crack a smile.

When the flight attendant walks by, Camden calls for her and orders two scotches. I lift my eyebrows as I look at him, and he winks.

"It's what you were drinking at the wedding. Figured you could use some liquid courage for the rest of the flight."

I groan and nod. He's right; I need liquid courage, but not because of the aircraft I'm on. I need the courage to sit next to this man for the next few hours and not break down, or jump him and become a member of the mile-high club.

Before yesterday morning, Camden and I would be totally normal, chatting and joking with each other. Sitting beside him wouldn't feel weird. I just need to go back to that. Channel the pre-one-night-stand Allyson and Camden and get over my embarrassment. So, I had sex with the guy. No big deal, right?

Turning to look at him, Camden holds his glass and tilts it my way. "Cheers."

I wish I could be as cool as him. I take a chug of the whiskey, the amber liquid burning my insides as I hold back a cough.

"Take it slow…" Camden says with furrowed eyebrows.

I nod and let the glass rest on the small fold-down table so some of the ice can melt and water it down a bit to make it easier to drink.

"What are you doing in New York?" I ask, hoping regular conversation will break apart this awkwardness that's settled over us.

"I'm helping with a new dating app system. I'm meeting with the owner and a buddy of mine who was hired for the job, to help them get a secure and effective system in place after they hit a wall in the creation of it."

"That's cool." I take him in. Camden could talk about computers for hours and not realize the other person has no idea what he's talking about. Once he starts, he gets lost and babbles on and on.

"How is life in Spain? Everything you thought it would be?" He lifts his eyebrows in genuine curiosity.

"It's been great. The first year was a little rough in the beginning with all the differences in culture and just general mindset, but I'm really getting the hang of it. Besides, Madrid is a huge city, so I've got everything I need within reach."

"That's good to hear." He nods pensively. "And the job is good?"

"Yeah, the new branch is basically up and running, and I've been responsible for the HR department. It's been a lot of work, but it's worth it."

the Right kind of Wrong

"How's the language barrier? Have you made friends?" He shifts in his seat, taking a sip of his drink while he waits for my answer.

"I've been learning Spanish. They've offered classes in the office for the few of us Americans that came with the company, so that's been great. As for friends, I've made a few, mostly colleagues. Fortunately, I already knew the co-workers who came from the Richmond office."

"Awesome, I bet the nightlife is amazing."

I nod with a smile. "It's definitely nothing like we're used to here in the States. Actually, the whole lifestyle is night and day. Noon cocktails, soccer games, ten PM dinners. It's an experience."

"Sounds like it."

I smile and drink my scotch, relaxing for the first time in over twenty-four hours. This is how Camden and I used to be. We'd talk, joke around, catch up in each other's lives—not this weirdness that's settled between us. Surely, two friends can sleep together and not let it affect their relationship. We wouldn't be the first or last to fall into bed together after a few drinks and remain friends.

Taking a healthy drink and a deep, calming breath, I risk telling Camden, "Listen, about yesterday or the night before, whatever," I'm already screwing this up by rambling. "What happened," I correct. "You know what I mean. Things don't have to be awkward, right? We can forget about it and remain friends as usual. No need to make a mountain out of a molehill. We're two consenting adults that scratched an itch."

Camden coughs when I say that, clearing his throat. "Don't worry about, Ally. You're still the same pestering girl I used to make fun of."

"Ha, ha, ha," I say dryly.

"Let's make a deal. One night won't ruin years of friendship." He holds his almost empty glass up. "Besides, as soon as you get back to your real life, you'll find a Spaniard to sweep you off your feet." I hear a hint of resentment in his tone, but I ignore it and blame the whiskey.

"Cheers to not letting it make things awkward." I tap my glass with his and take a drink. Then I add, "I'm not in Spain permanently, so getting into a relationship would be doomed from the beginning."

"You may want to scratch an itch," Camden bites back his laughter, rinsing it away with his drink. I glare at him, but he looks at me with a cocky smile. "Or… You could call me," he winks, and I fish out an ice cube from my glass and throw it at him.

"Hey!" He argues, reaching in his glass, but he realizes it's empty. "Payback will be served." He points a finger at me.

"Oh, I'm shaking in my boots," I joke, tossing my head back in laughter. That's when I feel something cold hit my throat.

I snap my head back and look at Camden, who whistles innocently. I look in my glass and find the other ice cube missing.

"Did you stick your hand in my drink?" I ask incredulously.

"I'd never. What do you take me as?"

"A pig," I murmur, waving down a flight attendant as if I were in a restaurant or something. When she stands next to me, I order another drink.

"Add it to his tab," I jut my thumb toward him.

the Right kind of Wrong

Camden laughs at the same time as the flight attendant says, "Business class doesn't have to pay for their drinks."

"Humor me, and make him pay for it. Make it a triple, so it costs him more."

The flight attendant grins and walks away, probably humoring me like I asked instead of actually charging Camden for my drink.

"No drink for me?" he asks with a pout.

"Order your own." I lean back with a victorious smile. Yeah, it's not a huge win, but at least I got the last say.

Camden mumbles something under his breath that sounds like, *I'll order you,* but I ignore it, blaming my wild imagination and the burning memory that won't abandon me.

By the time we land, I'm three scotches in and feeling the heaviness of the liquor in my bloodstream.

"How long is your layover?" Camden asks, reaching for my bag in the overhead compartment and handing it to me.

"Two hours."

"Eat something, or you'll feel like shit on your next flight."

"Aye-aye, captain." I salute him and giggle.

Camden groans and squeezes his eyes tightly.

I freeze when his hand wraps around my waist, and he presses into me. "If you want, you can submit to me as your captain and be at my mercy. It'll be a sure-fire way to burn off the alcohol in your system." His nose skims my jaw, and I suck in a gasp, stuck in place.

When Camden leans back and looks down into my eyes, his carefree smile is painted on his lips, framed in his stubble. "That should do the trick to sober you up." He chuckles mischievously, and my mouth drops.

"You're an ass." I slap his chest and step back, bumping into the armrest and almost landing my ass in the seat.

All he does is wink and step in front of me as the line in the narrow hall begins to move out of the airplane, other people sneaking in, creating more space between him and me. Damn him and his sex appeal. Not only am I sober now, but I'm also filled with desire. And the only person that can scratch this itch is the man who awoke it in the first place. The man that should be so off-limits I shouldn't even entertain the idea of pulling him into a bathroom stall and having dirty bathroom sex with him. The kind I've only ever thought was acceptable in books.

By the time I'm off the plane, there's no sight of Camden. He's disappeared into thin air, leaving his final words lingering worse than a scotch hangover on a turbulent plane ride.

Chapter 4

Allyson

I walk down the busy streets of Madrid, dodging tourists left and right as I make my way back to my apartment for my lunch break. I've been living here for two years, and sometimes I'm still thrown off by the two-hour break I get. I was used to a short lunch break back in Richmond, mostly consisting of eating at my desk or in the break-room.

Unfortunately, no amount of tourists have been able to make me stop thinking about Camden. Three damn weeks since I returned, and I was sure that throwing myself into work would do the trick, but human resources doesn't exactly provide the type of distraction I was hoping for.

I shake my head, bumping into someone, and I call out an apology over my shoulder in my best Spanish while I keep walking forward. This city is full of life. No matter the time of day or day of the year, there's always a crowd of people making it exciting.

I do wish the streets were a little less crowded with the heat wave that's consuming us these past weeks. It's like a fiery tidal wave, and I can't wait for the weather to cool down. I'll take a brutal winter over a burning summer any day of the week. I attribute it to being from the Wyoming mountains and having grown up with freezing cold weather. Virginia doesn't get as cold as Everton, my hometown, but it still gets cold.

By the time I make it up to my apartment, sweat drips down the back of my neck. One thing I definitely miss is AC. Nothing beats good old air conditioning in the summer—not even an ice-cold beer.

I heat up leftovers from last night and jump in the shower for a quick cooldown. I rinse my body and stop mid-way, leaning forward in the shower to listen to the noise coming in from the cracked open window. Is that? No way…

I chuckle, reminding myself I live in a city, not the country for goodness sake. Turning off the water, I grab my towel and wrap it around me as I step out, this time no shower head competing for the noise coming through my window. I squint my eyes and wait for the noise to come back.

Is that a rooster?

It's cock-a-doodle-doing in the middle of a metropolitan city. Sure, Madrid isn't New York, but some would argue it's better than The Big Apple. I've never been to New York, so I always have to keep quiet when that argument arises, which also means my comparison is null and void.

I shake my head, interrupting my inner-conversation, and step out of the bathroom. No time to figure out why a rooster is in a nearby apartment, I get dressed quickly, not caring one bit that I'll show up to the office in a second outfit, and grab my food from the microwave.

The pasta steams as I sit on the couch and open my iPad to call my best friends, Noel and Berkeley.

"Heyyyy, boo!" Noel calls out immediately.

Berkeley rubs her eyes and winks at me before she croaks, "Hey."

the Right kind of Wrong

"Are you still in bed?" Noel asks, furrowing her eyebrows. "Get up! Time to work. Let's go, let's go." She cheers her on with way too much energy considering it's eight in the morning in Richmond.

"I'm up," Berkeley sits up. "But let me grab coffee. It's my day off," she grumbles as she holds her phone and makes her way to the kitchen in her apartment.

"So, how's the big life in Spain?" Noel asks, without waiting for Berkeley's coffee to brew.

I smile at my best friend. "It's great." My lunch break has become our chat time since the time difference makes any other time a challenge between work and sleep schedules.

"Funny story, though…" I wait until I have both of their attention. "There's nothing like taking a shower with the window cracked open and a rooster cock-a-doodling. And you both thought I moved to Spain for the glamour. I moved for the cocks.

Berkeley sputters, her sip of coffee flying everywhere as she laughs. "That shit's funny." She wipes her mouth with the back of her hand before rinsing her hand at the sink. God, I love that girl, but she's a hot mess most days.

"I'm pretty sure it's called crowing. A rooster crows…" Noel corrects me, scrunching her eyebrows as if she were deep in thought. "I'm going to have to google that now to know for sure."

"I guess you really did move to Spain for the cocks," Berkeley adds, taking a seat on her kitchen table and setting her phone down. Knowing her, it's leaning against an empty jar she hasn't thrown away yet.

"Speaking of cocks…" Noel trails off, squinting her eyes at something. "Yes! It is called crowing." Her attention is back on us. "Anyway, cocks… What I was saying. Have you found your own *rooster?*" I chuckle at her use of rooster for a guy.

"I told you, there's one somewhere in my apartment building."

"Did you bang a hot neighbor you didn't tell us about?" She leans forward on her elbows, her brown eyes widening. "Wait, we are talking about a guy and not the real rooster you heard, right?" My comment dawns on her as Berkeley and I both laugh.

"Assholes," she mutters. "Seriously, Ally, you've been living there for two years, and you haven't banged a hot guy."

"Who still says *banged?*" I roll my eyes dramatically, sure that she sees my annoyance. Bless her heart, but she's dead-set on me meeting a hot Spaniard and falling in love with him.

"I don't know if I could date a guy who wears tighter jeans than me. Like, my ass wouldn't fit in his pants." I sigh and fall back on my couch, stuffing my mouth with pasta and keeping track of the time.

"Who said anything about dating?" Noel waggles her eyebrows, and Berkeley calls out in agreement.

"Besides, you said dating a guy with an expiration date wasn't what you wanted," Berkeley speaks up. "Have some fun. It's not like you've ever had a one-night-stand. You gotta have one before you turn thirty!"

I choke on my lunch, my eyes watering. *If they only knew…*

I hold up a finger and walk into the kitchen, grabbing a glass of water. "Sorry, it went down the wrong pipe," I say after collecting myself.

They both wave it off and then pry for more information. "There's gotta be a cute guy that's caught your eye. How about

the Right kind of Wrong

in that bar you always go to. What's the name of it?" Berkeley's curious eyes widen as she waits for my response.

"Toro," I say.

"Doesn't that mean bull?" Noel asks with a proud smile.

"It does."

"So, there must be a bull of a man there for you." I laugh at her corny joke.

I love having this time to talk to my friends. They've been with me since I moved to Virginia, helping me settle in after my move, making sure I fit in. They even said I was heaven sent because no "Mean Girls Club" would survive with just two members. They were anything but mean girls, so I always found that amusing. They did become my best friends, from high school to college to the real world, where we had to get real jobs and apartments and *adult*.

"I'll see if I meet someone this weekend," I lie.

"Mmhmm… You say that every week," Berkeley calls me on my fib.

If they only knew that my mind has currently been caught up on another cock… I mean, man. On another man. Whose cock I should *not* be thinking about.

Damn Camden for getting me all tied up in knots when I'm not supposed to see him as more than a friend, maybe even an older brother. I roll my eyes at myself. Yeah, Camden is so not like an older brother.

"Ally!" Noel's voice brings me back to the present.

"Yeah?" I look at their furrowed faces on the screen, my own is doe-eyed in confusion.

"I was saying that you should just let it flow. Be open to meeting someone—no expectations—and have fun. Don't overthink it, even if the guys there do wear super skinny jeans.

Take that as a clue into what their package would be like, and if they'll be worth a wild ride in the sack."

I giggle as I listen to Noel's speech.

"I'd high-five you if I were with you right now," Berkeley says.

"Hell, high-five now!" Both of their hands slam the screen, and I let out a deep, belly laugh at their ridiculousness.

"Okay, I gotta go. Thank you for the chat, and for waking up early on your day off," I say to Berkeley.

"For you? I'd wake up at four A.M."

"Love you," I tell them, waving at them until I realize that's not necessary.

We laugh as we end our call. I jump up from the couch, wash my plate, and put on my shoes so I can head back to work. Whenever I can, I stop at a café near the office to have a coffee and pastry. Thank goodness for all this walking, or I'd be rolling with all the puffed pastry and whipped cream I eat on a daily basis.

Thinking about what Noel and Berkeley said, I wonder if they're right. I am looking forward to the weekend, but more so I can veg out on my couch, read, and have a few beers. My friend supply here is limited, but I've never been one to have a huge group of friends. I've always believed a small, loyal, and loving group of friends is better than a huge amount of people you can't really count on. That's what acquaintances are for.

The only downfall to free time is that I continue to replay my night with Camden. I wish we had a choice to erase certain memories. Better yet, I wish I could go back in time and redo the past. Because I may have never considered Camden Steele to have a place in my love life, but now all I can see is him as the main character when it comes to the hero in my own story.

the Right kind of Wrong

And that is so wrong. So not going to happen. Easton aside, Camden isn't the guy that would ever really settle down. I've always imagined him as George Clooney, the forever bachelor (ignoring the fact that George settled down eventually). He has fun in his life, travels for work, gets what he wants with no real attachment holding him back. I mean, I get it to a certain extent, but that's not what I want.

One day, I'd like to have a relationship that will lead to a home together, marriage, and maybe kids. I hope one day to have a permanent travel partner and coffee date. Every time I see couples around the city, traveling together, a sense of longing washes over me. I've never had a serious enough relationship where we were at the point of moving in together, but a girl can hope that a guy will come around one day and sweep her off her feet.

I sigh and walk into the café, taking my coffee to-go today and skipping the pastry. I have a feeling I'm going to be hitting the junk food aisle after work. I'd much rather savor what I eat than stuff my face in a rush because I'm running out of time.

The rest of the day drags with a few messages from my mom and one from Easton with a picture of his view in Mykonos. Greece has always been a honeymoon destination I would love to have. Seeing his pictures makes it even more romantic. Luckily, my brother and Faith were able to take a long honeymoon since Faith works at the school and has summers off and my brother was able to weasel himself a four-week holiday. I'd do the same. It's a shame to fly to Europe for anything less than three weeks.

I hope one day I'll find a love like that. Until then, I'll be open to possibilities like Berkeley and Noel suggested.

Chapter 5

Allyson

I never thought the weekend would get here. While working in Spain is totally different than the US—it doesn't feel like the in and out hustle and bustle we're used to back home—I am definitely ready for a break. This week was never-ending, not to mention I had to deal with two co-workers and personal differences. Being in human resources, I'm the lucky chick who's designated as, usually, the office counselor, especially when it comes to starting an international office and merging two different cultures in one space.

Working in logistics in itself isn't exactly exciting, but dealing with people's personal challenges keeps me on my toes.

But, I'm finally home, lying on my couch with a bag of chips resting on my chest. Easy access for the lazy lover. *Ha! Lazy lover.* That sounds wrong. Like a person needs the other within reach because they're too lazy to put some effort into it. Not the kind of lover I'd want. I'd want...

Ugh! Now I'm thinking about Camden again and his non-lazy ways.

Shaking out of my thoughts, I take a deep breath and shove two salty chips into my mouth, crunching away as I compete to listen to the television. Reruns of an old American

the Right kind of Wrong

crime show I had never seen before moving here plays in the background. Since living here, I've discovered so many older shows I hadn't heard of. Spaniards seem to love all things drama, murders, and drugs it seems. Thankfully, I don't have a weak stomach, and my mind's a little twisted, too, or I'd hate the entertainment options here.

I hear the buzz of my apartment intercom and sit up, catching the bag of chips before it spills on the floor, and look around my apartment in confusion. I'm sure as hell not expecting anyone, which means it could be a mistake or some mass-murderer checking to see if there's a vulnerable person in their apartment.

Okay, maybe I should quit it on the crime shows.

I stand wearily and make my way to the speaker by my door, thankful they can't come in unless someone buzzes them.

"Si?" I speak into the system.

I hear whispering on the other side along with a giggle, but no one answers. Probably some punk kids trying to prank people.

As I'm walking away, it sounds again. "Si," I repeat, wondering who is downstairs and more irritated this time when I don't get an immediate response.

"Oh, someone is pissy," I hear a familiar voice say on a chuckle.

My eyes pop open, and my mouth drops. I press the button and speak into the system, "Is that you?" I can't believe it. I buzz open the door to the building as a huge smile fills my face.

Opening the door, I wait right outside of it to see if my imagination is playing tricks on me. When the elevator opens with a ding, I crane my head in the hallway to see Easton and Faith walking down the hall.

I swallow back tears and rush to them, hugging my brother and then my sister-in-law. "What are you doing here? Oh, my goodness! This is the best surprise ever," I'm talking a mile a minute, tears welling in my eyes. The last thing I expected was for them to come to Spain.

Easton chuckles, wrapping his arm around my shoulder as I lead them toward my apartment.

"We wanted to surprise you, which I guess we did. Faith thought you were on to us because I posted an airport picture on Instagram, but I guess you didn't realize it."

"No, I didn't catch on at all. How long are you here?"

"Just four days, then we had back to Everton," Faith says with a smile.

"Oh, my God. I can't get over it. You're really here!" I jump up and down, holding their hands. "My apartment's a mess. It's been a long week. I'm apologizing now," I rush them in, closing the door behind me.

"This is really nice." Faith looks around. "It's so airy."

I nod. "Yeah, I got lucky. After seeing other apartments my co-workers have, I hit the jackpot with this place." My apartment has big windows in the living room that allow natural light to come in. The kitchen also has a window, and I've got a covered balcony where I can sit and slide open the windows to create a more open space when the weather is nice.

"You guys are staying here, right?" I look between them.

"We actually booked a hotel nearby." Easton smiles. "It's within walking distance."

the Right kind of Wrong

"No way! You have to stay here. I've got a sofa bed I can stay on, and you can sleep in my room."

"No, we don't want to put you out," Faith shakes her head.

"You're not, honestly. Half the nights, I end up asleep on the couch anyway." I look at my comfy sofa. "Unless you want to… You know, keep the honeymoon going," I joke.

Easton scrunches up his face, and Faith lets out a deep laugh. "That's so wrong," my brother shakes his head.

I join Faith in laughing loud until I snort, which makes me laugh even more. "I'm kidding. You're more than welcome to stay here, but if you do want privacy, I understand as well."

"We'll stay at the hotel, but we plan on having you show us around. We made sure to come on a weekend, so you'd be free."

"Yes! I can't wait to show you all my favorite places. Let me take a shower, and we can go to a bar near here that I love. Good, cheap beer, believe it or not, and tapas. It's paradise." I rush into my room, grab my clothes, and take a quick shower.

I can't believe that they're here. So many different plans run through my mind as I wipe the steam off the bathroom mirror and brush my hair. Thank goodness I washed and straightened it this morning. Grabbing my makeup from the small organizer I have on the sink, I add the minimal makeup necessary, a bit of concealer under my eyes, a brush of mascara, and my magenta lipstick. I'm a simple gal, but there's nothing I love more than bright lipsticks.

I step out of the shower and see Easton and Faith out in the balcony.

"It's nice, right?" I ask them.

"Definitely. You've got a great view," Faith says, and my brother nods in agreement.

"I'm proud of you, sis," he pulls me in for a hug, the familiarity and comfort making my throat clog up with emotions.

Despite being four years apart and a man, my brother has always been there for me. While other people may wish to have a sibling the same gender as them, I wouldn't trade Easton for a sister. Never. Besides, Faith is my sister-in-law, and while I hadn't seen her in years, I always loved her and had a great relationship with her. That had proven to still be the case after seeing her again a year and a half ago when we spent Easter with my brother and Faith's family in Everton.

After giving my brother and Faith more of a tour around my small apartment, we head down to Toro, the bar near my building. As we walk down the street, they comment on buildings and stores, asking me questions about the city I've called home the last couple of years. I love that they're here and seeing where I live. I never thought I'd see the day they came to Spain. It's such a long way from Everton.

We walk through the open door of Toro, moving past the crowded tables and conversations that mingle and combine in the air. Once we reach the bar, Faith's wide eyes look around.

"This is insane."

"Right? It's a Friday afternoon, and it's summer. People are out and about, having drinks and tapas before dinner."

"You mean, they still have dinner after?" She checks the time on her phone.

"Yup, around ten in the evening."

"Wow," she breathes out.

the Right kind of Wrong

"It's crazy," Easton adds, taking in the wooden decor, frames of bullfighters on the walls, and Serrano hams hanging from the ceiling in the bar from hooks. It's so different than what we're used to, and yet I fell in love with this place as soon as I stepped in. I quickly became a regular, building a friendship with the bartender.

"Do you guys want beer or wine?" I lift my eyebrows as I smile.

"Beer," Easton says.

"Same," Faith nods.

I wave at the bartender, who smiles and tilts his head so he can hear me. "Tres cañas," I order three draught beers over the loud murmurs in this bar. With our drinks in hand and a plate with sautéed mushrooms and aioli potatoes, we clink our glasses together in a toast.

"This is good beer," Easton comments, looking at the glass.

"I know. It's pretty amazing. Try the potatoes. You'll love them."

We eat and drink while Easton and Faith tell me about their time in Greece, showing me more pictures than the ones they had sent while they were away. We order a second round of drinks, enjoying the extra round of tapas as well, and I tell them about work and make a plan to visit places tomorrow.

I'm on cloud nine having my family visit. It can get lonely at times, being so far from my family and friends, especially after my dad passed away three years ago. It was a shock to us all when we learned of his heart disease, and even more so watching him go. The only thing that consoles me is that I know I have him watching over me and protecting me.

I take a deep breath and nod when Faith suggests we take a picture. While Easton holds the phone in our direction, shameless selfie-style, we all smile and hold up our beers.

"Where to now?" Easton asks, clapping his hands.

"How about instead of sit-down dinner, we continue having tapas? We can go to a few different places. I'd suggest a corto instead of a full draught."

"What's a corto?" Faith asks.

"It's like a mini draught, so you won't get so full off of beer. Besides, it gives us more chances to eat tapas," I wink.

"Sounds like a plan." Easton guides us out of Toro after paying, and I lead the way to the next bar.

We laugh as we drink our beers, take a ton of pictures, and eat a lot more delicious food. This beats vegging out on the couch with my bag of chips. Having Easton and Faith here, even if for a few days, will help me get out of my recent slump and weird mood. Not to mention, it will distract me from Camden and the ghost of his hands I still feel on my body.

When Faith asks if I've met anyone, I shake my head with my nose scrunched up and take a sip of beer.

"There are cute guys, though." She looks around the current bar we're in, a more modern place that's filled with more tourists and a combination of different languages swirling around us.

"Yeah, but I haven't met anyone really worth getting to know."

"I'm sure you'll meet someone," she says with a smile.

"You're okay single. Don't settle for someone who isn't worthy of you," Easton pipes in, and I roll my eyes. Big bro protector kicks in, and I can't help but giggle.

the Right kind of Wrong

I'm an adult, and I've been making my own decisions for a long time. Besides, it's not like I've ever just fallen into bed with someone for the sake of it. Until recently… I remind myself that's no longer the case after the night of the wedding. I shiver at the memory and chug what's left of my beer.

Tonight is about family, fun, and more booze than I should consume, not about remembering a fling and getting caught up in emotions I have no business having.

Chapter 6

Camden

Fuck me. And not in the, *I'm fucking whoever I want and thoroughly enjoying it*. It's more along the lines of my life is a mess for the first time, and it has to do with the woman who's staring back at me from my phone screen, holding a glass of beer with her brother—my best friend—and his wife.

I haven't seen or heard from her since I walked off the airplane in New York. I've been so busy with work and helping Logan with Hotline Hookup, the dating app. When Mallory, Owen's business partner and girlfriend, found out I had flown to New York from Everton, she about jumped out of her skin with excitement, telling me how her cousin lives there. Her cousin, Lia, is Knox's sister-in-law. Small, small world. I couldn't believe it when she told me.

Now, I'm back in my apartment in Richmond, daydreaming about Allyson and her full lips and soft hands. I'm so hung up on her, I haven't so much as been able to flirt with another woman since the wedding. No one even catches my eye.

Instead, I'm following Easton's Instagram like a creepy stalker, looking for any glimpses of Allyson in his photos, wondering if she's slept with anyone else or if she's also thinking about me. Searching for her account, I check to see

the Right kind of Wrong

if she's posted any new pictures, and I groan when I see a photo from a few hours ago in her story. She's still in bed with the caption, *Someone bring me coffee and a pastry.* Her sexy pout lures me in, and her swollen eyes remind me of the morning she woke up freaking out because of what we did.

My fingers itch to send her a private response, a joke about repayment if I took her what she asked for, but I don't. I stop myself. Because as much fun as it was to tease her, I'm now torturing myself in the process.

Adjusting myself in my sweatpants, I make my own coffee and grab a banana. I have work to do, even on a Saturday, but all I can think about is hitting the gym in my building and burning some of this pent-up need.

Tonight, I'll go out for drinks and distract myself. There's no future for Ally and me, not even another night in the sack, so there's no point in holding on to a memory that will eventually burn to the ground in a pile of ashes. Or make my life go haywire like a spazzing computer on the verge of burning out. I'll end up in a pile of crap just like that computer if I even consider another night with Allyson. Easton will make damn sure of it. And I can't betray my friend more than I already have.

I pull at the roots of my hair, squeezing my eyes shut. It's all fun and games until you fuck your best friend's younger sister. I'm unsure of what's right or wrong—fess up to Easton and deal with the backlash or keep it to myself, risk him finding out, and make the betrayal even worse.

I finish off my coffee and change into my workout clothes, taking the stairs down to the gym as my warm-up — nothing like running down twenty-four flights of stairs to get your heart pumping and mind clear.

By the time I make it into the gym, I've built up a sweat. Stalking toward the treadmill, I begin running until Allyson is a distant memory and the only thing straining are my thigh muscles and my furiously pumping heart.

Allyson

I stare at his name on my story insights on Instagram. He looked at my pictures. He's been keeping up. That thought shouldn't excite me, but knowing that Camden has been thinking of me, at least enough to look at my Instagram account, makes me uncharacteristically giddy when it really shouldn't. I'm thousands of miles away. There's no real chance at anything, and even if there were, there's still the issue with my brother. I'm not sure how he'd react to me being with Camden, in any sense of the word. He knows Camden too well to probably be okay with me… dating him? Sleeping with him? I'm not sure what we'd even do.

"Hey," Easton's deep voice draws me out of my wild imagination.

"Yeah?" I look up at him with wide eyes. It's their first full day in Madrid, and we've been walking around after having breakfast at a café I love that has the best croissants.

So far, we've walked down the streets, taking in the historic architecture in this city, and passed by the Royal Palace of Madrid. The sound of cars whooshing by reminding us of the busy traffic this city has, but nothing competes with the amount of people filling the city streets. No matter where you turn, you find groups of tourists, families, young kids,

the Right kind of Wrong

older couples. It's fascinating and overwhelming all at the same time.

"What's that there?" He points to an archway crowded with people.

"Oh, that leads to the Plaza Mayor," I tell them, weaving through the crowds of people as we walk toward the main square. It's a magnificent square spanning out all around. I swear thousands of people could fit at one time.

"Wow," Faith gasps. It's lined with buildings that border the square as it opens up before us. Different cafés and restaurants sit on the ground floors of those buildings. Tourists wander around, taking photos and having a cold beer, coffee, or a glass of wine out on the terraces.

"Do those people live there?" Easton points up to a few balconies, where people look down at the square.

"Yeah, they're apartments. Isn't that crazy?" I look around, taking it all in.

"Do people spend their lives drinking here?" Faith asks, noticing the time. "It's not even noon."

"Welcome to Spain, where the alcohol flows more than the numerous rivers in this country."

"Damn," Easton comments.

"I know. It's crazy, really, but a mid-morning drink is part of the lifestyle. A lot of people drink vermouth—they actually call it the vermouth hour—but I don't really like it. Others have a beer, a coffee. Really anything you want. I love sitting on the terraces and watching people." I move around a man taking a picture of a family to not disrupt their photo.

We make our way around, Easton and Faith asking me about the statue of the man on a horse in the middle of the square.

"I honestly have no idea who that is. Maybe an old king?" I shrug. Giving them time to take photos, I take my own, including a video clip for my Instagram story. Social media has been heaven sent when it comes to keeping in touch with my family and friends, allowing them to experience my life in Spain alongside with me.

"Drink?" I lift my eyebrows when Faith and Easton head my way.

"When in Rome..." Faith laughs. Easton wraps his arm around her and looks at her with so much love that I feel a small pang in my chest. If I ever want a chance at what they have, I have to be willing to at least give a guy a chance. Who cares if this isn't my permanent home so long as I like the person. And who knows? Maybe I'll fall in love and end up staying in Spain forever.

The idea of missing out on nieces and nephews, being close to my family, makes me somber, but if love wants me here, then love will have me.

Internally shaking my head at myself, we walk to a terrace that has a table available and take a seat, ordering three beers to help cool off on this searing, August day. Sometimes I drive myself crazy with my own thoughts.

After our beers, Easton, Faith, and I make our way to Parque de El Retiro, a huge park in the city with beautiful gardens, monuments, and a lake where you can rent rowboats. It's all very romantic in retrospect, but it's also a great place to get lost when the chaos of the city becomes too much to bear. And some days, I need a break in a beautiful place to collect myself when I'm feeling stressed or homesick.

I let Faith and Easton row around the lake while I wander around the park. That way, they can do their cute, couple thing

the Right kind of Wrong

and still feel as if they're on their honeymoon and not have me third-wheeling. I take advantage of the time by photographing the gardens and observing the nature around me.

Breathing in deeply, I smile to myself as I watch the sun peek through the branches, heating us up like a burning flame. I bunch my hair in my hands and throw it in a ponytail, glad to feel the breeze against the back of my damp neck.

When I make my way back to the boats, I smile as I see Easton and Faith in the distance, laughing and taking pictures. I'm definitely going to miss them when they leave on Monday, but I'm so freaking grateful they popped over here on their way back home. Shaking away any sadness, I come up with our evening plans. Yesterday we took it slow with our tapas, but tonight I plan to show them Madrid's nightlife. First, we need to have lunch and a nap, because I cannot party like I used to when I was in my early twenties. And *fiesta* and *siesta* must rhyme for a reason.

Excited about tonight, I sit on a nearby bench and resist the urge to check my phone in case Camden has viewed more of my pictures.

Chapter

Camden

"What you're telling me is that you slept with Easton's sister?" I look at Luke's wide eyes as I take a drink of scotch. Luke and I have been friends for years, Easton also being a friend of his. We all met in college, and I'm not one bit surprised by the shock painted on his face.

No longer able to deal with my inner turmoil, I caved and called him up to meet at a bar and tell him what happened. I figured talking to someone about it would put things into perspective, but it's only confused me more.

"Sure, Allyson is hot, but man, Easton is going to kill you if he finds out. I do think it's best that he hears it from you. What if Allyson caves and tells him, or worse, he finds out from someone else. You said the owner of the bed and breakfast saw you guys in the morning, and she's friends with his wife." Luke's eyebrows remain raised as he shakes his head.

"I know, I know. I'm just not sure what he's going to say or how he'll react. He's like a brother, and the idea of losing him because of this has me in knots."

"If I may…" Luke nods once and purses his lips. "From what you've told me, this is more than guilt for sleeping with Allyson. You're hung up on her."

the Right kind of Wrong

I shake my head. "Nah, it was one night."

Luke scoffs, a deep sound coming from the back of his throat. "Yeah, and I'm engaged to Jennifer Aniston. Your denial is as unbelievable as me marrying her. Dude, maybe you should be honest with why you're all tied up and go from there. If you've got feelings for her, then maybe you can work it out."

"No, she lives in Spain. That's a whole ocean apart. Not to mention, she isn't the kind of girl that would go for me—"

"And let me guess, you're not the kind of guy to settle down in an actual relationship. I've heard you spew that shit more than once. To be frank, it's getting kinda old now that we're in our thirties. If you want the girl, go for the fucking girl." He slaps my back in what is supposed to be encouragement, but I cough up the whiskey I was swallowing. Whether it's because of his slap or the truth in his words is what I'm unsure of. I'm guessing it's a combination of both. I have nothing against settling down. I just haven't found someone who makes me want to take that step. Could Allyson be it?

"If you do," Luke continues, sharing his words of wisdom. "Talk to Easton first. Let him know what's going on."

"Maybe I should talk to Ally first before I make a big deal out of it and get a big, fat rejection." Usually, I'm the one turning women down, not the other way around.

"Say what you want, brother, but you've got it *bad*." His emphasis only fuels me more, wanting to prove him wrong. I spin around in my barstool, looking at the people lingering around.

"If you really don't care, pick a woman and take her home," Luke taunts.

"You're a fucker," I grunt, which causes him to laugh. None of these women appeal to me, and it's all because of that green-eyed beauty I shouldn't want.

Paying for our drinks, I leave the bar and grab my phone once I'm seated in my car. Opening Instagram, I look at Allyson's pictures before sending her a message.

I inhale deeply, slowly releasing my breath. *Here goes nothing.* I have no fucking clue what I'm doing, but I'm hoping this is one of those learn as you go moments, because I could use the trial and error.

@CamIAm: Hey

Okay, I was hoping for something better than that. Smoother even. I haven't spoken to her in four weeks, and all I have to say is, *Hey*? Also, when the hell did I create my Instagram handle to be @CamIAm? Was I going for some Dr. Seuss twist of Green Eggs and Ham? Shows how much I actually use the app.

Going into my settings, the first thing I do before sending her a follow-up message is to change my name to something more mature and professional than a fifteen-year-old's idea of cool. Ready to write her another message, I give myself a pep-talk and type.

@CamSteeleIT: How are you?

Now, I wait for her response. I'm not sure what the time difference is, but she very well could be sleeping. All I know for certain is there's a reason why I haven't been able to get

the Right kind of Wrong

her out of my mind. No woman has lingered for longer than a few days after having sex with her. Maybe it's because I know Allyson as more than a woman I slept with, or it could be the guilt I feel for keeping this from Easton. I ignore the nagging feeling that the real reason is something deeper and drive home, ready to head to bed and wake up with a clearer mind.

@AllyinSpain: Hi…good and you?

I stare at her message, nothing spectacular, but she responded. Rubbing the sleep out of my eyes, I type back.

@CamSteeleIT: I'm good…great actually. Work's got me busy. I saw Easton and Faith were visiting you. That's great. I bet you had fun with them

Her response is almost immediate.

@AllyinSpain: It was a nice surprise and fun to show them around.

@CamSteeleIT: Happy to hear that. Just wanted to see how you were doing

@AllyinSpain: I'm good, you don't have to feel obligated to check in. Really, I'm good

@CamSteeleIT: I don't feel obligated, I really wanted to see how you were doin

@AllyinSpain: Oh ok… Thanks then

@CamSteeleIT: Anytime

@AllyinSpain: I shoud get back to work... Don't want someone walking in and accuse me of spending time on social

@AllyinSpain: oops... I meant should

@CamSteeleIT: I got you... Have a good day or rest of the day. Bye

@AllyinSpain: Bye

I stare at our conversation, as platonic as could be but also awkward as fuck if you really dig deep, knowing our history.

Getting up and ready for work, which really means make coffee and turn on my laptop, I check my emails to make sure there aren't any updates from my current clients and get to work. All the while, my conversation with Luke from last night ringing loud and clear.

If I do feel something more for Ally, then I should figure out what that is and what it means for me and us, if there even is an us. I mean, she lives in a different country for fuck's sake. I'm insane to think anything could come from it if I haven't even been in a relationship with someone local in years. I've dated, fucked, and wooed women, but I haven't had an actual girlfriend in years. What makes me think I can handle long-distance relationships?

I must be insane.

After hours of work, I stand and stretch my tense body and jump in the shower, so I can grab a quick bite to eat. I'm not really in the mood for leftovers or frozen pizza, and a walk outside would be nice to clear up the fog of adware, SEO, and bandwidth. I love what I do, but sometimes I need to take a

the Right kind of Wrong

step back before I start thinking as analytical as a computer does.

As I sit at a table in Meat Me, my favorite sub shop, I replay my conversation with Ally. Googling the time difference between Richmond and Madrid, I make a mental note of what she might be up to at seven in the evening and smirk to myself when I see the poll on her Instagram story asking people if she should have a beer or glass of wine. Forgoing the poll, I go straight into our chat, asking her straight up which one she went for, seeing as she posted the poll over an hour ago.

@AllyinSpain: <picture of wine glass>

@CamSteeleIT: Good choice although I'd go for the beer

@AllyinSpain: Typical guy

@CamSteeleIT: More than just a typical guy <wink emoji>

@AllyinSpain: <eye-roll emoji>

@CamSteeleIT: That's not a denial tho

@AllyinSpain: That's true but you're still annoying

@CamSteeleIT: Annoying but sexy *waggles eyebrows*

@AllyinSpain: LOL jerk

@CamSteeleIT: I think you're sexy too

@AllyinSpain: Camden…

@CamSteeleIT: Ally…

@CamSteeleIT: You're just gonna ignore me? I can see when you read a message

@AllyinSpain: Ugh! You annoy me from afar too

@CamSteeleIT: Can't help that you've been on my mind

I watch the typing bubbles appear and disappear, wondering if I pushed too far. I shift on my chair and take a bite of my sub while I wait for her to respond. This back and forth was fun until I'm on the receiving end of silence.

@AllyinSpain: What's your deal?

@CamSteeleIT: Blunt and straight to the point huh?

@AllyinSpain: I'm not one to be caught in games

@CamSteeleIT: No games, sweetheart

@AllyinSpain: Really? How many girls have you called sweetheart before?

Busted.

@CamSteeleIT: You're right. No games, Kiwi

@AllyinSpain: Kiwi? WTH?

@CamSteeleIT: Yeah cuz your eyes are as green as the inside of a kiwi

@AllyinSpain: …

@CamSteeleIT: So KIWI no games. You wanna know the truth?

the Right kind of Wrong

@CamSteeleIT: I really can't stop thinking about you. You're on my mind at all times and it's fucked up because you're Easton's little sister and he has no idea what we did

@AllyinSpain: First of all I'm not a kid. I'm a damn adult despite being his younger sister. Secondly he doesn't have to know. It was one night and that's it. No harm no foul

@CamSteeleIT: What if I don't want it to only be one night?

I hold my breath as I wait for her response, waiting for the message that will follow the bubbles that never appear after she's read it. Rejection doesn't taste so good when you're on the other end of it.

Chapter 8

Allyson

I stare at my Instagram feed, and my eyes flicker to the small paper airplane icon where my messages are. One week I've avoided Camden's message. He is insane. I've decided it. Who in their right mind thinks they want to go another round in sexyville when they live thousands of miles away from the other person? *Crazy*.

And Camden of all people? Puh-lease. As if he really hasn't already been with a few other women these last five weeks. Things would get messier than an unsupervised toddler with a rainbow of permanent markers in a white room if anything more happened. I'm sure the only reason it isn't messier than it already is is because Easton now lives in Everton, and Camden doesn't see him every day.

And yet, after all these thoughts, I still think about his unanswered message. It's best to leave some things to die in a social media abyss, and this is one of those things. The chances of me seeing Camden in the near future are slim. I'll be home for the holidays when the time comes, but my mom and I will fly out to Everton for most of my vacation time.

I'll be safe from the Camden charm. Who knows? Maybe by then, I'll have met someone, and Camden will be the distant memory of my first one-night-stand.

the Right kind of Wrong

A text message notification drops down on my screen, stealing my attention from my Instagram feed. Opening the message, I smile as I read Rubén's message. He's a co-worker and one of the people that has become a friend these last couple of years. He's a riot to hang out with, and every time I'm with him, I'm guaranteed to laugh until I pee a little.

Typing back quickly, practicing my Spanish as I do so, I let him know that I'll meet him at Nos, a bar near Plaza Mayor. I head to my room and get changed, swapping my sweats for a short, floral dress and sandals. Throwing my hair in a sleek ponytail, I grab my purse and lock up behind me, making the walk to the bar. My favorite thing about Spain is that you've got bars that serve drinks and tapas, and then you've got your club-type bars with music and drinks that have a more low-key vibe than a full-on club.

When I walk into Nos, I see Rubén, Vanesa, another co-worker, and Dawn, one of the girls that worked in our Richmond branch who also took the opportunity to work in Madrid. Rubén and Vanesa have been heaven-sent friends. Sometimes it's not so easy to make friends with the locals, and they've taken us under their wings, introduced us to their friends, and guided us when it comes to living in this city.

"Hey," I take a seat on the empty chair waiting for me.

"Sexy." Rubén's deep accent comes out as he waggles his eyebrows.

"It's just a dress," I tug at the hem noncommittally.

"And the hair is…" He snaps his fingers. "How do you say…sex kitten."

"What?" My eyes pop out of my head as I laugh. "No way!"

"You're looking for…" He trails off, but his dancing eyebrows give away exactly what he means, his heavy English accent adding to his charm.

I laugh and shake my head, Vanesa and Dawn looking at us with amused expressions.

"How about we get drinks, yeah?" I nod, picking up the cocktail menu, although I know I'll order a glass of wine. But what the hell? Maybe tonight is different. Maybe tonight I want to go a little wild and drink a martini or something. I scan the menu, seeing if anything calls my attention, and my eyes land on margaritas.

After we order and toast, I take a sip of the margarita, sighing as I close my eyes. This is much better than I anticipated, the perfect balance of tequila, sour, and sweet flavors.

"Tequila… A qué te pone?" Rubén's eyes sparkle, and I furrow my eyebrows.

"What?" I ask in confusion.

Vanessa laughs, holding her stomach. "Rubén," she scolds. "Ignore him. You know how he is."

"What does 'qué te pone' mean?" Dawn asks, her own curiosity getting the best of her.

"It means it gets you horny," Vanesa chuckles again.

"Rubén!" I squeak. "Margaritas do not do that to me."

"I don't know, but something is different about you." He points at me, squinting one eye as if that will give him a better view into my soul or something.

"Whatever," I shrug him off and take another sip, enjoying the cocktail while we wait for the few tapas we ordered to arrive.

the Right kind of Wrong

Music plays in the background, just loud enough to be heard but not enough to disrupt the flow of conversation. The white and black bar buzzes with people out on a Saturday night. Spain is a social country, and I learned that firsthand when I wandered alone to have coffee once after first moving and saw a ton of people at tables with friends having coffee together.

There's always an excuse to celebrate and get together, and gatherings aren't the short events I'm used to in the United States.

A lunch here can run as long as six hours, and even then, you move on to a bar for drinks since, by the time you leave, it's already time to have a glass of wine. It's fast-paced in the city and yet slow-living, where you can really enjoy the moment and the company. It's a fascinating mindset and way of living when you really think about it.

Rubén tells us about his recent failed date. The guy is as social as they come, but he's been in search of his happy ending since he was seventeen and came out to his family. He told me once that he assumed his parents knew he was gay, but it was about him having the courage to state it, take a step toward his true identity, and I admire him for that. Few people dare to show the world who they truly are without pretenses or covering up their vulnerabilities.

We continue to drink and eat, thoughts of Camden slipping further from my mind after each sip I take of my margarita, and each ridiculous comment Rubén makes. Leaning back on my chair, I look around and smile. I never imagined I'd live outside of the United States, but this has been one hell of an experience.

"Let's go," Vanesa calls over the music, now pumping louder as the bar transitions into a lounge. I stand and hold on to the chair to get my footing as the three margaritas I drank hit me at the same time, causing me to sway.

"Whoa…" Dawn loops her arm in mine. "Are you okay?" Her eyebrows pop on her forehead.

"Yeah," I nod. "Come on." Using her guidance, I follow Vanesa and Rubén to some bar I've never been to that's full to the brim with dancing bodies and deafening music. The dim lighting makes it hard to make out the people, or it could be the margaritas blurring my vision, but I do see Vanessa hug some people and Rubén dance in excitement.

After quick introductions, we're all dancing and singing. My inhibitions drop, and I sway to the music in time with the guy that's dancing behind me. I turn around with a lazy smile.

"Hola," he leans in and whispers his greeting. Despite the loud music, his one word sounds clear and deep in my ear. I look up at him and see shaggy hair, a stubbled jaw, and smiling eyes.

For all I know, he wants to have some fun between the sheets and leave before the sun rises, but what harm does dancing with him do? Besides, Noel's advice rings loud and clear over the overwhelming music and thumping beats, so I decide to let loose and have fun. Camden begone, and *hello* sexy Spaniard.

Taking my movements as a hint, his hands land on my hips, and he moves closer, grinding into me. I swallow my surprise and look down. There's one benefit of tight jeans — holy cobra pushing into me. Yeah, it's safe to say he plans to take this dance off the dance floor and straight into a bed. I'm sure he couldn't care less whose bed it is.

the Right kind of Wrong

When Dawn winks and hands me a beer, I gratefully take it to wash down the surprise of this guy's erection against me, and I realize I don't know his name.

Calling out loudly, I ask him.

"Sergio," he calls back. "Inglesa?" he asks if I'm British, and I shake my head.

"Americana," I correct him.

"Ahh…" he smiles, spinning me around, and I almost drop my beer in surprise.

That one spin does me in, and my hand flies to my mouth, hoping to keep down the contents in my stomach. Holding my finger up, I turn around and race to the bathroom, hoping it's in the direction I'm going and that there's an empty stall.

I must look like shit because the girl who is about to walk into a stall moves away and urges me in. Unashamed, I throw up with the door open until tears burn my eyes, and my throat is dry. Heaving one last time, I feel heat cover my neck and cheeks as I turn around to an audience staring at me with wide, concerned eyes.

Goodness, could I be any more of a mess right now?

This is a first for me, and I vow to make it the last time I puke in a bar with an audience because of too much alcohol. Rinsing my mouth and washing my hands, I slowly walk back to my friends, ready to tell them I'm heading home. Everything spins, and when the next wave of nausea hits, I want to be hugging my own toilet in PJs.

I wave off Rubén when he offers to walk me home, but he's stubborn and a good friend who ignores my dismissal and makes sure I get home safe.

fabiola francisco

After getting ready for bed and standing still in the bathroom in case I need to puke again, I lie in bed, watching the ceiling spin until I fall asleep.

Ugghhh... I turn on my bed, groaning as my dry tongue sticks to the roof of my mouth. My brain slams in my head, killing me with the pain. Lord, what in the world possessed me to drink so much last night? Let loose, my ass. I went drunk crazy. I should've known too much tequila would be a bad thing. I've always been a lightweight when it comes to it.

Turning onto my back, I squeeze my eyes shut as I replay the night before. Pieces of the puzzle coming together with missing spaces where all I see are black flashes. Unfortunately, my puking fiasco is not one of those lost memories.

Covering my face with my hands, I sit up slowly, my stomach churning. Liquor before beer, have no fear, is a damn myth. I bet that last beer I drank was the tipping point.

I grab my phone to check the time and groan again. I need greasy pizza and a Coke to cure this hangover. Thankfully, it's almost lunchtime, so it's acceptable to pig out on cheese pizza. I call in an order for delivery because there is no way my hungover self is walking out into the light of day so that the sun can shine the hangover on my face for everyone to read like some invisible ink revealing itself.

After ordering lunch, I jump in the shower and wash away last night, the alcohol in my blood still pumping as I sway and hold myself up on the shower wall. Thankfully, it seems like I released everything last night in the bathroom, and my stomach only complains a bit.

the Right kind of Wrong

That shower was a blessing. Combing my hair and dressing in cotton shorts and a t-shirt, I wait for my food to arrive. Plopping on the couch, I turn on the television, lowering the volume, and have my ibuprofen ready to swallow as soon as my pizza arrives.

Opening Instagram, message notifications catch my eye right away, sending my heart into my throat as I wonder if Camden got tired of my silence and is pushing for some kind of response.

I read his last message with confusion until I scroll up and freeze, heart-stopping nausea washes over me, and this time it's not because of the alcohol. Actually, I could totally blame the alcohol for this. When the hell did I send him a message last night? I can't remember doing that.

Oh, my goodness, I'm going to puke again. Checking the timestamp, I realize I was still at the first bar when I sent him this. *Foolish, traitorous margaritas!* I read what I wrote, trying to decipher my drunk texting.

> @AllyinSpain: I hte yip n thst stypd smie you thnk yoy csn tll me you wnna hve sex w me agin n grt awsy w it
>
> @CamSteeleIT: Sorry to disappoint but I'm not fluent in pig latin or whatever that is supposed to be
>
> @CAmSteeleIT: Although I do see the word sex so I take it you're thinking about my Steele of a cock
>
> @CamSteeleIt: Get it? lol
>
> @CamSteeleIT: They say when you're drunk the truth comes out <wink emoji>

fabiola francisco

I drop my head back on the couch and close my eyes, wondering if I wish this drunken message away it will miraculously disappear. I peek one eye open and still see it on the screen. This is worse than my hangover, and I haven't been hungover in a *long* time.

I take a deep breath and collect myself. I'm about to write back when my doorbell buzzes from downstairs, and I leap from the couch, thankful for the interruption. When the delivery guy makes it to my door, I pay him and thank him, grabbing a plate and cup on the way back to the living room. With the television in the background and my mouth full of cheesy, greasy goodness, I begin typing on my phone.

@AllyinSpain: I was drunk

@CamSteeleIT: It seems that you being drunk brings out the truth. The wedding, last night… I can't wait to see what comes next

@AllyinSpain: Nothing. No more damn drinking for me.

@CamSteeleIT: Sure… Then what excuse will you use to write to me?

@AllyinSpain: I should block you

@CamSteeleIT: If you feel you need to block me it's bc you're too tempted to send me a message. You should look into the real meaning behind that

I inhale deeply, calming myself before replying. He's driving me insane with his know-it-all attitude and self-confidence as if I've been pining over him.

the Right kind of Wrong

@AllyinSpain: What are you? Some psychologist now? Reading into hidden actions

@CamSteeleIT: So you admit I'm saying the truth

@AllyinSpain: Ugh! I hate you

@CamSteeleIT: You don't but you're thinking about my cock and hate that but def not me since I'm the owner of said cock

@AllyinSpain: Cocky

@CamSteeleIT: You see… You can't stop thinking about it

@AllyinSpain: Goodbye

@CamSteeleIT: Aw come on be a sport and have some fun

@AllyinSpain: If I were really thinkin about you I wouldn't have been with a guy last night

I throw that out there, a half fib. I was dancing with a guy, even if it ended right before I almost puked on him, but Camden doesn't need to know that. All he has to know is that I'm not thinking about him.

I smile to myself when he doesn't respond and continue eating my pizza, happier than a pig in mud.

Chapter 9

Camden

> @AllyinSpain: If I were really thinkin about you I wouldn't have been with a guy last night

I re-read Allyson's last message, grinding my teeth. What fucking guy was she with? She's not the kind of girl to sleep around.

Except she slept with you.

Pacing around my room, I run a hand through my hair. I meant it when I told her a week ago that I'd want more than one night with her. Sure, the situation isn't ideal, and she's not exactly the woman I should be pursuing, but damn it, I want her. I'd never paid much attention to her in this way since she's Easton's sister, but after having a taste of her, I know I'm going to need more to quench my craving.

Unsure if she's telling me the truth or not, I send back a reply with a smile, mentally giving myself a standing ovation for my smart-ass comment.

> @CamSteeleIT: If you were with a guy you wouldn't have sent me a message about sex

> @AllyinSpain: Camden... I don't know what you're doing or what you think you'll win out of this but there's no point. I live

the Right kind of Wrong

in Spain and even if I didn't I wouldn't sleep with you again. One night…that's all it was

@CamSteeleIT: One damn good night

Who knew Allyson Locke would wrap me around her little finger and hold on tight? I sure as hell didn't think so. Yet here I am, convincing her of giving me another chance, albeit by ruffling her feathers a bit when she's across a fucking ocean.

She's right, it's pointless in a sense, but I can't get her out of my mind. I don't want anyone else to warm my bed but her. I haven't even tried to sleep with another woman since I slept with her, and my hand is tired of pumping my own dick to the faded memory of Allyson beneath me with her hair sprawled out in a mess. She looked like sweet perfection on that bed, and I made damn sure to commit that to memory before I thrust into her hard and fast, giving us both what we were seeking.

When she doesn't reply again, I stand and go for a run, hoping that will calm my damn mind and insanity. I'm not sure how all this would play out if she still lived in Richmond, but I'd bet all of my money that we'd end up in bed again at least one more time.

Shaking all thoughts of Allyson from my head, I focus on the pavement beneath me as I run down the street and make a right, sweat trickling down my neck.

With each pounding of my heel on the ground, I tell myself to forget her. Until I almost believe that I could…

fabiola francisco

"Hey," I smile as Charlene, Easton and Allyson's mom, answers the door. After my run, I showered and grabbed some pastries from a shop she loves and decided to go visit her. Easton's parents became second parents to me when I met them in college, and I spent many evenings at their house, having dinner and doing laundry when we lived at the dorms.

When Easton's dad passed away a few years ago, I would visit Charlene whenever I could. After Easton moved, I went kind of lax on visiting her until Easton had to come from Everton to check up on her because she wasn't acting like herself. We discovered she was overwhelmed with grief and struggling to keep up with bills and responsibilities that Mr. Locke used to take care of.

I promised Easton I'd come to visit her whenever I could, even though he assured me it wasn't necessary. It's the least I can do for all the dinners they invited me to and for making me feel like family for over ten years.

"To what do I owe this pleasure?" Charlene smiles, opening the door to her apartment so I can walk in.

"I thought I'd drop by to see how you were doing and bring you some of your favorite pastries." I lift the pink box in my hand, drawing attention to it.

"You didn't have to." Her smile grows, and she pats my arm. Charlene is a professor at the University of Virginia, and a tough one at that. I once had her as a teacher, and she made sure to show zero preference because I was her son's best friend.

I follow her into the small living room, placing the box on the coffee table and taking a seat on the sofa.

"I'll make coffee." She walks into the kitchen, and I look around. Standing, I walk to a family photo I've seen hundreds

the Right kind of Wrong

of times, but this time I look at it with fresh eyes. Ally smiles wide and carefree, with one hand in the air. I chuckle as I find another picture from when she was younger, dressed in some nineties get-up.

"I always love to reminisce," Charlene startles me.

I turn around, putting my hands in my shorts pockets. "It's fun to remember the old times. How are you doing?" I walk back to the sofa and sit.

"I'll tell you what I told my son. I'm doing *great*," she emphasizes. "I don't need you to check up on me as if I were some helpless toddler."

"That's not why I came," I shake my head, sighing dramatically, which causes her to laugh. "I was out for a run and saw Bakeology, so I decided to buy you some and head over."

"Thank you." She places a tray with two coffee mugs, sugar, milk, and coffee. "How are you?" She looks at me intently. "You know... I could introduce you to a Teacher Assistant that started this semester. She'd be perfect for you," she gives me her devious smile.

Shaking my head, I lift my hands. "I'm okay the way I am, Char. I don't need anyone setting me up on dates." If she only knew the woman consuming my thoughts is her own daughter. I shrug that off and prepare my coffee.

"Your momma is going to want grandchildren soon."

"Sammy could give her some," I shrug, throwing my sister under the bus since she's not around to defend herself.

Charlene laughs, catching on to my game. "She'll want some from you. Your sister shouldn't be the solely responsible child to do so."

fabiola francisco

I chuckle and take a sip of coffee. I don't know what she puts in it, but her coffee is some of the best I've ever had. Since my parents lived further away in Virginia Beach, visiting Easton's family always gave me a sense of home. When my mom and Charlene first met, they hit it off and became fast friends. They still keep in touch, and I'm sure this conversation has come up more than once.

"Think about it. I'll be happy to introduce you to Rose if you want me to," she nods. I assume Rose is the TA she mentioned and smirk.

"I'll make sure to do so, but honestly, I'm good the way I am. How's work?" I switch topics.

I spend the afternoon with Charlene, talking and keeping her company for a while. She's felt lonely without her husband, and I make sure to pay my due since I'm close enough to drive over on the weekends.

Just when I thought I'd spend the rest of the day not thinking about Allyson, I come to the one place that's plagued with memories of her.

Charlene's phone rings, interrupting our conversation about the football season starting at the university. Smiling, she says, "It's Allyson. Let me answer quickly, or she'll worry something happened, call Easton terrified that I've fallen, and he'll send an army over to check on me," she jokes, but she's not far off from the truth.

"I should go," I move to stand, but she firmly motions for me to stay seated as she answers the phone.

"Hi, sweetie." Charlene holds the phone in front of her as Allyson's voice rings loud and clear.

"Hey, Mom, how are you?" I inhale her sweet voice.

the Right kind of Wrong

"I'm good. I'm here with Camden, who brought pastries from Bakeology." Charlene turns the phone to me, and I see Allyson on the screen. I smile and wave.

"Oh, hi…" Her green eyes widen, and I recall the nickname I gave her, my smile growing. Her hair is thrown in a messy bun, much like my sister does when she's home and doesn't feel like combing it through.

"I can call you back, Mom." Charlene turns the phone back to her.

"We can talk. Is everything okay?"

"Yeah, I was just calling to see how you were doing. Call me later, okay?" Allyson's voice is even, but her eyes were filled with curiosity when they looked at me.

"Okay," her mom agrees, and they hang up with goodbyes.

"She's doing so well over there, but I do miss her." Charlene smiles sadly, taking a bite of a cream-filled eclair.

"I bet it's difficult having her so far away."

"Yes, but she'll be home for the holidays, and that keeps me happy. Besides, technology is so advanced nowadays, it's almost as if she were here talking to me."

"That does help." I nod, picking up the conversation about the university's football team as time passes.

By the time I say goodbye to Charlene and get in my car, I have a notification from Allyson. Smiling like a fool, I open it and read it before responding.

@AllyinSpain: Why were you there?

@CamSteeleIT: Because I wanted to. I visit her whenever I can. Told Easton I would after everything that happened.

@AllyinSpain: Ok

@CamSteeleIT: She's proud of you

@AllyinSpain: Yea

@AllyinSpain: I'm gonna call her

I let her have time to talk to her mom. I'm no one to keep her from that, even if I selfishly want to continue my conversation with her. I turn up the music as I pull out of the parking lot in the apartment complex and drive back home.

I'm in deep water when it comes to Allyson, and I don't see how I can do anything but try to forget about her. She may be beautiful, smart, funny, and a bit of a mess, but she's also Easton's sister and lives in another country. The fact that she's Easton's sister alone should be enough for me to slam on the brakes of this thing we have going on, yet I find myself pulled to her like I've never felt before. Some kind of draw and it has to do with a lot more than her tight pussy.

Chapter 10

Allyson

My foot rests on the coffee table as I lean over my bent leg and paint my toes. The Spanish translation of *Pretty Woman* plays in the background as I continue to try to figure out why Camden was at my mom's house the other day, and more importantly, I can't get over the fact that it's a recurring thing.

After my dad passed away, it was hard to watch my mom live alone. Soon after, my job sent me to Spain, and Easton was researching the possibilities of moving to Everton—both encouraged by my mom. She always wants the best for us, but it doesn't mean it is easy being away from her. I worry; however, knowing that Camden checks in on her makes me feel…calmer.

I sigh and wipe a smudge of paint that landed on the side of my toe as I tried to paint the edge and look up at the television, not really interested in the movie. Lately, I'm not interested in much. I've been feeling weird, chalking it up to homesickness and my attempt at processing everything that's happened with Camden since that fateful night.

Our chats may seem playful or even annoying from my end, but there's a deeper reason he keeps writing, and I keep responding. A reason I'm not sure I want to explore. Now or ever. I thought I'd arrive back home after the wedding and be over sleeping with Camden in a week's time. Wham, bam, thank you ma'am style and move on. I'm still stuck on the bam part of that, and I don't see how I can move on if I'm obsessively thinking about him.

I switch feet, painting the toes on my right foot when my phone rings with an incoming video call. I answer Noel's call and lean the phone against a candle on the table so I can continue my pedicure.

"Hey," I look over at the screen and smile.

Noel squints her eyes. "Girl, you need to shave your legs. I can see your prickly hairs from here."

"Asshole, I shaved last night." I drop my leg from the table. I'll continue my pedicure after I hang up with her, so she won't go on and on about how a lady should always be prepared for the unexpected, AKA sex.

"What's wrong with you?" Her face gets closer to the screen as if that would give her a better view of my face.

"Nothing," I shrug.

"Are you staying in tonight?" Her eyebrows furrow.

"Yeah, I feel kinda blah. I don't know what it is. Besides, it's Thursday."

"You're grouchy..." She scrunches up her nose. "You've gone out during the week in the past. Maybe you should order pizza and some dessert and just pig out. That always helps."

"Yeah, it must be PMS, but my damn period won't show up already."

"Did you have sex recently and not tell me? You're holding out on me!" Noel's voice rings with amusement.

"No!" I answer automatically because that would usually be the case. Until it dawns on me...

the Right kind of Wrong

"Ohmygod, ohmygod, ohmygod, ohmygod!" I jump and start flapping my arms like a wild woman.

"What?" Noel interrupts my freak-out. "Wait... Did you?" Her eyes widen as big as saucers, and her mouth drops open. "You little skank. And you kept it a secret from me?" She slaps the table next to her laptop, her eyes bright.

"Shut up." I drop on my couch. "Oh. My. God." This can't be happening. I drop my face in my hands, leaning down on my elbows on the table.

"Hold on..." Noel's voice now rings with worry. "If you slept with someone, and now your period is late—"

"Stop talking," I cut her off. "It could just be a coincidence. It can't be... I-I can't be... Fuck," I groan.

It's impossible for me to be pregnant. We used protection, right? I squeeze my eyes shut and try to remember the foggy memories from a few weeks ago. Between the few drinks I had and the heady feel of his hands on my hips, I can't recall what we did in terms of condoms.

"Who's the father of your possible child?" She breaks up my thoughts.

When I lift my head to meet my best friend's eyes, I cringe. "Camden."

"Holy shit-balls on fire. Camden Steele?" I nod. "Your brother's going to kill you."

I cover my mouth with my hand, nodding as tears run down my cheeks, and my entire body trembles as I release a shaky breath. I check the time on my phone and notice most pharmacies are closed already, but there's always one that's open through the night for emergencies, and damn it, this is one big emergency.

"Ally?" Noel whispers, her voice small and concerned, so unlike her. "It'll be okay. Take a test before you have a panic attack over stubborn hormones. When I travel, it throws my period off, so it could be that."

"I'm over five weeks late. I was supposed to get it right after the wedding because I remember praying it wouldn't come while I was on the plane."

"Oh, yeah, no one wants to bleed out of their vajayjay while up in the air with those tiny and gross bathrooms."

"I gotta go," I leap to my feet, grabbing my phone as I search for my purse. Where the hell did I leave it? Not in my room, not on the couch. I check the hook by the front door and exhale a relieved breath when I see it. Slipping on flip-flops, I couldn't give three fucks if I'm dressed in pajamas.

"I'll call you back," I tell Noel and hang up, googling the pharmacy that's open tonight, and wave down a taxi as soon as it drives by. Slipping into the backseat, I tell him where I'm headed and incessantly tap my fingers against my legs. My heart is threatening to leave my body and flop around on the ground, mocking me, since I feel like, at any minute, my life could be over.

What if I am pregnant?

I've never had to consider that question. I'm always careful, and I've only ever had a handful of partners, all guys I was dating or in a relationship with until now. It very well could be what Noel said—traveling always throws my body off, too. I'm sure I'll get my period soon. If not, I have no idea where to even begin making decisions. Starting with, do I tell Camden? And how do I approach him?

I swallow back my tears as the taxi pulls up to the pharmacy. Asking him if he wouldn't mind waiting, I ring the

the Right kind of Wrong

doorbell on the outside of the door for the pharmacist to open for me. I'm all about precaution, especially in a big city like Madrid, but damn if I don't want to wait outside.

As soon as I'm inside, I ask for the pregnancy tests while the pharmacist purses his lips and gives me a once over. I roll my eyes exaggeratedly so he can see my reaction since apparently, we aren't hiding our honest opinions about the other, and demand the test. While he walks through a back door, I wander around the small space. I don't know why they don't have these things displayed, so someone can just grab them and pay.

Instead, he returns with three different tests, explaining the difference between each one. I peek out the glass door to make sure my cab driver is still out there and point to the test he said shows the earliest results. Paying him, I run back into the taxi and head home, where my fate awaits me.

My body is trembling, emotions haywire at all the different possibilities my life could go. My furiously beating heart pounds like an angry lion banging against his cage. I blink back tears with deep, even breaths.

Once I'm back in my apartment, I pace back and forth in front of the bathroom, the hallway feeling like it's closing in on me. Times like this, I wish I didn't live alone in a foreign country. A silent sob rips through me, and I lean against the wall, dropping to the floor to sit. One test is in my hand, but I can't draw up the courage to open the cap and pee on the taunting stick.

My fate will be sealed—two pink lines—or I'll continue living the same way I have, this just being a scare along the way.

I jolt when my phone rings. Answering it, Noel's worried face is front and center on my screen.

"What happened?" she rushes out. I hold up the test in silence. "What does it say?" Her eyebrows lift on her forehead.

"I haven't taken it yet. I'm scared," I admit. It'd be one thing if I knew for sure we used a condom, but honest to God, I can't remember.

"I'll talk you through it. Come on, I'm right here with you." I nod, standing, and my legs tremble as I walk into the bathroom.

"Don't look," I warn, which is silly. Noel's seen me pee hundreds of times.

"Puh-lease." She rolls her eyes playfully, making me crack a smile.

"Here goes nothing." I pull the cap from the test and place it where it needs to go as I tell myself to pee. After a few minutes, I'm covering the test again and washing my hands.

"Noel, what am I going to do if the test is positive?" I hiccup.

"Shhh… We'll cross that bridge when we get there. Is anything showing up?"

I bite down on my lips and shrug. I can't look. Maybe because deep down, I know the probability is high. All types of worries and concerns hit me at once, like Miley Cyrus coming at me on that wrecking ball. Scary as hell.

When I look down at the test, resting on the sink, my hand covers my mouth, and tears flow freely from my eyes. Noel doesn't need to ask what the result is by seeing my reaction, but she does anyway.

the Right kind of Wrong

"Pregnant," I whisper, holding the test up. I feel like I'm in a dream, floating around as if I'm witnessing someone else's life.

"Everything is going to be okay," Noel tries to console me, but I'm too far gone.

"What do I do?" I ask myself, but she replies.

"Make an appointment with your doctor tomorrow morning. You have a gynecologist there, right?" I nod. "Great, call the office and tell them you need to confirm a pregnancy. Whatever you need to do, so they will see you right away. After that, we'll make a plan. I'm here for you, babes." Noel offers a small smile, and how I wish she were here so I could cry on her shoulder.

I've got no one to lean on right now, and for the first time in two years, I feel truly lonely because I decided to take this job.

When I wake up, my body is tense, and my muscles are tight. I stretch my arms over my head and yawn as I come to. I feel out of it, dazed, as I fully wake. My throat is dry from crying myself to sleep last night, and the memory of a positive pregnancy test slaps me awake. Forget caffeine; the reality that you're carrying your brother's best friend's baby from a one-night-stand is enough to make your heart rate higher than a caffeine overdose. Not to mention that I've drank alcohol and haven't exactly been eating the best.

I climb out of bed and to the bathroom, where the box with the second pregnancy test mocks me. Grabbing it, I rip the wrapper open and take the second test. I once read that the most effective time to take a pregnancy test is first thing in the morning, so I might as well try. For all I know, last night's positive was a false alarm.

I jump in the shower while I wait for the test to do its thing, skipping washing my hair and trusting dry shampoo to do the job for today. It's Friday, so that's acceptable, right? Besides, if I really am going to have a kid, I better get used to dry shampoo, quick showers, and coffee on the go. Who am I kidding? I don't need a child in order for me to have my coffee on the go.

With a stammering heart, I step out of the shower and wrap myself in a towel before looking at the test on the sink. It's like a replay from last night—two pink lines, bright and obvious, confirming what I already knew. My hand instinctively goes to my stomach as my throat closes up, trapping every single emotion trying to find its way out.

I sit on the closed toilet seat lid, body quivering, and finally, the tears come in silent trails that burn down my face. This isn't a dream, something that would disappear if I fell asleep. It's damn real, and I have no idea what it means for my career, my living situation, and my life.

Reaching for my phone, I call the office and let them know I'm sick and not able to go into work today. There's no way I can focus on anything in the state I'm in. Needless to say, my face will have my emotions written all over it. I've never been great at hiding what I'm feeling, and this isn't the moment to start experimenting with acting skills.

Walking numbly to my room, I throw on another set of pajamas and climb back in bed. I'm not sure if I'll be able to stay working here if I'm pregnant. I'm sure the same rules as our American office are put into practice here, but for all I

the Right kind of Wrong

know, my boss will replace me with someone who could be around and won't need to take maternity leave. Though I don't think that's legal.

And how the hell do I tell Camden? Do I even tell him? Yes, of course, I do. What kind of question is that? I hug a pillow to my chest and bury my face in it, wishing away this crazy nightmare.

I should call my doctor, but I need some time to digest this before I can have her triple confirm it. I'm also worried about the drinks I've had, although I'm sure many women drink alcohol before they know they're pregnant and their kids are just fine.

My breath catches in my throat. My body trembles with my cries. How am I going to do this alone? The baby may have a biological father, but for all intents and purposes, I just became a single mom.

Chapter 11

Allyson

I'm not sure how I got so lucky, but my gynecologist had an opening this afternoon, and I rushed over for an examination.

Diagnosis: Definitely with child.

Cure: Birth it.

Dilemma: Tell the father he's going to be my baby daddy.

I sigh, walking down the warm streets of Madrid. With this weather, it doesn't feel like early September, and I'm counting down to the start of fall. I could use a climate change to go with the change my body's experiencing.

I swipe my cheek, removing any evidence of the emotions choking me, and wander around the city I've come to call home. My arms wrap around my midsection, and while I may not have a clue what I'm doing, the idea of getting rid of this baby paralyzes me. In this moment, everything in my life seems as if it's hanging upside down from a frail thread that threatens to unravel by breathing the wrong way.

I have no idea when I should tell my boss about this, or my family. *God,* Easton is not going to take this well. The mere idea of having to tell him closes up my throat and brings a fresh wave of tears to my eyes.

I don't know anyone who has been in this situation to seek advice from. I cross an old, stone bridge without a clue

the Right kind of Wrong

as to where I am or where I'm going, which is symbolic of my life. Stopping midway and placing my hands over the hard stone, I look down at the river before lifting my gaze and taking in the city before me. The palace sits in the nearby distance, tall and regal, the perfect personification of the royal family.

The cool stones beneath my hands do little to extinguish the heat within me. For the first time in my life, I'm terrified of the future. I'm scared of what will happen with my job, my living situation, and with Easton and Camden's friendship.

With one final deep breath, I turn back and walk in the same direction I came. When I see a café a few blocks down, I head inside and order a decaf coffee. The doctor gave me a list of dos and don'ts, and while coffee isn't a complete don't, she did say to limit my intake. I figured I could cut back and take care of myself since I didn't know I was pregnant and went a little wild with those margaritas the other night, which she assured me the baby was fine.

While I let the coffee cool, I check my phone. Noel sent me a message earlier, asking how I was doing, but I haven't written back. I need to figure out how to tell Camden since an Instagram message isn't exactly ideal. Unless I send him a baby daddy gif and let him come up with his own assumptions. *Avoidance at its finest, ladies and gentleman.*

I haven't heard from Camden since the day he was at my mom's house. It's not like I expect to receive messages from him every day. He has his own life to live, a job, friends. He isn't thinking about me, unlike me, who now has a permanent reminder of the night we spent together, *like it or not.*

I drink my coffee, failing at my attempt to come up with a way to talk to him since I can't exactly ask him to meet in person. My phone lights up with an incoming call from Noel, and I realize it's still in silent mode from my doctor's visit. Hitting the side button, I end the call and send her a quick message, letting her know I'll call her as soon as I get home. Then, I pay for my coffee, chug what's left, stand and leave, taking the subway back to my side of town.

Plopping on the sofa once I'm home, I call Noel back.

"You do not look good, boo," she says as soon as she answers the video call.

"Thanks, I'm with child," I deadpan, rubbing the worry lines on my forehead.

"About that... I need to add Berkeley to this call. I didn't tell her what happened, but I saw her earlier for coffee, and she noticed I was holding something back. When I told her it wasn't my story to tell, she demanded even more. I think she feels left out. You know, since I'm your number one best friend and all." Noel shrugs as if it were annoyingly obvious, and Berkeley should know this when in reality, they've known each other longer than I have known either one.

"I guess you should call her. If not, I'll probably hear from her soon."

"B-R-B," she calls out, and I chuckle. As the ringing comes from both sides, I chew on my bottom lip. Once I tell Berkeley, this will be true, and right now, I've been in denial, pretending this is a nightmare that will go away come sunrise.

"Hey," Berkeley finally answers, sitting on her couch and shifting as she angles the phone the way she wants it.

"Hi." My voice is quiet, strangled, as I hold back tears.

"What's wrong?" Berkeley's eyes stare into mine as if she were sitting in front of me. When I remain quiet, they shift to the other side of the screen, looking at Noel.

the Right kind of Wrong

I tell her about my pregnancy, sleeping with Camden, our back and forth. I let it all out everything that's happened these past weeks. By the time I finish, I'm crying, and my words are inaudible—a bunch of sounds that make no sense. My chest heaves as I try to hold it all in, but it's useless. Reality is sinking in, and I'm drowning in it.

"You should send him a balloon that says, 'Pop,' and then the message is inside," Noel interrupts my sobbing conversation, and I chuckle humorlessly. Leave it to her to try to make me smile.

"Or those people that show up at your door singing out a message. Make them dress like a baby," Berkeley adds. They're both ridiculous, but I listen as I wipe my face with the hem of my shirt.

"Order a cake from Bakeology, have them write, *Congrats! You're gonna be a dad!* and deliver it to him. Oh, you should keep it anonymous for a bit so he can freak out, wondering who he got pregnant." Noel's eyes gleam deviously.

"That's not helping, Noel." I groan, dropping my head back.

"Fine, keep the cake idea and send a note with your name." She rolls her eyes as if I ruined her best idea yet.

As much as I appreciate them bringing humor into this conversation, none of their ideas are actually great for the seriousness of this situation. They keep tossing ideas back and forth while I zone out, freaking out internally about how monumental this is. Me. A mother. Living in a different country where I'm not fully familiar with their laws and with a father who has never had any intention of settling down—not that I think we should become a couple simply because I'm pregnant with his child.

"Or... Are you listening to me?" Noel interrupts my thoughts. "I feel like I'm being ignored." She raises a perfectly arched eyebrow.

"Sorry."

She waves me off and continues speaking. "You could use the Instagram feature that allows you to call someone and actually talk to him."

"I didn't realize they had a call option."

"Well, it's a video chat, but that's even better! Makes it feel more personal and all that jazz."

Noel is a badass influencer and blogger, and it's thanks to her that I have my love for Instagram and always check out their new features right away. It's been a great way to journal my time here in Spain.

Now, her knowledge of all the social media trends is becoming my downfall. How the hell am I going to video call Camden like it's all good?

"That is the most mature suggestion," Berkeley agrees with a serious nod as if she wasn't the one who came up with the dancing and singing adult baby.

"I need to think." I rub my temples, closing my eyes to prevent another wave of tears from falling. I'm tired of crying, but I have a sense that from now on, it will be full-on cryfest.

"No matter how long you delay it, the truth will eventually come out. Your family will find out you're pregnant, and word will get back to Camden, who will suspect he's the father. Rip it off like a Band-Aid. The sooner this is off your chest, the more you can focus on having a healthy pregnancy. I'm sure the stress of this isn't good for the baby," Noel grows serious, sharing wise words that I know in my heart are all true, but the fear is gripping, and my stomach flips at the thought of

the Right kind of Wrong

looking at Camden and telling him the truth. And I'm not talking about the kind of stomach-flipping butterflies that bring me joy. This is more full-on nausea. Though, that could be a side effect of the pregnancy.

"Yeah," my voice squeaks.

"I know it's scary, but the sooner you talk to him, the better you'll feel." Berkeley smiles softly, and I wish they were both here so I could hug them. I can't even have a virtual happy hour with a glass of wine while we discuss this.

"Yeah, thanks, ladies," I say, defeated. My mom and brother need to know about this too, and I cringe at the idea of telling Easton what happened. I've never wanted to disappoint him, and I have a feeling this will make up for all the times I didn't disappoint him throughout the years.

"I'm gonna go," I tell the girls, feeling a whole new breakdown coming.

I hang up before they finish saying their goodbyes and lie on the sofa, clutching one of the throw pillows to my chest as I bury my face into it and release every ounce of pain, fear, and worry. I cry until my throat runs dry, and my eyes sting.

I can't tell Camden. There's no freaking way I can randomly video call him and be like, *Hey, I'm pregnant, and you're the dad, by the way.* Yeah, not gonna happen.

I sink deeper into the sofa and just stare at the wall, clearing my mind as much as possible. I'm so overwhelmed, I don't even know where to begin making a plan. I'll definitely wait until I'm through the first trimester to say anything at work, so I guess that's a start at a plan.

However, I don't think I can wait until Christmas break to show up at my mom's doorstep five months pregnant. Not exactly the best pregnancy announcement for your family, and

I highly doubt I could use the excuse that I didn't know I was pregnant like those women on that reality show.

I reach for my phone on the coffee table and unlock it, opening my Instagram account. No messages are waiting for me. I haven't heard from Camden in a few days. A few *long* days if I'm being honest with myself. I was getting used to our back and forth banter.

I finally spot the video camera icon that allows calls, my finger hovering over it before I close out the app and throw my phone down by my feet. I'll worry about it tomorrow. Today is for me to digest this news and wallow. I wish I had dark chocolate brownies with chewy centers to binge eat. The doctor didn't say anything about not having sugar, so I'll be making double fudge brownies tomorrow. Maybe I'll get drunk enough off chocolate to build the courage to talk to Camden. I'm sure tomorrow everything will seem more hopeful. It has to.

Chapter 12

Allyson

No matter how many hours pass watching reruns of Gossip Girl, it doesn't erase what I have to do. I woke up this morning, made tea, and had breakfast, all the while giving myself a pep-talk to woman up and tell Camden that I'm pregnant. Just the mere thought of it made me puke said tea and breakfast, and my heart race like a wild stallion feeling attacked. Of course, the throwing up could've been morning sickness, but it's easier to blame my nerves.

Sitting tall on the couch, I grab my phone off my lap and take a few deep breaths. No matter how scary it is, I need to tell him. He has a right to know. And like Berkeley said, once I tell him, I'll feel like a weight's been lifted. Telling my family is a whole different story that I'll get to once I've talked to Camden. He should be the first to know.

I stare at the video camera outline in the chat, my finger trembling as I press on it. I stare at it with wide eyes and hang up immediately. I can't tell him like this. I run a hand through my knotted hair, shaking my fingers in between the strands.

My fingers begin typing as I chicken out, but a written message is still better than not telling him at all, right?

> @AllyinSpain: Hey…what's up? Listen I need to talk to you about something

I focus on my breathing while I wait for him to respond, curious if he's aware of his phone or not. When the word, *Seen*, shows under my message, my breathing becomes erratic, and tears sting my eyes. This is it.

> @CamSteeleIT: What's going on? Did u just call me?

> @AllyinSpain: Ignore that. Okay, so...I don't know hwo to say this but I'm pregnant

I hit send without re-reading or thinking twice because I know I'll delete it and completely chicken out. I groan when I spot the typo but figure it's acceptable considering the bomb I just dropped on him.

I wait for Camden to reply, seeing as he read the message, but instead of typing bubbles, I get silence on the receiving end. My stomach drops, and hot tears roll down my face. I wasn't expecting a ton of exclamations and happiness, but I was expecting a response, anything that would make this less heavy, less scary and lonely. Tying my hair in a knot, I sink into the couch and drop my head back, closing my eyes.

I trap the tears, but some manage to escape from between my lashes. Camden isn't my happily ever after, but the silly girl in me was hoping I'd have the father to help ease the fear and worry that are twisting my stomach like a tight-rung towel.

When I continue to receive silence from Camden, I get up to work on the brownies I planned on making today. Today's secret ingredient—salty tears.

I can't believe he didn't respond at all. I slam the spatula into the bottom of the bowl and furiously mix the ingredients as my frustration increases. He could've at least acknowledged it, said something like, *Hey, good for you, but I'm not taking care of*

the Right kind of Wrong

it. Anything would've been better than ghosting me. I'm here, scared shitless and alone, and he's got the balls to ignore me. Typical Camden, never taking responsibility for his damn actions so he can continue to live his carefree life.

After I've placed the brownies in the oven, I pace around the kitchen. When my legs give out, and my anger turns into sadness, I sink onto the floor, hugging my legs and burying my head between the nook of my knees and thighs. In this moment, it all crashes down on me, and I sob into my pajama pants, soaking them.

Every bit of denial I had is stripped from me, and I'm left with the cruel reality that I'm going to be a single mom. But I can't abort. I refuse to. Maybe I can look into adoption, give a couple that's been hoping for a baby their answered prayer. I could be the light in their life. The only thing I'm unsure about is if I'll be willing to let the baby go after having him or her growing inside of me for nine months.

I rub a hand over my stomach, sucking in a breath as I attempt to stop the tears. My chest trembles as I bite my bottom lip, inhaling the sweet chocolate scent that wafts through the kitchen. It calms me just enough to stand and check on the brownies before grabbing my phone and video calling my mom.

"Hi, sweetie." As soon as I hear my mom's voice, my lips tremble, and my face contorts as I begin crying. "What's wrong?" My mom's worried voice hits me in the chest, and I shake my head, covering my mouth with my hand as tears fill my eyes.

"Allyson, talk to me." I see my mom lean forward, her face closer to the screen.

"Mom…" I cry out. "I-I-I'm pregnant." I suck in a breath, hiding my face with my hands. I can't stand to see the shock on her face, so I rather hide.

"What?" my mom whispers. "Allyson, look at me." I peek up at her, my palms wet with tears. "Tell me what's going on." Her soft voice calms me enough to take a deep breath.

"I'm so sorry, Mom. I didn't mean for this to happen." I shake my head, feeling as if I'm five again after I broke her favorite vase full of flowers because I took a corner too sharply.

"Don't apologize. Start from the beginning." She talks to me slowly, patience oozing from her, and I wish she were here or me there. I wish we were having this conversation in person instead of calling her in a bout of sorrow and spilling this news like this.

I tell her what happened at the wedding, as embarrassing as it is to tell my mom I had sex. By the time I get to the part about Camden's silence, her eyes are filled with tears. I remove the brownies from the oven as I watch a mixture of emotions flicker through her face, her salt and pepper hair pulled back in a bun giving me a clear view of them.

"Camden is a good person, and he'll do right by you." I open my mouth to argue, but she keeps talking. "That doesn't always mean an engagement, but I'm sure he'll help with the baby."

"I always thought when I got pregnant, I would be married, in love, and ready for it." I shake my head, tucking my lower lip between my teeth.

"You can still have that in life. This one situation doesn't mean your life is ruined. It's a blessing. Look at it that way.

the Right kind of Wrong

And heck, you're gonna make me a grandma," my mom's voice wavers. Then, she chuckles to herself.

"What's so funny?" I wipe my cheeks with the back of my hands.

"I was just telling Camden the other day that he should consider settling down. Oh, the irony of life." She shakes her head as if this were the most amusing thing in the entire world.

Once I get her to focus again, I tell her all my worries and how I have no idea what will happen with my job. Then, I mention that I don't know how to tell Easton, nor do I want to ruin his friendship with Camden because of this.

Although my mom assures me everything will work out as it should, and my brother will not be upset, I can't help but feel angry butterflies in my stomach attempting to break through and cause havoc. I'm not as confident as she is.

It was a quiet weekend after my meltdown, my talk with my mom, and getting over the fact that Camden never replied to my message. Instead of quiet, it was actually a rough weekend, but quiet sounds better, more fulfilling. I did, however, have to dodge text messages from Rubén and Dawn, asking why I was staying in on a Saturday night.

If they only knew.

I want to keep this to myself, especially with co-workers, until I have a solid grasp on what's going on and move through the early weeks of this pregnancy. That means I'll have to play the sick or tired card a few times to avoid going out and being asked why I'm not drinking. I can only fool my friends for so long.

fabiola francisco

Speaking of, Dawn peeks into my office as I'm settling in. "Hey, how are you feeling?" She smiles genuinely.

"Better, thanks." I called in sick on Friday with no details of what exactly I was feeling. Although my pale face and sour expression are enough to prove I feel ill.

"I'm happy to hear that. Have a good day." I sigh when she leaves my office. My head drops onto my hands. It's going to be a long day.

The best way to make the hours pass is work, so I check on what I missed or left pending for Friday and start catching up on what needs to be done first. Thankfully, that keeps my mind busy as the morning passes in between paperwork, curriculums I've received, meeting with employees, and a call with my boss in Richmond. Before I know it, it's time to head home for lunch, and I'm looking forward to getting some fresh air as I walk home.

Madrid has shifted from crowded tourists to a routine as kids go back to school. I see different children dressed in their uniforms, talking a mile a minute to their mothers as they also head home for lunch. A pang hits me in the pit of my stomach as I watch them, wondering if I'll raise my own child here or in the States.

As I approach my apartment building, I squint my eyes and then shake my head to remove the tricks my mind is playing. Ever since I got back from Everton, I've been seeing doubles—men who look like Camden and remind me of him. It's annoying as hell, more so today when I just want to forget about him and move on.

The man I thought was Camden stands as I reach my door, smiling sheepishly. My eyebrows furrow, blinking rapidly.

the Right kind of Wrong

"Hey."

My heart jumps to my throat, pulsing against the base of it like a techno beat. This is the last thing I expected when I got home. He looks tired, his eyes rimmed in red, and his hair sticking up all over the place from running his hand through it. His worn jeans have a relaxed fit, and I'm so damn happy to see a guy in jeans that are not skintight.

"What are you doing here?" So much for my mind playing tricks on me. No confusion here; Camden is standing outside my apartment building with a small suitcase. I cross my arms so he doesn't notice that they are trembling.

"Can we talk?" He points to the door.

I'm so mad at him that I want to send him back home and never speak to him again, but I know that's not the right thing to do. We do need to talk because, like it or not, I'll have a tie to Camden forever. Even if he decides he wants nothing to do with this baby, every time I look at him or her, I'll remember Camden.

"Yeah." I unlock the building door and walk in, holding the door open. Camden walks in behind me, both of us waiting for the elevator in silence.

I fidget with my keys as it dings open and step inside, every drop of nerves hitting me at once until I'm fighting against them in a losing battle. As if I were swimming upstream against a violent current.

The entire ride up to the fourth floor is filled with more silence, only amping up my anxiety. I can't even think about what he's going to say, but I'll let him speak first. I already told him what I needed to, but I won't force him to play Dad if that's not what he wants. I'm not looking for someone to pity me. If he wants to be in this baby's life, we'll make it work.

"The place is a mess, and I'm not just saying that to fish for compliments about how non-messy it is. You won't walk into a spotless apartment, especially after this weekend." I open the door and walk in, allowing Camden to enter behind me. He places his small suitcase by the entrance and sticks his hands in his pockets.

He must catch me eyeing his bag because he says, "Don't worry, I booked a hotel."

I swallow thickly and nod. "Good, because I only have one bedroom, and I'm not giving up my bed," I shrug.

"I would never ask that. Jesus…" He mumbles the last part as he runs a hand through his hair.

"So, what can I do for you?" I cross my arms over my chest and arch an eyebrow. Camden gives me a dubious stare, something mixed with insanity, too, as he furrows his eyebrows.

"Uh… You kinda dropped a bomb on me, and I wanted to talk in person." I can't believe he's here.

"And you dropped a bomb in me," I grit out, pointing to my stomach.

Camden snorts, trying to hold back his laughter and failing, which only causes me to glare harder. "Sorry, Kiwi, but that's kinda funny. I guess my sperm is uber-fast and determined."

"Camden!" I rake my hands through my hair and turn around, blinking to dry up my tears.

"Hey," his voice is soft, and I tense upon feeling his hand on my shoulder. "I was just joking, trying to lighten the mood a bit. Trust me, I'm as scared as you are."

I shake my head and turn around. "No, don't come at me with that. You aren't the one carrying this baby. You aren't the one living in a foreign country, questioning how the hell you're going to overcome this. You're the one that gets to choose to walk away and wipe your hands from this…this…this thing," I'm at a loss for words as my emotions spike.

"I flew over here to talk, to work this out. I'm not going to leave you alone and abandon you to deal with this." His jaw ticks.

"Fine," I surrender because he's right. He flew all the way over here, and he doesn't deserve my attitude of doubts.

"Are you hungry? Let's go eat since I know you have to get back to work, and we can talk. We can meet once you're done to discuss more if you want to.

"Wait… How did you find out where I live?" My eyebrows pull together as it dawns on me that I never told him.

He looks at me out of the corner of his eye with a lifted brow. "I'm a computer whiz. I know how to hack into systems and get the info I want."

"You hacked a computer to get my address? That's creepy, Camden." I cross my arms. Goodness, this is the father of my child.

"What you call creepy, I call efficient." He gives me a boyish smile, and my tension begins to melt away as I laugh. I hold my middle, manic cackles taking over at what my life has become.

"Uhh… Are you okay?" Camden's wide eyes stare at me, which causes me to laugh harder. I nod before throwing my head back, tears prickling the edges of my eyes.

"Oh my God…" I try to catch my breath. "Be right back!" I race to the bathroom before I pee my pants, still laughing as I sit on the toilet.

Camden flew all the way from Richmond after ignoring my message, so we could talk in person. Then, he hacks a system to get my address instead of being a rational adult and telling me he's coming and wants to talk. This poor kid is in trouble with parents like us.

My hand lands on my stomach, my giggles turning into cries that clutch my stomach. I swallow them back, but it's no use. My vision clouds as I stand in front of the sink to wash my hands. I look at my disheveled reflection, which only makes me cry more. I try to control my emotions and wash my face. I guess mood swings are very real in pregnancy.

When I walk back to the living room, Camden is looking around the space. Turning around, his face instantly scrunches up, worry lines forming around his eyes and forehead.

"What happened?" He strides toward me.

"Nothing." I shake my head. "This is just a ridiculous situation."

"Were you crying?"

"Mood swings," I shrug as if it's no big deal.

"Ally…" He reaches for me, wrapping his arms around me in the most comforting hug I've ever experienced. "We're gonna be okay," he promises. I nod against his chest, finally wrapping my arms around his waist.

When his fingers comb the long strands of hair that cascade down my back, I sink into him, grasping as much of the comfort as I can. For the first time in days, I feel relaxed. And if I'm being honest, it's the first time in weeks. Sleeping

the Right kind of Wrong

with Camden not only left a physical reminder but an emotional impact. I haven't been myself ever since.

"Let's eat." He gives me one more squeeze before I step back and nod. "There's a deli around the corner."

"Perfect. Can I leave my bag here until we finish? I need to check into my hotel, but I came here first, so I wouldn't miss your lunch break."

"I'm not even going to ask how you got a hold of my schedule." I shake my head, grabbing my purse, and heading out of my apartment.

"That was easy. Your company website has it listed."

"Well, that does bring down your stalker status by half a point," I deadpan, which causes him to laugh.

Chapter 13

Camden

I'm pregnant. Those words will forever stay in my mind. When I saw the notification for Allyson's message a few days ago, I remember grinning to myself, thinking she'd contacted me instead of the other way around. I gave her space and stopped writing, not wanting to come off like a douche by continuing to bring up the night we spent together.

The last thing I expected was for that night to change everything in our lives.

I sat and stared at the message for well over thirty minutes. I couldn't process it or understand until it hit me—caught up in the moment, we never used a condom. Then, I did the one thing I could think of and book a flight over here to talk in person. After an overnight flight with two layovers, I'm exhausted, but seeing Allyson in the flesh after all these weeks thinking about her is worth it.

She looks beautiful, even with bags under her eyes and fear written all over her face. Never in my wildest dreams did I think life would take the two of us to this moment or that I'd one day crave her more than I do my evening scotch. But I do.

"This way," Ally finally speaks as we walk toward the deli she mentioned. I open the door for her, allowing her to walk

the Right kind of Wrong

in before me. Her sweet perfume hits me, and I inhale like a starving man. Forget the hunger in my stomach; around Allyson, I've got a hunger for things I've never wanted in my life.

"What do you recommend?" I ask, unsure what half of the ingredients are on the overhead board.

"I've got it." She finally gives me a smile, albeit a weak one but a smile nonetheless.

"I'm in your hands." I rock back on my heels, placing my hands in my pocket as I smile.

Her chest rises and falls with each deep breath she takes until it's our turn to order. I'm impressed by her Spanish, lifting my eyebrows as she is in total control of the conversation with the attendant at the counter.

Once our food is ready, I grab the tray and follow her to an empty table. The place is full of people waiting in line to order while others sit at tables, engaged in conversations—such a change from back home. Since I got off the plane, I've been noticing the differences between both countries.

"I have to be back at work at four, although you probably already knew that." Allyson takes a sip of water before unwrapping her sandwich, which is made with French bread, and instead of cold cuts, it has grilled chicken.

"Yeah," I nod. "So… Anyway," I pause, trying to collect my thoughts.

"Honestly, Camden, you don't have to take on this responsibility. Don't feel like you need to step into a Dad role just because I'm pregnant. I didn't tell you because I expected something from you, but I did think you had a right to know, even when I'd rather have kept this to myself." She leans forward on her elbows, her face serious as her eyes stare into mine to emphasize her point.

"I'm not going to propose just because you're pregnant, but I do want to be a part of this. That kid's mine, too." I don't back down. If I flew all the way over here, it's to tell her I plan to be in this child's life. I know that jumping into a marriage just because of a baby isn't exactly a solution, but I'm going to be there for Allyson and this kid. If it means spending more time with her, then lucky me.

Allyson mutely blinks a few times. She finally nods and begins eating her lunch. I've got about an hour and fifteen minutes before she has to be at work, and I refuse for them to be silent awkward moments.

"How are you feeling?" I ask right before I take a bite of my own sandwich. The chicken is juicy and perfectly seasoned and covered in melted cheese. "This is really good, by the way." Almost as good as the subs I love from Meat Me in Richmond.

"I love this place." She wipes her mouth with a napkin. "I'm okay. I haven't one-hundred-percent processed it yet."

"I get that," I nod. "I mean, I'm not in your shoes, but it's kinda hard to believe."

"Yeah," Allyson sighs. "I'll be okay. I should mention, though, that my mom knows."

My eyes widen, and my stomach falls into a dark pit. "Huh?" My eyebrows lift as Allyson looks at me with narrowed eyes.

"You're panicking," she points out.

"I'm not." I tug the collar on my t-shirt, taking a deep breath.

"Uh, huh." She nods, her lips pinched.

the Right kind of Wrong

"What did she say?" I hold my breath while I wait for her response. The last thing I want is for Charlene to hate me.

"She said everything would work out." Allyson's lips press together.

There's so much I want to say, and nothing is coming out. We sit in silence for a few minutes, eating our food. This is a mess because of my relationship with her family, and I know Easton is going to kick my ass when he finds out. But I made my choice, and now I have to deal with the consequences.

When I can't take the awkward tension that's settled over the table, I clear my throat and say, "Have you gone to the doctor?"

"Yeah, on Friday. I wanted to make sure the pregnancy tests weren't damaged and giving me false positives. Wishful thinking at the moment, but I'm pregnant. Everything looks okay."

"Do you resent me?" The question spits out of my mouth faster than I can catch it, but hearing her say it was wishful thinking she wasn't pregnant made me think she might. It isn't ideal, I get that, but does she hate me because of this?

Allyson shakes her head. "If I resented you, then I'd have to resent myself. We both did this, so I'm not pointing the finger at you and playing innocent. We made a choice, and well," she rubs her stomach, "we got an unexpected surprise." Her eyebrows rise and fall in a quick motion.

"I won't have an abortion, even if you ask me to. I can't do it." Allyson shakes her head sadly, and my heart goes into overdrive.

"I'd never ask that. If I didn't want to be in the baby's life, I'd tell you and move on. I wouldn't force you to make a choice that you don't want."

fabiola francisco

She's talking as if she doesn't know me at all. Although, I guess when it comes to relationships and women, she doesn't know me and is probably using her judgment of what she thinks my bachelor life is like to judge this situation and my reaction.

"I did think about adoption and giving a family who's always wanted a child their happy ending."

"What?" I jump in, more forceful than I mean to. Allyson's eyes bug out as she leans back on her chair.

"Sorry, sorry." I settle down. "Here's the thing, I want this baby. I'll help you. I can't imagine knowing a child of mine is being raised by another family when I'm capable of raising him."

"Or her," Allyson interrupts me.

"Or her," I echo. "What I'm saying is that yes, this is totally out of my element, but knowing I have the means to raise this baby and then giving that up isn't what I envisioned."

"So, you're saying that you really do want to be a part of this?" Her chin tilts toward her chest, and she looks at me with raised eyebrows.

"Yes, that's what I said earlier." I lean forward, placing my elbows on the table. "I'm here for this." I reach for her hand and squeeze.

Allyson's gaze falls to our hands and then back to my eyes, her face serious and shoulders tense. I've been wanting to touch her again. Teasing her over messages is fun, but it's not what I want since we woke up on the same bed together.

"How do we do that? I live here, and you live in Richmond." I've tossed that question in my mind over a hundred times.

"We'll figure it out. I promise." I nod with a small smile.

the Right kind of Wrong

Allyson releases a deep breath and her eyes water. I give her hand one more squeeze in an attempt to comfort her.

"We should get going," Allyson says softly, and I hate seeing the sadness in her eyes.

Nodding, I grab our garbage and throw it away before following her out of the deli, my hand in the small of her back.

As we make our way back to her apartment so I can grab my suitcase, I ask, "Can we get together tonight when you're done with work?"

"Yeah, sure. I guess we still have a lot to talk about. What hotel are you staying in?"

"It's called Hotel Real. It was the closest I could find to here."

Allyson giggles at my response, and I furrow my eyebrows as I wait for her to tell me what's so damn funny.

"Sorry," she says, shaking her head. "It's Re-al," she corrects my pronunciation of the hotel, saying it in Spanish instead of real in English as in this is a real shit-show. "It means royal."

"Well, it's a good thing I brought my Spanish-English dictionary with me."

"Did you really?" Her nose scrunches up.

"Yup." I open one of the compartments on the outside of my bag and pull out my dictionary. Allyson laughs again, and I don't give three shits that she's laughing at me so long as I can see the light around her green eyes return.

"This will help me navigate these streets and not look like a complete ass," I defend.

"And paging through a dictionary makes you look as if you know what you're doing?" She quirks an eyebrow and gives me a smart-ass smile. Fuck, in this moment, I want to try that baby-making skill again. She's already pregnant, so why the hell not?

"Also, I'd expect a tech whiz to use technology for translations, not a physical dictionary," she giggles.

Taking a step toward her, I hold up my dictionary. "This is how the cool kids do it. Besides, I'm going to need a crash course in Spanish if I'm going to be around. Unless you want to give me some one-on-one courses." I lower my head, whispering the last part. Allyson gasps, and her full lips part. Her silence and frantic, wide eyes telling me she isn't as immune to me as she'd like me to believe.

"I need to leave." Her voice is soft.

Stepping back, I nod and grab my bag. "I'll come by when you're home." When I lean in to kiss her cheek, she freezes. It takes everything in me not to wrap her in my arms and hold her, keep her safe and calm. As much as I want to, I also don't want to make her uncomfortable.

But if there's one thing I'm certain about, it's that this baby is mine, and so is she... I just need to make her see that.

Chapter 14

Camden

After a much-needed shower, I grab my handy dictionary, despite how much Allyson laughed at it, and head out of my hotel. My room is spacious enough for me, and the entire hotel has a modern feel that caught me by surprise since the exterior seems as if it's from another century, and if I knew anything about art history or architecture, I could probably name the time period. Regardless, it was a contrast to the interior and a nice surprise.

I walk around the city with no real direction. I didn't exactly come here with the idea of being a tourist, but I can't stay stuck in that hotel until Allyson finishes work. So many things have been crossing through my mind these last few days. The first one is how we're going to co-parent when we live in different countries.

I wasn't joking when I told Allyson I wanted more than one night, and now it seems as if in some capacity, we'll have a lifetime. As much as the idea of something like this would have made me run in the opposite direction in the past, this situation isn't as scary as I thought. One look at Allyson and I want to protect her. This isn't about me; it's about something greater. Something I never put much thought into.

fabiola francisco

I'm out of my element and traveling into unknown territory. Bachelorhood? I've got that down pat. Relationships? Not so much. Parenthood? I don't have a fucking clue. But hell, I've never been afraid of a challenge, and there's no time like the present to grab the bull by the horns and ride it out.

I look up at the buildings I walk by, cars and buses buzzing by as locals move around me in a hurry. I chuckle to myself when I walk by a Dunkin' Donuts and continue going until I come across a terrace full of people.

I take a seat and order a beer. While I wait for my drink, I open the dictionary and look up random words in an attempt to give myself a crash-course in Spanish, which I know is a flawed plan. I thank the waiter when he brings my beer and pay him on the spot.

With a refreshing sip of my beer, I lean back in my chair, watching people walk by. My mind wanders to Allyson and what her life is like here. I only get a glimpse based on what she posts on social media, but I can't help but imagine her living the day-to-day here. Grocery shopping, lounging in her apartment, taking the subway.

I wouldn't ask her to leave her job to move back to the US because we're having a baby together. We're going to need a plan. One where I'll visit every chance I get since I can work from anywhere, and maybe have Allyson fly home during the holidays. So many scenarios run through my mind—missing milestones, the child not recognizing me, not being present if something happens, not reading him or her bedtime stories.

I've been turned inside out with this news, and all I can think about lately is being a father, of things I'd want to do with the kid, ways to protect him or her, what I'd want to

the Right kind of Wrong

teach as the baby grows. I never thought about things like this before. Now, I can't get it out of my mind. It's non-stop.

When I finish my beer, I stand and continue walking, getting a feel for the city, and stopping at any place that calls my attention. When I'm tired of walking, I head back to my hotel room and do some work in hopes that the last hour before Allyson gets out of work goes by faster than these last two hours have.

I take the elevator up to Allyson's apartment after she confirmed she was home. My heart is racing, although I'm usually calm and confident. This is different, and I know we're going to have to tell Easton soon. He's going to kick my ass, but I'll be lucky if he stops at that instead of completely writing me off.

Inhaling deeply, I run a hand through my damp hair and knock on the door.

"Hey," Allyson opens right away.

"Hey." I smile as I walk in, closing the door behind her.

When I told her the hotel recommended a restaurant for dinner, she got super excited, telling me she loves the place. A ton of exclamations marks followed her response. But right now, seeing her in tight jeans and a low-cut shirt, all I want to do is walk her back to her room and test the rumor about pregnancy making women crave more sex.

"You're going to love La Finca. They've got fresh food, all locally grown and raised." Allyson is talking, but I've been staring at her instead of paying attention.

"Camden?" She lifts her eyebrows. "Are you ready?"

That's when I notice she has her purse flung over her shoulder and keys in her hand.

"Oh, yeah, sorry." I open the door and lead her out of her apartment, waiting while she locks up.

"How was your afternoon?" I ask, focusing on our conversation.

"Good," Ally smiles. The worried woman I came face-to-face with earlier is gone, and the woman I've always known is back. God, she's gorgeous. "How about you? Did you look around the city?"

"I walked a bit, had a beer on a terrace, and then went to the hotel to do some work."

"As long as you don't hack any more of my private information," she jabs, and I chuckle. I much prefer her like this—easy-going and funny. I know our situation is awkward, having slept together when I've known her since she was a teen, and now the pregnancy, but there's no reason we can't be ourselves while navigating all of this.

"I promise," I place a hand over my heart. Allyson rolls her eyes, the hint of a smile tipping her lips up.

"How long are you here for?" She looks at me out of the corner of her eye.

"I got an open-ended ticket."

"What? Really?" She turns to me, her eyebrows pinched together, causing her nose to scrunch up in the cutest way.

I tap my finger on her nose. "Yup. We've got a lot to discuss, and I'd like to meet the doctor if that's okay."

"Oh, yeah, of course." Allyson scratches her forehead as the lines between her brows deepen.

the Right kind of Wrong

I stop walking and turn to her. "I mean it when I say I'm all in for this. I don't want you to feel like you're doing this alone. I've even been thinking about names," I smile wide.

"You have?" Her voice shakes.

"Yup. I've got options for a boy and girl, although I've got a feeling I'm going to have a football player."

Her face turns to stone, as if the realization of everything hits her at once. "I haven't even begun to think about any of that. I haven't even wondered what gender it is. I've been so caught up in my worries and fear of having to tell you, my mom, and my brother, that I feel as if this is still a dream. Names?" She shakes her head, turning and walking forward again but slower this time.

I jog up the few steps to reach her and place my hands on her shoulders to stop her, turning her to face me. "Hey, you've got a lot on your plate right now. I'm not the one growing a child inside of me. You don't have to have it all done at once. We'll go little by little."

"You're really going to help me?" She looks up at me through her long lashes, her stunning green eyes pleading for support as they mist over.

I pull Allyson in for a hug, burying my face in her hair, taking in every sweetness she'll give me. "You aren't alone in this, Kiwi." When her arms wrap around my body, and I hear soft sniffles, I vow to make this as easy for her as possible.

"Thank you," her strangled voice cuts through me.

"Don't thank me. It takes two to tango, so it also takes two to clean up afterward."

She giggles softly, shaking her head. "That doesn't make much sense, but oddly enough, I understood it."

"We're gonna be all right." I drape my arm around her shoulder and continue on to the restaurant. In this moment, we're two lost people in search of some light to shine down and guide the way. What I know for sure is that having her by my side to experience this with makes it better.

I enjoyed my time with women and then moved on when we went our separate ways. Until the moment a message like that comes through, and you feel as if the rug's been pulled out from under you, I never really wondered what would happen if a woman I slept with ended up pregnant.

I'm still trying to get my footing after that, but it all feels okay with Allyson here. As much as a thought like that might scare another man, it excites me. And I'm certain it's because of the woman walking beside me, who has yet to pull away from my hold. I smile at that thought, knowing she's letting me comfort her.

When we arrive at the restaurant and are seated, Allyson asks me for the names I came up with.

I lean forward a bit, the tablecloth wrinkling where my arms press on the table. "If it's a girl, Chloe, Amelia, Lynn, Alaina, Olivia, or Annabelle. For a boy, I was thinking Jasper, Isaac, Liam, or Camden, after me, clearly." I smirk, and Allyson narrows her eyes. Camden wasn't an option, but I'm sure it would annoy her that I thought about naming the baby after me and not her.

"Not gonna happen." She shakes her head.

I tip my head back and laugh. "I'm just messing with you."

"I know," she rolls her eyes.

"In all seriousness now," I begin, so tempted to reach for her hand across the table but hold myself back, "I did think that if it's a boy, we could give him your dad's name as his middle name."

Allyson's eyes soften as a sad smile marks her face. If I didn't know any better, I'd say she was feeling something here.

"That's really thoughtful, Camden. Thank you." She nods, biting down her lips as her eyes water.

"You don't have to thank me." This time I don't back down from reaching for her, and I grab her hand, giving it a gentle squeeze. The look that passes from Allyson to me speaks volumes, and I'm starting to believe this could be more than two people on the journey to co-parenting.

Chapter 15

Allyson

If someone had told me that one day I'd be sitting across from Camden at a restaurant, talking about our child, I would have spit wine all over their face as I laughed at their absurd suggestion. And yet, here I am.

After telling me he'd use my dad's name for our son's middle name as a way of honoring my dad's memory, I about melted into a puddle of goo. I'm still in shock seeing Camden here, and now he's telling me all this, throwing out baby name suggestions as if we've had years to prepare for this, as if it's something we've both been waiting for.

I stare into his dark eyes as the rough pad of his hand tickles mine. I allow myself a second to pretend that we aren't two friends gathered to discuss our child like a business meeting. But that's all we are and will ever be, friends. I'm not sure when I started to want more from Camden, but a small voice inside of me tells me it was before we even slept together. If I had never thought about it, not even a subconscious slip, I wouldn't have slept with him.

"When do you find out the gender?" Camden interrupts my deep thoughts.

"I'm not sure yet. I think by twelve weeks, they may be able to tell me when they do the prenatal testing." I slip my

the Right kind of Wrong

hand from under his and grab my water glass, taking a drink. I need something to cool me down and a break from his touch.

"So, in about six weeks?" He lifts his eyebrows in question.

"Give or take," I nod.

My stomach growls loudly, and I press my hand against it in an attempt to quiet it, but it's no use. Camden chuckles and opens the menu.

"Let's get you fed."

Once we order, Camden tells me about his job, the work he did for the dating app he mentioned when we flew back from Everton to New York. As I listen to him speak, I smile. All afternoon, I've been on some kind of cloud, pinching myself. As shocked as I was when I saw him standing by my apartment, as the afternoon went by, I started to feel less alone.

He has no idea what it means to me that he flew over here to talk in person and simply offer the comfort I'd been missing. It's going to be a long road, but I believe we can work together to make this as easy as possible.

"Does Easton know?" Camden says after swallowing a bite of his steak. The food here is delicious, and the aroma has been amping up my hunger since we walked in.

I shake my head. "I wanted to talk to you first. The only reason I told my mom was because you never replied to my message, and I had a meltdown. I called her on impulse and spat it out."

Camden nods, pensive. "I know he's your brother, so if you want to tell him alone, I'll respect that, but I'd like to tell him together. Even if it's through a video call. I owe him that

117

much." He scratches the scruff on his jaw, his eyes darting around the restaurant.

"We can do that," I agree. "He's not going to kill you," I add when I notice the wrinkles on his forehead and tight jaw.

"Funny," he chuckles dryly. "Trust me, Easton is going to rip me a new one, so I'd like to be there when you tell him. I'd rather show my face than have him think I'm a coward."

"Camden, look at me…" I wait until his eyes land on mine. "I'm sure Easton is going to be confused, but I won't let this ruin your friendship."

"It might already be ruined without him knowing it."

This time I reach for his hand to comfort him. "Trust me," I whisper, but everything else I was going to say dries up in my throat when I stare into Camden's eyes. They pierce through me, heat and affection combined. The way he's looking at me digs deep in my heart and claims a piece of it.

"This is kinda a shit-show, right?" He gives me a crooked smirk that makes him look younger.

"I guess, in a way, it is," I laugh.

In between bites of dinner, I catch glimpses of Camden. The guy I thought I knew has been replaced with a version of him I could see myself falling for. He makes me laugh when he needs to and comforts me when he senses I'm going to fall apart. He's been considerate all day. The perfect gentleman, really, which is a category I had never placed Camden into.

When we finish dinner, we head out into the cool evening, and I point out different places to Camden. My phone keeps buzzing in my purse, but I'm ignoring it as best as I can, assuming it's Noel.

"You can answer the phone," Camden says finally. So much for trying to be slick.

the Right kind of Wrong

"Sorry, it's probably Noel. She's been worried about me." I fish my phone out of my purse, confirming my assumptions.

"Yup, it's her." I show him the screen before answering.

Her eyes narrow, scrutinizing me before she opens her big mouth. "Where are you? You look pretty. Are you out on a date? Getting some and forgetting about that douche bag baby daddy?" Her eyebrows dance on her forehead as she smiles deviously.

"Noel!" I scold her and widen my eyes, wishing she could read my damn mind. Instead, Camden leans in closer to me, making sure his face appears on the screen.

"Hello, Noel, long time no see." I see the cocky smirk reflected back at me on the small frame in the call.

"Oh… Uh… Hi," she squeaks, staring at me like a deer caught in headlights. "I was talking about another douche bag baby daddy," she says, schooling her features.

"Uh, huh," Camden nods. "Sure…" He pinches his thumb and forefinger together in an *okay* gesture.

"A little warning would've been great, Ally." Noel rolls her eyes.

"Now it's my fault? You're the one with the huge mouth. Imagine if I *were* on a date, and you said that. The guy would've heard you!" I argue.

Noel opens her mouth to say something, but we both look at Camden when he growls.

"Whoa…" Noel says. "That's kinda hot." When I look at her again, she's fanning her face. "Gotta go!" She smirks and winks before hanging up, leaving me alone with the man who looks like he wants to eat me for dessert. The idea alone causes tingles to travel up and down my spine while at the same time, terrifies me.

"I'm sorry you thought I didn't care and thought I was a douche bag. I wanted to see you in person was all." He steps forward, holding my hands. "But you aren't going to have any other douche bag baby daddy if I can help it." My heart drops into the pit of my stomach as I stare at him, searching his eyes. I'm sure I look like a lunatic as I figure out exactly what he means.

I take a deep breath to slow my sprinting heart. When I collect myself again, I say, "I guess that's a title that only you can truly handle."

"Fuck," I hear him mumble before releasing my hands and running his fingers through his hair.

He takes a step closer until our chests are flush, and his heartbeat is racing against mine. His hand combs through my hair as he holds the side of my face. My breath catches as I stare up at him, swallowing thickly while I wait for his next move.

"Ally," he whispers, his breath tickling my lips.

I throw every excuse I've been feeding myself for the last six weeks out the window and lean into his touch. His lips touch mine in a careful kiss at first, a soft brush that's tentative, waiting for my reaction. Camden inches back the tiniest bit and stares down at me.

When I don't argue, his fingers curl into my hair as he holds me possessively in place. His tongue swipes against my lips, probing and begging for me to open for him. We deepen the kiss, standing in the middle of a sidewalk in Madrid, and I don't even question it. I grip onto Camden for dear life, hoping he'll always keep me afloat the way he did today.

As our tongues dance together and my heart thumps against my ribs, every worry melts away. In this moment,

the Right kind of Wrong

nothing else matters but Camden and me. I sigh into the kiss, clearing my mind as his prickly stubble scratches my face. His roughness against my softness—it's a perfect balance. My body reacts, nipples tightening and core clenching as heat swims through me. I moan into the kiss, and Camden takes my lower lip between his teeth, tugging.

He brushes his lips against mine, slowing us down as we catch our breaths.

"I've been wanting to do that since you ran out of my bed in a panic," he confesses with a full smile, all pearly whites, and one dimple.

"I wanted to kill you that morning. I was so confused when I woke up, and when I turned and saw you next to me, all hell broke loose."

"I know. You were worse than my shrilling alarm clock."

I smack his arm and glare at him. "It was *so* not what I was expecting, and you were very arrogant."

"I'm always arrogant, but with reason." He winks, and my body shivers. From what I remember, he has every right to be confident.

"I meant what I said." His hand lands on my stomach and butterflies fly wild. "Let me show you that I'm here for you. Give me a chance to prove myself."

I can't tell if he's asking for a place in the child's life or mine, but the way his eyes stare into mine with sincerity makes me nod.

"I haven't been with anyone since the night we spent together. Even if I wanted to, I couldn't. You were stuck in my mind, as wrong as that may seem to others." His confession catches me off-guard. Camden is always with someone, dating, sleeping with them, flirting. And I've always been his best friend's little sister.

"Well, this is awkward. Clearly, I've been on a ton of dates," I shrug apologetically, pursing my lips.

"Allyson," Camden growls, and Noel is right, that is kind of sexy.

A slow smile covers my lips as I look up at him through my lashes. "It was a joke," I throw out with a roll of my eyes.

"Mine," he says through a clenched jaw.

"What are you, a caveman?" My eyebrows bunch together as I stare at him.

"No other man is going to raise my baby," he says possessively. "And as for you, no other man will touch you but me if I can help it."

My eyes snap open upon hearing him—laid bare with no more questions or doubts.

"This may be a complicated situation, but just hearing you being out with another man does things to me I've never felt before. Hell no, Allyson," he shakes his head. "I want a chance first."

I cock my head to the side and narrow my eyes as I assess him. He's completely serious, but I don't know if he realizes what all that entails. "Are you capable of having a stable relationship with a woman? One-hundred-percent loyal? This isn't about testing out and seeing what happens. Now, there's a child involved, even if it's not born yet, it will affect its life if we date and things end badly." I try to explain the best I can, make him understand this isn't a game.

"He."

"What?" I scrunch up my face.

the Right kind of Wrong

"Not it, but he. You keep calling the baby it," Camden shakes his head as if it were obvious.

"What if it's a girl?" I lift my eyebrows.

A slow smile creeps on his face that should tell me to turn and run, fast. "Let's make a little wager." My heart leaps. "If the baby's a boy, you go on a date with me."

"And if it's a girl?" I arch an eyebrow.

"No need to add more terms to this bet," he says confidently, an easy smile on his lips and his hands in his pockets. Damn him for being so good-looking. His mussed hair and bright, brown eyes that are always smiling. His stubbled jaw and sexy smile add to the dangerous mix.

"So all this talk, and you're willing to wait *at least* six weeks to see what will happen?" I cross my arms over my chest.

"These six weeks will just prove to you I can be faithful." He winks, his smile growing.

Arrogant jerk.

"Six weeks is nothing in the span of a lifetime. From now on, Camden, you and I are linked."

"I know, Allyson. Don't you think I've thought all this through? I can't stop thinking about you. You've got me so twisted, I don't even care to look at another woman if she's not you. And now you're carrying my child. It may be a life I never thought I'd have or want, but now that it's hanging in front of me, I want to grab it and protect it."

I don't know what to say to that, so I just stare like an idiot, focusing on my breathing—*in and out, in and out.*

"And by the way," he adds, "I'm staying until we find out the gender. I'll have a bet to win, and I want to make sure I'm here to reap the rewards." He begins walking.

Just like that, he leaves me standing in shock, staring at his back, questioning what the hell I've gotten myself into.

"Are you coming?" He looks over his shoulder and asks. My feet begin moving toward him, although my mind is filled with messy thoughts and questions. Can Camden be more than just the father of my child?

Chapter 16

Allyson

True to his word, Camden has stayed in Madrid, working from his hotel room or a café while I'm at work during the day. It's been five weird days since he arrived, and I've gotten used to seeing him day in and day out. But since he usually waits for me outside my apartment building in the evenings with some kind of treat to quench my cravings, I'm okay with him being here.

Okay with him being here, I scoff at myself as I stretch in bed. I'm definitely more than okay. Who am I kidding? After that kiss on Monday night, all I can think about is Camden. His possessiveness, protection, and care. He's stepping up to the plate, and it scares me.

I get up from bed and race to the bathroom. I have to stop waiting until the very last minute to pee.

Once I've relieved myself, I drag my body to the kitchen and heat up the milk to make my decaf coffee, a gift from Camden, along with the kettle and a bunch of teas. He's seriously become overprotective, and it's sweet and annoying at the same time, but that could be a cause of my chaotic hormones.

As I take a sip of my steaming coffee, someone knocks on my door. With furrowed eyebrows, I walk to look through the peephole since I didn't buzz anyone in. I open the door with pursed lips as I hold my mug to my chest.

"Good morning," Camden says with a smile. "I brought breakfast. I'm starting to realize Spaniards don't eat breakfast the same way we do in the US, although I did see a couple places advertising brunch." He walks in as he talks on and on about going to brunch tomorrow.

"Camden," I stop him.

"Yeah?" He turns around with lifted brows.

"I already have to drink decaf coffee; give me a sec to take a sip before you continue talking a mile a minute."

He smiles, his one dimple making an appearance as he looks me up and down. "You look sexy."

I bring my free arm up to cross over my chest, resting the one holding the mug over it.

"Uh-uh, don't cover yourself now." He takes the few steps toward me, closing the space between us, as his hand holds my chin. "You really do look amazing," he whispers before his lips kiss the corner of my mouth. I hold my breath and wait, frozen by his bold move. Since Monday evening, Camden has been more upfront about what he wants, and he's determined to prove himself.

"Thanks," I choke out, which only causes his smile to widen.

"Come on, I brought croissants from that bakery you showed me the other day." He grabs my arm and pulls me into the small kitchen, setting the bag on the tiny table.

"Did you bring anything else?" Curiosity gets the best of me, and I peel open the bag to peek inside while Camden grabs two plates.

the Right kind of Wrong

When I look up at him, I notice he's placing a glass of milk in the microwave. "You can have regular coffee," I tell him.

"I'll join you in the decaf world today," he smirks and spoons the instant decaf into his steaming milk before taking a seat at the table with me. "And there is something else in there," he winks.

A smile takes over my face, curious if it's the puff pastry filled with whipped cream I got the other day. Before I can get to the sweet goodness, Camden steals the bag from my hands.

"You need to eat a real breakfast first."

"Are you already preparing for your Dad role?" I tease, biting down my smile.

He leans forward with an arched eyebrow. "Let me take care of you," his husky voice washes over me. My heart spikes, still not used to his gentle side, so I nod.

"Good. Do you have eggs?" Camden stands, opening my fridge before I can reply. "Get ready for The Steele Breakfast."

"The Steele Breakfast?" My eyebrows pinch together as I snort in laughter.

Camden turns to look at me, the sleeves of his Henley tee scrunched up on his arms. "You laugh now, but when you try it, you'll be begging me to make this every morning."

I watch him crack eggs into a bowl while I drink my coffee, patiently waiting. I'm not complaining about the view; the muscles on his toned forearms flex with each movement. When my stomach growls, I stand and lean beside the small section of counter next to the stove and watch him scramble the eggs.

I smile when he looks over at me, confidence oozing out of him. Camden walks around my kitchen, grabbing ingredients he needs as he goes. The savory aroma wafts around my kitchen, and I inhale deeply, mouth watering.

"Do me a favor?" He lifts his eyebrows as he looks at me.

"Sure." I nod and move away from the counter.

"Toast the croissants." I nod and turn on the toaster oven while I cut open the croissants the way Camden instructs. After putting them in the oven, I refill our mugs with milk and prepare two more cups of coffee.

"Ready?" Camden looks at me over his shoulder, shielding our plates with his body.

"Uh, more than ready. I'm starving." As if my stomach thought I needed to emphasize my hunger, it growls on cue. Camden's deep chuckle echoes around the kitchen.

"Tell that kid to be patient," he jokes. When he turns around, my eyes widen. Two croissants stuffed with scrambled eggs, melted cheese, and pan-seared ham.

"That looks freaking delicious." I lick my lips and lean back on my chair. Once Camden is seated, our plates in front of us, I smile at him and say, "Thank you for this."

"You're welcome. Cooking helps ease my nerves, and I'm honestly scared to talk to Easton today." He frowns, his confident armor slipping as our plan to tell Easton about my pregnancy silences us.

I'm terrified of telling him, although my mom continues to assure me it will all work out.

"Yeah, I'm nervous, too," I tell him.

"You're his sister. That makes you irreplaceable. But I'm his friend, and friends are always easily replaced." He looks

the Right kind of Wrong

down at his breakfast with a dark expression. "Especially now that he's in Everton."

I hadn't realized that Easton moving had affected Camden this much. Noel, Berkeley, and I do our best to keep our friendship strong, and I figured they did as well. Guys are different, though.

"I promise I won't let this get in the way of your friendship. I'll do everything in my power to make him realize it was a mistake and not intentional to hurt him." Camden's eyes snap up to mine, his scrutiny making me feel tiny as his jaw ticks. "I—"

Camden interrupts me. "Maybe it was unplanned, but that night was not a mistake." His tone is hard.

"Okay." I let my one-word reply linger between us as I take a bite of my croissant.

"Sorry…"

I shake my head. "Don't be. I should be more careful with my choice of words."

Silence settles over us as we finish our breakfast. You could cut the tension with a knife, and it's definitely not sexual tension.

Camden clears our plates when we're done, probably to keep himself busy. "You can have your surprise now," he says seriously, his back to me as he rinses soap from a plate.

I don't know how to handle a situation like this. He isn't my boyfriend, so it's not exactly like I can walk up to him, hold him, and kiss his worries away. This is different, and while an attraction between us is clear, we haven't fully crossed that line.

"Do you mind if I jump in the shower first?" I stand from my seat when Camden turns around, wiping his hands on the dishtowel.

His eyes burn into mine before they scan my body. Heat prickles my skin as I hold my breath and wait for him to say something. Once he clears his throat, he says, "Go for it."

"I'll be quick."

"Take your time. I'm going to check my email."

I nod and walk toward my room, grabbing what I need before heading into the bathroom. Under the warm spray, my mind wanders in different directions. Easton could take the news well, or all hell could break loose. For Camden's sake and mine, I hope my brother is at least understanding and willing to hear us out.

Since Camden found out about the baby and showed up here, he's done nothing but be present and caring. Easton just needs to see that. But I also know that he knows Camden in a different way—the man who dates a lot, never settling down.

I have the same image of him, yet this week I've gotten to know a different side of him. A side that I never expected from Camden but, if I'm being honest, I like a lot.

I turn off the shower and wrap my body in a towel, then wipe the mirror free of the steam. As I comb my hair and get dried off, I hear a ruckus somewhere in the apartment.

"What is he doing?" I murmur as I get dressed and walk out of the bathroom. I find Camden in the living room, moving furniture around.

"What's going on?" I cross my arms and lean against the wall.

"Oh, shit, sorry. I'll put everything back where it was. I took pictures beforehand, so I remember where it all goes."

the Right kind of Wrong

My sofa is pushed back, the coffee table is nowhere to be found, and the television is on the other side of the small living room.

"What are you doing?" I repeat.

"Well, if you're still going to live in this apartment when you have the baby, he'll need somewhere for his crib and clothes. I thought that half of the living room can be converted into his room. A dresser here," he points to one wall, "and the crib on this side." He points to the middle of the space he opened up.

"We can even get those dividers to block off the space and keep it private."

I bite down on my lip as I listen to him, watching the furrow between his eyes deepen and the tip of his tongue peek out of the corner of his mouth as thinks.

"Camden, take a break. You're on overload. At first, the baby will sleep in my room in a bassinet. I'll put his clothes in my dresser and armoire. I'm going to get rid of my desk in there and put in a changing table." Anxiety begins to spike as I speak; this pregnancy is becoming more and more real by the minute.

Camden must notice because he walks over to me and grabs my hands. "Are you okay?" His eyes stare into mine as if he were reading me like his favorite book.

"Yeah," I sigh. "It just shocks me at times. It's like I'm on automatic and yet have not fully taken in the information."

"I get that, but you'll be okay. I'll visit as much as I can." He nods and rubs his thumbs over the tops of my hands. The soothing back and forth helps bring me down from my panic as I focus on deep breaths.

"Thank you." I look up at him, rolling my lower lip between my teeth.

"I've got you." He pulls me in for a hug, and I allow his warmth to blanket me and provide the comfort he is so keen on giving me.

When my arms go around his back, he sighs, his breath tickling my ear. Camden looks down at my face, one hand cupping my cheek as his thumb brushes across my lips. His eyes lock on mine, something passing through us that I've never felt before, and it makes me want to cry and smile at the same time.

Taking a deep breath, I close my eyes and lean my face into his palm.

"Ally…" Camden whispers.

When his lips land on my forehead, I melt into him and bask in the sensation of his stubble against my skin. My fingers clutch his shirt, wanting to feel this new emotion for longer. I'm afraid when we break apart, it would've all been a momentary glimpse in time that will never repeat itself.

The buzzing of my phone cuts the moment too short, and Camden steps back with a boyish smile. He reminds me of the eighteen-year-old I first met when my brother brought him home one evening to do laundry. I was the annoying fourteen-year-old that stared at him over the top of my book while I pretended to read.

And now here we are, about to become parents to the same child, and he's still that handsome boy, now a man.

"You should get that," he says, clearing his throat.

"Yeah." I step around him and the mess of furniture. My heart stops when I see Easton's name on the screen. He's calling *way* earlier than I expected. Although if I know him, he barely slept, curious about why I wanted to talk to him. That was my mistake, sending him a message yesterday to ask if he'd be free to talk today.

"It's Easton." I hold my phone up.

"Fuck," Camden mumbles, running a hand through his hair. "Pick up. It's now or never," he says, sitting on the sofa.

I swipe my phone to answer the call, waiting for the video to come up.

"Hey, big bro." I smile at his sleep-filled face.

"Hey," his deep voice comes through gruff from waking up. "What's going on? You said you wanted to talk."

"Uh, yeah…" I feel like puking. My heart is racing, and my palms are sweating. I bite down my lips, tears coming to my eyes that I blink away before Easton can notice.

I take a seat on the sofa next to Camden and hold the phone far out enough that Easton can see him. "Um… Actually, we both wanted to talk to you about something." My voice wavers.

"What's going on?" Easton sits up straight, his eyebrows bunching together as he narrows his eyes.

"Hey." Camden's voice sounds small in comparison to a moment ago. I sneak a hand on his knee to help comfort him.

"Here's the thing…" I begin talking.

"Are you two together?" Easton interrupts me, his jaw ticking.

"No… Well…not really," I stutter over my words.

Camden takes over. "Listen, man, the night of your wedding, Allyson and I slept together."

"The fuck?" Easton growls his interruption.

"Please let us talk," I beg my brother.

"Are you fucking kidding me?" Easton keeps going, shaking his head.

"Easton, I'm pregnant," I spit out. That gets his attention because his eyes snap to mine, anger and confusion darkening his green gaze.

"You're kidding," he leans back on his couch.

"No," I shake my head. "I found out about a week ago. I told Camden, and he flew over here so we could talk in person and figure this out."

"You should've told me." His glare is directed at Camden.

"I wanted to, but I didn't know how. Then, Ally told me this news, and I had to talk to her first." Camden shrugs, his fingers blindly finding mine on his knee and linking with them, holding on to me.

"We just wanted you to know. I didn't know how to bring it up, and I don't want this to ruin your friendship with Camden. He's your best friend, and it'd kill me that years of friendship would be destroyed because of me." I look at my brother, hoping he's listening.

"It wouldn't be your fault if it was ruined," he spits out. "That's my fucking little sister," he throws at Camden.

"I know, but… Fuck," Camden runs a hand down his face. "It wasn't planned. It just happened, and then I couldn't stop thinking about her. Now, we're here."

"You're gonna fuck her over." He shakes his head.

"Easton, no, he won't. It's not like we're getting married. We're going to be parents, and we have to work together to be the best for this child."

"So, what are you going to do? Date other people and warn them beforehand. I'm having a child with someone else, FYI?" He shakes his head as if he doesn't understand.

the Right kind of Wrong

"We're figuring it out."

"If it were up to me, neither of us would date other people," Camden adds. I turn to look at him with wide eyes while Easton scoffs and chuckles humorlessly.

"Easton, stop being a jerk. We wanted to tell you, have you be a part of this. It's not exactly easy for either of us, but damn it, we're trying." I blink back tears.

"I don't know what to say." Easton softens a bit when he sees me wipe my cheek.

"Just say you won't stop being friends with Camden," I tell him. The guilt of ruining years of friendship because of this is greater than anything I've felt before.

"I...I need to process," my brother responds. "We'll talk later, okay?" He looks at me, his jaw set straight.

"Okay," I nod, saying goodbye and hanging up. I can't help the tears that roll down my face, but Camden's there to wipe them away before they free-fall down my chin.

"He'll come around," he says, although he doesn't sound convinced.

"I'll never forgive myself if you two are at odds because of this."

"Hey." Camden holds my face. "This isn't your fault. I refuse for you to carry this weight. We made choices, and they have consequences." He smiles sadly, and I nod. Camden may be putting on a brave face, but I see the worry marking his face.

"Let's go for a walk." He stands, reaching his hand out. "Fresh air will help break up this funk."

"Okay." I reach for his hand and stand. "Thank you," I hug him quickly before heading to my room to put on my shoes.

When I get back, Camden is by the door, ready to head out. "Why don't you show me that park Easton and Faith went to?" He talks about Parque de El Retiro.

"That'd be fun," I smile up at him, locking up and heading down to the street. The mood is heavy as we walk, but with each breath I take, the more I begin to relax.

After a few minutes, I receive a text message from Faith. Opening it, I read it aloud.

> Faith: HOLY MOLY! Your brother just told me the news. Congrats! I think. You are happy about this right? I can't believe Camden is going to be a dad

"I feel like I should be offended by the amount of people that doubt my ability at fatherhood."

"I mean, you are the most unlikely person. It's kinda a shock," I shrug.

"I can't wait to prove everyone wrong," he says, his shoulders squaring in determination.

"You've already started to prove me wrong," I admit. That catches his attention, and the smile he gives me awakens the butterflies in my belly.

I write back to Faith, quickly letting her know I'm okay and getting used to the idea. I make sure to tell her Camden has been great so far, and we're working through a plan.

I pocket my phone and continue walking in the direction of the park when Camden tugs my hand and drags me into a store.

"What the…" The rest of the phrase trails off when he holds up a onesie.

the Right kind of Wrong

"Isn't this the soccer team logo?" The Real Madrid logo with the initials in a circle and the crown on the top stares back at me.

"Yes."

"I'm getting it. My boy is going to end up being a soccer fan if he's raised here, but I'll still teach him about American football." Camden wears a proud smile as he reads the size and walks to the register to pay. I stand in awe, my eyes watering. When he turns around after he's paid, his eyes soften as a smile paints his lips.

I get myself under control with a deep breath and a quick wipe of my fingers under my eyes. "If this baby is a girl, she's going to be a sports fan no matter what," I joke.

"It's a boy," he says with conviction.

He wraps his arm around my shoulder, and his other hand lands on my stomach. The feel of his touch makes my heart gallop like a wild horse in the Wyoming mountains. A sense of home comes over me as I smile at the thought of my hometown—a place I left behind years ago, yet lives inside of me.

"When will you start showing?" he asks, his hand moving in circles.

"I don't know. I read on the internet that it would be after the first trimester, so I still have a few weeks, although I feel swollen."

"You look beautiful to me." Camden continues walking as if his comment were the most natural thing in the world, but to me, it's still a shock to hear him talk to me in that way. It makes my heart leap.

I may be scared about having this baby and the uncertainty about my job and living situation if they ask me to move back to Richmond, but having Camden near me has made me feel like I can do this. It's not so scary when you've got someone by your side, encouraging you. I have no idea what will happen when he returns back home, but I know that I'll miss him.

Chapter 1

Camden

Allyson has me wrapped around her pretty, little finger, keeping me hooked, and I doubt she's even aware of it. Spending time alone with her has allowed me to get to know her on a different level, learn her quirks, what gets her fired up, and what makes her laugh. I've learned that she chews on the inside of her cheek when she's watching TV and that she picks her nail polish without realizing it.

She may have been burning a hole in my memory since that fateful night, but this week that I've spent with her, she's started to sear her name on my heart. I've known her for years, and I've never taken the time to truly get to know her, which is a shame because she's one hell of a woman.

Allyson is strong, determined, and beautiful, but above all, she's caring. The way she reached over to comfort me today when we told Easton what was going on—when she must've been as stressed if not more than me—spoke volumes. I didn't expect Easton to jump for joy and send us a congratulatory gift basket, but I was optimistic, so I wouldn't chicken out.

This isn't something I can take back because he doesn't want it to happen. And now that I'm here in my life, on the road to fatherhood, I don't want to walk away. I've never been the kind of guy to visualize a wife, kid, and a whole happy family. I thought one day it could happen, but it wasn't something I was searching for. I guess it's true what they say; things come when you aren't looking for them. Because Allyson and I just became an instant family without either one imagining this could happen.

"Are you okay?" Her quiet voice moves through my clouded thoughts like sunshine breaking through after the storm. *Shit, she's even got me being poetic and crap.*

"Yeah," I smirk. "Show me this park," I add when I realize we're already here.

Allyson guides us down the path, looking at the flowers holding on to their last breath of summer, and she points out a fountain and a building. When we get to the lake area, I rent a small rowboat without questioning it and guide her in.

She doesn't fight it. She takes my hand and climbs in, sitting on one side and holding the oars. When I settle in, I take hold of them and begin rowing through the water, passing by ducks that are floating around us.

"This is nice," I say as I look around, couples, families, and friends on other boats.

"Yeah." Allyson smiles, holding the sides of the boat before tipping her head back and closing her eyes. The sun beams down on her despite the slight chill in the air, highlighting her face.

My jeans grow tighter, and I swallow down the lump forming in my throat. I want to lay her down on this boat and drive her wild, not a care in the world if we rock the boat hard enough to tip us over.

When she lowers her head and blinks her eyes open, a light blush covers her cheeks. "What?" she asks, scratching her chest.

the Right kind of Wrong

I shake my head and continue rowing, taking a deep breath.

"Tell me," she demands, narrowing her eyes in the cutest way that I can't take her seriously.

"Nothing," I smirk, which rewards me with an eye-roll. I still can't get over being here with her. So many years knowing each other, and never once realizing how amazing she is.

Allyson's eyebrows pop on her forehead. "What is so funny?"

"It was nothing, really." I'm not about to tell her that I was admiring her beauty and wishing we were alone so I could have my way with her. We're having a great day, and I want to keep it up, especially after the stress of telling Easton.

Without warning, I feel water land on my shoulder. My mouth drops open as Allyson laughs.

"You aren't going to want to start this, Kiwi," I warn.

She crosses her arms over her chest and smiles confidently. I dip my hand into the water and splash her, accidentally wetting her more than I planned.

Allyson gasps, and her eyes widen. "That was... Oh, my God."

In between laughs, I apologize.

"You aren't one bit sorry." She pretends to be angry, but the smile on her face is proof she's forgiven me.

"I really didn't mean to—" My hands fly up to cover myself from the water she sends my way as if that would protect me.

"The oars!" Allyson calls out. "Crap." The small boat rocks as she leans over to grab one of the oars that fell into the lake.

"Careful," I warn, trying to keep us from tipping over.

141

"Got it," she cheers, holding one of them and placing it again through the loop on the side of the boat.

"The other one?" I ask, looking around until I spot it floating a few feet away from us. "Damn," I mumble.

"Can you row with just one?" Allyson's nose scrunches up.

"We're about to find out." I do my best to get us to the oar, carefully reaching for it. Allyson claps when I grab it, and pride swells in my chest. If I could make her this happy everyday...

"We should probably behave before they kick us out. Truce?" She holds her hand out.

"Truce, Kiwi." I clutch her hand, holding on longer than necessary as I stare into her eyes. Allyson's lips part as she inhales, and she's the first to blink and look away, placing her hand under her thighs as she sits quietly.

"Are you cold?" I ask when I see her shiver.

"Just a little. I'll warm up soon."

"Here." I hand her the oars, and she lifts a brow.

"You want me to row so that I'll warm up?"

"Just hold on to them a second." I roll my eyes playfully as I smile, taking off my jacket and handing it to her. "Put this on. I don't want you to get sick."

Her face relaxes as she looks at me with soft eyes. "Thank you," she whispers, slipping her arms into the sleeves of my jacket and wrapping her body in it.

By the time we're done with our boat ride, I'm drunk on Allyson's energy. This feeling is foreign to me. I've always been up for a good time—having fun, telling jokes, using my charms—but what I'm feeling now is different. It's a combination of pride, protectiveness, and fear.

the Right kind of Wrong

My life is changing in a huge way, and I hope I'm ready for all it entails. Playing Dad and buying the baby its first outfit is very different than being a dad, and I'm not sure I've got what it takes to be the best dad in the world. I sure as hell want to try, though.

"Where to now?" I ask her as I swing my arm over her shoulder and walk out of the park.

"I could so go for some coffee," she smiles up at me.

"Decaf." I lift a finger in warning.

"Yes, sir." Her teasing smile tells me she's joking, but the idea of her surrendering to me is anything but a laughing matter. I wouldn't mind hearing her use those words in the bedroom.

I promised I'd wait until we found out the gender of the baby to win our little wager, but she's making it damn hard to keep my hands and lips to myself.

By the time we finish our coffees, Allyson suggests lunch. We spend the day together, walking the streets of Madrid, her wearing my jacket and my arms holding her. Anyone who sees us would think we're a couple. As for me, I have no fucking clue what we are.

The only thing I'm certain of is that eventually, my time here will be up, and I'll have to head back home to Richmond. I can't live in a foreign bubble with her forever. We'll have to figure out a real plan so I can see the baby once the time comes. That is if her job doesn't make her move back to Richmond like Allyson worries they might. Selfishly, that would be the best solution, but I don't want her to give all this up if it's what she truly wants.

We make it to her apartment building, and I walk her up to her place. Allyson turns with a smile when we reach her door.

"Thank you for today. It was exactly what I needed. Easton will come around. I'll make sure of it." A sad smile lifts the corners of her lips.

"He will," I agree, even if I don't fully believe it myself. I don't want to disappoint her.

"I'll talk to him," she nods.

"Give him some time to process," I suggest. "He may just need a day or two to fully understand."

"Yeah, you're probably right. Lord knows his lawyer's mind is working overtime." Allyson means this as a joke, but my heart stops.

I take a step toward her, closing the gap between us and reaching for her hands. "We can work out a plan without having to get into all that. We don't need a lawyer, which is probably a good thing since we share the same one," I throw in to lighten the mood, but I don't want her to think we'll have to get legal advice.

"I want this to work, and I'll do anything you ask. Just let me be a father to this child."

Allyson's chest rises with a deep breath, and her eyes mist over. "This is all new to me, but I've known you long enough to know you won't take this child away from me." My eyes follow her hand that falls to her stomach.

"I promise," I whisper.

Allyson nods silently, and my lips touch her forehead, lingering longer than necessary. When I stare down into her eyes, I see an array of emotions swimming in those big, green eyes. I take a step back to give us both some space to think clearly.

"Here you go." She shrugs out of my jacket and hands it over.

"It looked good on you," I wink, which causes her to shake her head while she bites down her smile. I reach for her trapped lip and tug it away from her teeth with my thumb.

"We'll talk later. Get some rest. I know you're dying for a nap."

Allyson chuckles and nods. "I'm so tired."

I nod and rub her belly. "Bye, baby boy." I speak to her stomach before looking back at her. "Bye, Kiwi." I kiss her cheek and walk to the elevator, putting my jacket on. Her sweet scent immediately envelops me, as if she were still walking beside me.

I have no idea how I'm going to leave her when the time comes to fly back home, and I don't see any option that will allow me to stay here throughout the entire pregnancy since I'm not a Spanish resident or citizen. Ninety days isn't nearly enough, though.

Chapter 18

Allyson

Today has been surreal. Nothing could've prepared me for Camden and his presence in my life. I grab the onesie from the bag and shake it open. A smile takes over my face as my eyes mist over. I was surprised when he pulled me into the store, and my heart stopped when he said he was buying this for the baby. I had never experienced overwhelming emotion than I did at that moment, and I did my best to swallow it down and not cry like a baby in the middle of the shop.

I hold the onesie to my chest. My life right now is tilted, everything in an unfamiliar perspective. I'm not sure if I'm standing upright or lying down. It's scary to feel as if you're not in control of your own feet, as if you can't stand firm. However, today everything seems all right. The choking panic subsided as I walked with Camden, teasing him, being around him.

I see him in a different light, and it's scary because eventually he'll leave, and I'll stay. And while we'll have a child that bonds us, that's not the sole reason to be with someone. So much more goes into a relationship, and two people shouldn't jump into one just because they're having a child together.

the Right kind of Wrong

But maybe that child could be the reason that brings them together to form a deeper relationship.

I shake my head and walk into my room, folding the onesie and placing it in the empty drawer in my dresser. I started reorganizing and clearing out things I no longer wear so that I can have room for this baby. It may not be the ideal home, but we'll make do with the space we have.

I don't expect Camden to get down on one knee and ask me to marry him because I got pregnant, but I always imagined this part of my life to be full of crazy, can't-live-without-you love, and a home shared with someone. I never imagined I'd be a single mom, and while Camden is here, at the end of the day, I'll be alone.

I bite down my lip and blink away the tears starting to cloud my vision. Lying down on my bed, I grab one of the extra pillows and clutch it to my chest. The reality of this pregnancy hits me in spurts, taking me down a whirlwind of emotions where I can't figure out what's up and what's down.

As much as I try to distract myself and pretend I'm okay, the deep-seated fear of what's going to become of my life is ever-present. I've worked so hard to get to this point in my life and career, and the sudden possibility that I could lose it all makes my heart accelerate faster than a race car flying down the track in Daytona.

That's not to mention Easton's reaction to the news. I've never seen him grow so serious so quickly in my life. My brother is my rock, he's always been there for me, and the idea of not having his support on this kills me. I need him in my life.

I bury my head into my pillow, my anxiety spiking as different scenarios cross my mind. I take a deep breath, attempting to control my emotions, but the pounding in my chest only intensifies.

From somewhere in my room, my phone buzzes, but I choose to ignore it. I'm not in the mood to talk to anyone, especially if it involves questioning my pregnancy, my relationship with Camden, and how I'm feeling. It's not easy being away from home and my loved ones, but I do love what I'm doing. However, now that I know a baby is on the way, I'm questioning everything. How will I balance working and taking care of the baby? I don't have many people here that I can count on, much less to take care of a baby.

How long would my maternity leave be since I'm in Spain? Do the same regulations apply here as they do in our Richmond office since it's the same company? I would assume so. Would my baby be an American or Spanish citizen if I have the baby here?

First, I need to talk to my boss, but I want to do the prenatal tests I have coming up to make sure everything is okay before I do so. That will put me into my second trimester, which would be a good time to start announcing it.

The buzzing of my phone keeps going, competing with the incessant thoughts in my mind, both driving me crazy. I shift on the bed, holding the pillow tighter, and close my eyes, focusing on my breathing to see if that helps calm my nerves and the tears that don't stop welling in my eyes.

When my apartment buzzer shrills through my home, I curse. By the time I get up and make my way to the door, it rings again.

"I'm coming!" I yell, even though the person can't hear me.

"Si?" I ask, speaking into the system.

the Right kind of Wrong

"Ally?"

I close my eyes and expel a breath.

"What happened, Camden?" I lean my head against the wall above the intercom.

"Can you open up?" I buzz him in and open the door, waiting for him to make his way up to my floor.

When he rounds the corner, he sighs. "I called you, and you wouldn't answer. I got worried."

He stands before me, wrinkles around his eyes, and creases on his forehead.

"I was trying to sleep," I lie.

"Were you crying?" Camden reaches up and swipes his thumb across my cheek. I guess my eyes missed the memo that they had to keep up with my lie.

"No," my voice cracks.

"Come on." He steps into my apartment, closing the door behind us, and pulls me into his arms. I breathe him in, all masculine and woodsy mixed with the smell of fall on his shirt.

Silently, Camden guides us to my bedroom and motions for me to lie down.

"I'll make you a cup of tea. Relax." I nod and get under the covers.

He returns a few minutes later with a steaming mug and places it on the nightstand next to the bed. Then, he sits on the edge and removes his shoes before lying next to me. I eye him cautiously, my heart rate kicking up and body tensing.

Camden is oblivious to my reaction as he begins to speak, his words hitting me in the center of my chest. "I know you're scared. I am, too, but we're going to be all right." He brushes strands of hair from my face.

"If I had to choose a mother for my unplanned child, I'd totally pick you. You're strong, smart, beautiful, and kind. There's no way this kid isn't going to have the best life and qualities being yours." My stomach contracts at the feel of his hand landing over it.

"The uncertainty of everything is scary," I confess. "No matter how okay I try to make myself feel."

"Ally, I think even people who have been waiting their whole lives to have kids get scared. Even couples who have prayed for a baby have their moments of weakness." His thumb brushes back and forth over my belly.

"It's normal because we're all human trying to do the best we can. And now being responsible for another, tiny human who depends on us adds to the importance of our role in this world. We have to keep that person alive, healthy, loved, and sometimes it's difficult to do that for ourselves, let alone someone else," Camden continues, a vulnerability I've never seen in him before shining through his features.

He continues talking, though, not shying away. "But I'm here for you. You aren't doing this alone. I'll provide for you and this baby, even if I have to live thousands of miles away." His hand moves over my waist to my back, pulling me to him.

His body against mine causes me to tremble. The way he holds me, protective and possessive, it's what I've always wanted to find in a man. Except, Camden isn't really mine.

"Thank you," I gaze up at him.

He moves his hand up my ribs toward my face to cup my cheek and runs his thumb across my lower lip. His caresses move tingles up and down my spine. "You don't need to thank me. This is my responsibility, too. You weren't some random one-night-stand, and even if you were, I'd stand up

the Right kind of Wrong

for that kid, but you're...you're my Kiwi." A hint of a smile ghosts over his lips.

Maybe for this moment in time, he can be mine.

I drape my hand over his waist and scoot closer, burying my face into his neck as I allow his warmth to wrap me up in a blanket of safety.

"Ally..." Camden's strangled voice lands on my ears, his hand coming back around my waist and his fingers sneaking underneath my shirt. I shiver at the gentle caress of his featherlight touch against my skin.

"How did we get here?" I look into his eyes as I crack myself open.

"I'm not sure," he whispers, his lips centimeters from mine as his fingers continue their trail around my lower back. "I don't think I care how we got here..." His palm flattens on my back, pressing my body to his.

I stiffen when I feel his erection against me, and my lips part.

"All I care about is that we did. It may be unconventional, unexpected, and complicated, but what good thing isn't? And I think we could be a good thing."

I hold my breath as Camden leans his head down, but instead of kissing me, he runs the tip of his nose across my cheek. These are words I've always wanted to hear; I just never thought they'd come from him. Yet here we are, lying on my bed, self-control barely holding on, vulnerable and honest.

"You always smell so good," his gruff voice adds to the tension building between us. "So sweet."

A surprised gasp escapes my lips when his teeth graze my ear lobe, and my body erupts into flames feeling his mouth anywhere on me, his lips skimming the skin below my ear.

"Fuck, Ally," he growls, lifting his head to stare into my eyes. "I said I'd wait until we knew the gender to take you out, a little wager more for my own self-control than anything else, but I don't know if I can…" his words trail off as his eyes flicker back and forth between mine.

I don't wait. I don't think. I just act—on impulse and lust.

I tilt my chin up enough to catch his lips. Camden is right there with me, matching my desire, need-induced kisses claiming me as my heart slams against my ribs. I part my lips when his tongue traces the seam, and our tongues tangle, creating a dance that's guided by the beat of our hearts.

I breathe him in, weaving my legs through his, and groan when I feel his hardness so close to where I want him. My memory of our first time together may be clouded, but I'll make sure to commit this one to memory.

One of Camden's hands grips the back of my head while the other sneaks further up my back. His touch sears my skin, and his possessive kiss ignites a fire so hot that I feel like flames are licking my skin.

I moan and arch into him, pressing my lower body against his. Damn it, the feel of him has me wild.

"Need more," I say between kisses, trailing my lips down his jaw to his neck, nipping his skin as his stubble scratches my face. He's all man.

A deep growl sounds from the back of his throat. Camden brings his hand from my back to my ass, squeezing and pulling me to him.

"I can't stop thinking about you. The way you felt against me, beneath me, all around me. I'm lost when it comes to you. So fucking lost, but I don't want to be found."

"You need to stop talking to me like that."

the Right kind of Wrong

Camden leans his body up, holding himself with his hands on either side of my body. "Why?" His eyebrows furrow in concern.

"Because I like it way too much." I shift so I'm underneath him and wrap my legs around his hips, tugging him down onto me. I catch him by surprise, and he lands on me harder than I planned.

"Fuck, the baby," his voice is laced with concern as he leans up a bit and places his hand on my stomach. "I didn't crush him, right?"

I giggle and shake my head. "No. He's okay." My hand lands on his. We stare at each other for a few beats until a cocky grin appears on his face.

"You said he." Camden nuzzles my neck .

"You're contagious," I try to argue.

When he lifts his face to look at me, his smile is less cocky and more…emotional. "I just want the baby to be healthy. Are you sure you're okay?"

I smile and nod. His concern and attention get to me. Hell, it turns me on. Who am I kidding?

"Before we go any further, I need to say this because I don't want to leave any room for worry in your mind. I'm clean. I know I should've brought that up before I got you pregnant, but I don't want that to worry you. I never would've slept with you if I wasn't. Not the most romantic thing, but considering the situation…" He runs a hand through his mussed hair.

"Thank you."

"I guess since I already got you pregnant, we can…" His eyebrows waggle.

I try to hold back my chuckle, resulting in sputtering all over him, and heat creeps up my neck.

"Sexy," he winks, using the hem of his shirt to wipe his face and giving me a peek at his abs. "Like what you see?" My eyes snap up to his, and I find myself staring at a crooked grin and arched eyebrow.

"I'm too turned on right now to feel weirded out that we're about to have sex again, so yeah, definitely like what I see."

Camden growls again, thrusting his hips into mine, causing a moan to slip from between my lips.

"I love your honesty," he grits while his hands desperately lift my shirt. I arch my back to assist him and lift my arms so he can remove it completely.

I lie before him in my nude, cotton bra. My hair is a mess all around me. But Camden, he looks at me as if I'm some kind of gem. I shiver when his finger runs over the swell of my breasts, and he smiles. Wordlessly, he dips his head and begins kissing down my neck to my chest, lowering the cup of my bra before swirling his tongue around my nipple.

My body is sensitive, every touch and lick amplifying my desire. He moves to my other breast, repeating the same motion but this time taking my nipple between his lips and flicking his tongue over the hardened peak.

"I wonder if you're as wet for me as you were our first night together," he says in his deep, gravelly voice.

"More," I moan and lean into him.

His hands travel up and down my body, no real direction except for the purpose of touching me anywhere and everywhere.

"More?" he questions.

the Right kind of Wrong

I nod, looking into his eyes.

"I'll be the judge of that," he winks, unsnapping the buttons on my jeans and sneaking a hand in the waistband.

Camden doesn't hold back. He inches his fingers into my underwear and groans when he feels my slickness against his skin. "So damn wet," he groans, leaning back on his legs. "Need you naked." He peels my jeans off my legs along with my underwear.

The hunger in his eyes speaks volumes as they sweep up my almost naked body. Then, he leans over, sneaking his hand under my back and unsnapping my bra, removing it from my body and throwing it on the pile on the floor.

"Much better." His hands roam down my body, teasing and tweaking my nipples, leaving them pebbled and screaming for more as he scoots down the bed. Camden drops a kiss on my stomach, his eyes looking up at me with the sexiest smile I've ever seen.

"Mom and Dad's turn to play now." He winks at me and kisses down to my pelvis, my body tensing with anticipation.

"Can't wait to taste you. It's my one regret that I never had the chance to."

I moan and squeeze my eyes, waiting for what I know will be a mind-blowing sensation. When his tongue swipes up my pussy, my hips buck off the bed.

"Whoa…" I groan.

"Eyes open, watching me," he commands with authority.

I open my eyes and look down at him. Camden dips his tongue again, flicking my clit before closing his lips around and sucking. My body tenses and relaxes in spurts, moving around as he begins to fuck me with his tongue.

I lose track of all that he's doing to please me with his mouth and fingers as I surrender to the warming sensation taking over my body. Every stroke, lick, and kiss build me higher and higher. I'm a prisoner of his pleasure, thrashing my body as if I were chained in a desperate race to chase this orgasm begging to be released.

"Fuck," I moan.

"So sweet," he murmurs against my body, the vibrations buzzing over me, and I free fall as he continues to pleasure me with his mouth, the crash leaving me exhausted and satisfied.

My chest heaves as I try to catch my breath. Camden crawls up my body, his mouth an inch from mine.

"Taste yourself." His lips collide with mine, tongue demanding and assertive as he pushes through my lips in search of my tongue. I barely register the taste as I lose myself in the kiss, wrapping my arms around his body and bringing him flush against me.

In a desperate attempt to get him naked, I push his Henley up his body. Camden sits back and finishes the job for me, throwing his shirt on the floor. My eyes roam down his body, watching as his muscles twitch and flex with his movements.

"This what you want?" he asks with his hands still on his jeans. I sit up, nodding, and move his hands away. I palm his hardness over his jeans before unsnapping the button and lowering the zipper.

"You feel so good touching me," he says gruffly.

"Ditto," I wink with a smile.

Camden chuckles until my hand wraps around his length in the constraints of his jeans. He hisses through his teeth and stares at me.

"No going back," he says.

"You already got me pregnant. I'm pretty sure this is permanent in some capacity of our lives."

Camden gives me a bruising kiss, leaning me back on the bed as he kicks off the rest of his clothes. I reach for his cock, stroking him, but he stops me.

"Need in you now." He brushes his hair with his hands. "Shit, wait. You could have sex, right?" His eyebrows pinch together, and I dip my head back in laughter.

Wrapping one arm around his back, I lift my hips up to his, rubbing against his erection. "Yes," I barely breathe out before Camden turns us over, and I'm on top. I shriek and laugh at the surprise until I'm straddling him.

"Ride me," is all he says with a challenge.

I smirk and hold his gaze as I lift my body and position myself over him. I allow myself to sink onto him slowly, watching his face morph from cocky to awe. His hands land on my hips as I go lower, feeling him so deeply this way.

"Damn, Kiwi, you feel fucking fantastic."

"Yeah," I moan, adjusting to his size. "You, too." All intelligible thoughts have flown out of my head, and I'm left with half phrases and moans.

I begin to ride him, my hands on his abs and hair falling over my face. It's too much and not enough at the same time. Camden groans and holds me, guiding my body up and down his length, both of us working together.

"This feels… I feel everything. It's unreal," he says raggedly.

"So good." I lean down and kiss him, uniting in all ways possible as we get lost in each other, in our bodies, in our pleasure.

As my eyes close and my orgasm takes over, I see a life with Camden, raising our child, late nights on the sofa, and evening strolls as a family. I trap the tears that build, holding on to a dream that has no real possibility of manifesting.

Chapter 19

Camden

I'm in deep. Deeper than my dick was in her the other night. So fucking deep that Allyson has consumed my life. I hear her laughter when she's not around, feel the ghost of her hands on my body. Fuck. Me. Never in a million years did I expect this.

I hold on to the straps of my backpack that sit on my shoulders and walk the short distance to the café in between my hotel and Ally's apartment.

As soon as I take a seat, the woman behind the counter smiles and waves before asking if I want my usual. Coming here each day has helped me understand Spanish a little better, but my handy dictionary does the rest for me.

I open my laptop and tap the space key a few times to wake it up. Once the screen lights up, I begin reading emails and working through my tasks for the day. I thank the server when she drops off my black coffee and focus back on my computer.

Time flies as I work on a gaming application and drink another coffee.

"Hello?" I answer my phone when it vibrates on the table.

fabiola francisco

"Camden, hi, it's Jim. Our app is acting up, and I need you to take a look." I lean my forehead on my free hand and close my eyes.

"I'm out of the country," I sigh because I know that it won't matter to him.

Jim has been one of my long-standing clients, and I've been his computer engineer since he started up his company, and he hired me to create his business application. He runs an automotive company where he wholesales car parts, and his application allows clients to make orders through it and schedule appointments—sales at the tip of your fingers.

"What's going on with it?" I start tapping keys as he explains how the orders aren't going through, some clients are getting billed twice, and inventory is showing up that's been discontinued for some time.

"Crap," I mumble. "I'll see what I can do from my end."

"I'd prefer it if you can come to the office and we look at it together. You can also see if there's something else with our system that's making trouble."

I breathe heavily and shake my head. Jim's been great to work with, but he's definitely the hands-on kind of guy, and he needs to be present to see what's going on. In other words, he's a visual learner that needs to be shown step by step, even if he isn't the one directly working with the app.

"Let me see what I can do. I'm currently abroad, but I'll see if I can book a short trip there and back." My brain starts to spin different ideas, but if he needs me there, I know I have no choice but to fly to Richmond for a few days and work this out.

"Let me know," he says before hanging up.

the Right kind of Wrong

I scrub a hand down my face as my cheeks puff with my deep breath. I'll hate to leave Allyson right now when things are going well between us, and she has the pending prenatal tests, but if I'm quick enough, I can go and come back in time.

Before I can get back to work, a text message pops up on my phone. When I see Easton's name on the screen, my heart stops. We haven't spoken since Saturday when we told him the news. I have no idea what he's going to say, but one thing I do know about Easton is that the longer he stews, the worse it is.

Swiping my phone unlocked, I read his message.

Easton: Hey, I'm not sure what exactly is going on between you and Ally but we should talk

Camden: I agree. I'm finishing up some work and will head back to my hotel room. I can call you

Easton: When will you be back in Richmond? I rather talk in person

Fuck. I scratch my jaw as I think about this. What does he have to say to me that he can't say over the phone?

Camden: I may have to fly back for a few days, so I'll let you know

Easton: Sounds good. I'll try to meet you there

I finish up some more work before packing up and heading back to my hotel room. After Easton's messages, my concentration has been shot. For all I know, he wants to talk in person so he can punch me for knocking up his sister.

Once I'm back in my room, I call the airline and find out if there's a flight in the coming days. My best bet is to buy a round trip flight and leave my other ticket open since I plan to come back.

I'm going to hate telling Ally that I have to leave, but it's the reality of our situation. She lives here, and I live in the US. Regardless of what we're building between us, unless one of us changes our lifestyle, we'll always be faced with these predicaments.

I place a twenty-four-hour hold, so I don't lose the flight. After I talk to Ally tonight, I'll finalize my reservation. It's important that I'm here for her prenatal test, so I want to confirm the date to make sure I will be back by then, and I'm not confident the date I remember is the correct one.

Then, I take advantage of the hotel's gym and head down for a workout. Nothing is better to release stress than push-ups and some miles on the treadmill.

"Hey," Allyson smiles as she walks up to her building.

I push myself off the wall by the door and walk toward her, grabbing the back of her neck and kissing her. We may not have labeled our relationship, but in my eyes, we're together. The other night changed things for me in more ways than I could've imagined.

The feelings I'm having toward her are more than lust-induced. Allyson is more than a woman I met at a bar.

"How was your day?" I ask, still holding the back of her neck and touching my forehead to hers, breathing her in.

the Right kind of Wrong

"It was good. Same ole, same ole." I chuckle and grab her keys from her hand, turning the lock and holding the door open.

"Let's get upstairs."

As we ride up the elevator, Allyson places her head on my shoulder. I hold her, rubbing a hand up and down her arm. The words are on the tip of my tongue to tell her about my trip, but I hold back. I don't want to cause her any disappointment, and this moment is perfect.

When the elevator dings open, I hold her hand and walk to her apartment, entering. I watch as she kicks off her shoes by the front door. I smile at her ease as she walks around her apartment, going through her routine of opening windows and turning on lights.

She turns around and smiles shyly, watching me as I lean against the frame that leads to the living room where she's standing. A light blush covers her cheeks.

"Do you want something to drink?" Allyson scrunches her nose a bit, making a cute face that I want to grab and kiss.

"No," I shake my head. "I actually need to talk to you about something." I grab both of her hands and lead her to the couch.

"What's wrong?" Her voice immediately rises, and her eyes search mine.

"Nothing," I promise. "I got a call from a client, and I need to fly to Richmond to solve a problem he's having with his app. I'll be back in time for your next appointment."

She gives me a small smile, her eyes looking at me sadly. "Duty calls. We knew this would happen. It's not like you could live here forever." She puts on a brave face, but I read the disappointment in her eyes.

"I'll be back. I wanted to confirm the date of your appointment before finalizing my flight. Make sure I've got time to come back."

"It's on the twenty-third."

I do the math in my head. That gives me a couple weeks to go, fix Jim's problem, and fly back. If I don't find any major issues, it should be enough time.

"Okay," I nod. "How about we grab some dinner?" I smirk.

"How about we order in and watch a movie? Ronan Connolly's new movie is on Netflix," she gives me her best smile, and I can't turn her down.

"What do you want to eat?" I ask, leaning in to kiss her temple.

"You." The one word comes out with a deep tone, her eyes dancing with mischief.

"Kiwi," I growl, pulling her onto my lap. "*I* want to eat you, but we'll save that for dessert. I need you fed and with energy. I've got plans for us tonight if I'm flying back home in less than forty-eight hours." She shivers against me, and I smile knowingly.

"I'm going to miss you," I whisper against her lips. "It's crazy, but I am."

"I've gotten used to you being here," she pouts.

"I'll be back." I brush my lips against hers.

"But what about when you aren't able to come back? When your time to visit is up, and they kick you back to the US, what will happen then?" She blinks rapidly, most likely hiding the fact that she wants to cry. My sister used to do the same thing when we were younger, and she'd get upset over something.

the Right kind of Wrong

"I don't know," I shake my head, and my lips fall into a flat line. "We can work something out." I tell her what I've been saying since I arrived, hoping that it's true that we'll be able to have a fool-proof plan in place, but I'm not exactly sure how or what it will be unless she moves back to Richmond. Without a visa, I can't be in Spain for longer than ninety days, and each day I spend here is one less I'll have with her.

"Let's focus on right now," I suggest, tapping her thigh and putting a smile on my face. "I'm here with you, and we've got all night."

Allyson nods and moves off my lap. "I'm just going to change, and I'll be right back."

"What do you want to eat, and I'll order?" She looks at me with raised eyebrows before she tips her head back and laughs.

"What's so funny?" I cross my arms and stand.

"I want to hear you order our food." Her cackles resonate around the living room.

"Handy dictionary, remember?" I arch an eyebrow.

Wiping under her eyes, she tries to catch her breath. "I do need to hear this. Go on." She tips her chin toward her phone on the coffee table. "Call them. I'll wait." She leans against the wall, crossing her foot over her ankle and placing her hands in her pant pockets.

Confident, I grab her phone and repeat, "What do you want to eat?"

"Indian, their number is saved on my phone."

I search for the restaurant name and call, taking deep breaths. When the person answers and shoots off a phrase faster than I can catch it, I swallow thickly and try my hand at ordering dinner for us.

"Hola, um… Delivery? Eh…casa" Allyson snorts and attempts to hide her laughter with her hand. "Dos chicken masala…" I lift my brows to make sure she wants that. When she nods, I continue. "Y… Naan."

I sigh in relief when the man understands my order in a broken Spanish mixed with English. Covering the mouthpiece on the phone, I ask Allyson for her address. I repeat it to the man and hang up.

Slow clapping fills my ears. "I'm impressed, although some of those words are in English."

"I'm sweating," I admit, and then I laugh. "I did okay, though, right?"

"Yeah, you did more than okay." She slowly walks toward me with a sexy smile. Allyson wraps an arm around my back, and her smile grows. "It was kinda sexy, actually, watching you talk in Spanish. But you know what I think?" I shake my head. "You might need some one-on-one tutoring."

My dick stands at attention, volunteering to receive said one-on-one time. Clearing my throat, I smirk. "I've got some other ideas we can do that require no talking." I skim my nose against her cheek. Ally sighs and leans into me, bringing her other arm around my back.

"You're not the man I thought you were."

Her confession catches me off-guard. "I'm glad." I lean my head back a bit to look into her eyes. "I may not have been the best example of what settling down looks like, but I promise I'm determined to be the best father to this child and a partner to you if you give me the chance."

the Right kind of Wrong

Allyson tilts her head. "I want that, but I don't know how we can make it happen. I have three years left living in Madrid before I decide if I want to stay in this office or move back to Richmond. A long-distance relationship with a child just isn't ideal."

"Shhh…" I kiss her. "Day by day."

She nods quickly and takes a deep breath. "Okay."

I smack her ass. "Go get comfy. I'm going to turn on Netflix." I kiss her deeply, erasing every doubt swimming in her head and replacing them with memories of me, of us, of how good we could be together.

Chapter 20

Allyson

It's been three weeks since Camden flew back home. What was supposed to be a five-day trip has become uncertain as he tries to work with his client—something about a bug or hacker that I didn't quite understand when he explained it to me.

He missed the appointment I had for my prenatal testing. When the doctor asked me if I wanted to know the gender once the results came in, I said no. It felt wrong knowing without Camden, even if I never expected him to be such a big part of this pregnancy as he's become.

I miss him, though. I miss what we could be if life hadn't taken us down different paths. But somehow, we meet in the middle of our journey before moving along again. Except, this baby is forever. I feel split between two lives. I can only do so much. The choice would be to leave my job and figure out as we go, but doubts about resentment and failed relationships sneak into my mind.

I reach for my phone and find Noel's name in my contact list and call her. I chew on my bottom lip while I wait for her to answer, hoping she isn't busy. After numerous rings, I hang up and try Berkeley. I get the same result.

I sink into the couch and grab the remote as if surfing through channels would make a difference. Any other moment of my life, I would be heading out for dinner or drinks with my friends. Now, I'm home, questioning life while my friends are questioning me why I've imprisoned myself at home lately.

It's not like me to turn down their invitations, but until I tell my boss that I'm pregnant, I don't want to tell my co-workers. Thankfully, I have a video conference with my boss this week. I'm over the first trimester, so it's safe to share this news. The only thing stopping me is what will happen with my job. Obviously, women go on maternity leave all the time, but I'm the only person in the Madrid office that does my job, and that is the clear communicator between this office and the one in Richmond.

I take a deep breath to slow my racing thoughts.

"Everything will be okay," I say aloud.

My phone rings, and I quickly reach for it, grateful for the distraction. I smile, seeing Camden's name on the screen.

"Hey," I answer, putting the phone on speaker and placing it on my chest as I get comfortable on the couch. My feet rest on the coffee table, and I slouch down, sinking into the cushions.

"Hi, how are you?" His familiar voice soothes me, and a smile brightens my face.

"I'm good, and you? How's work?"

"It's okay. I hate that it's taking longer than I thought it would. I should've been done weeks ago and been back there with you." Camden sighs, the frustration evident in his hard tone.

"It's okay," I whisper. I don't even know what exactly we are or our limits.

"It's not, at least not for me, but I'll let you pretend you're okay with this." I could almost hear him roll his eyes.

"This would've been the plan all along. I live here, and you live there." How does he not see that this is our life? We don't get to be one big happy family, even if we wanted to unless one of us made a sacrifice.

"Kiwi, I don't want what would've been. I want what I want, and that's you," he says firmly.

"So what do you expect? I leave my job and move back there? I can't exactly ask for a transfer. I signed a contract committing to five years here."

"Breathe," Camden says softly, and I obey him. "I'm not asking for any of that. I would never ask you to leave your job for me. We just need time and a plan," he placates.

I take a few deep breaths, closing my eyes. "Yeah."

"I know that *yeah* was dismissive, but I'll forgive you because you're pregnant and hormonal," his tone turns teasing.

"Don't tell a pregnant woman she's hormonal unless you want to be on the receiving end of said hormones."

"Babe, I'll be on the receiving end of whatever you want to give me." My stomach flips, and my body reacts to his words, my core clenching.

"Camden…" I whisper, blinking back tears.

"I mean it." He's serious now.

I want to tell him so many things, but they all get trapped in my throat.

"Now," Camden lightens up. "Let me talk to my child."

I smirk and move to lay back on the couch, placing the phone on my swollen belly. When he sees me, he's going to be surprised.

the Right kind of Wrong

"He's all ears. Well, not literally since they haven't developed yet, but you know what I mean," I babble.

Camden chuckles and begins speaking to our baby. He's been doing this every time we talk, wanting to make sure the baby recognizes him even if he's not physically here. He wants to create a bond, and hell if I don't become a ball of mush hearing him speak to our child.

"Hey, baby boy." I snort when I hear him.

"If this baby is a girl, she's going to have an identity complex," I joke.

"Remember, we still have a wager pending. I guess we'll have to wait to find out the gender, but I'm confident it's a boy."

"I'm pretty sure you claimed the prize of that bet tenfold."

"And I'd do it again in a heartbeat," his deep voice grows husky.

Flashbacks of our times together have been forefront in my mind. The way he feels, his touch, his gruff words, and the gentle way he holds me. Everything about Camden has been a surprise, and what I'm feeling for him is deeper than I could've prepared for.

"Now, let me talk to my child." I hold the phone on my stomach and smile as I listen to Camden tell the baby about his job, Richmond, and his family.

"I'm gonna teach you to throw a football, and I'll take you to games," he promises. "Can't wait to see you wearing your first sports outfit I got you."

My eyes water, and I don't blink back the tears this time. They flow down my cheeks in a combination of joy and sadness.

"Your momma is taking good care of you, and I'll be there soon," Camden continues talking as my emotions swirl like a tornado. He must notice when I breathe in loudly because he stops talking for a moment.

I rub my belly with my other hand, grateful that he's at least being a part of this journey somehow. I close my eyes when he starts talking again, telling the baby all the plans he has. It's overwhelming, and each time I hear him speak to my stomach, I get choked up in emotion.

"Kiwi," he says.

"Yeah?" I whisper in a shaky voice.

"Wish I was there."

"Me too, Camden." There's no need to deny it. I want him here with me. He knows it, and I know it.

"Soon," he promises like he has each time, but being in town means that more clients are trying to get a hold of him to see him in person, which is making it even more difficult for him to fly back. It's his job to work for them, so I don't expect him to turn them down and rush over to me.

"What do you have planned this weekend?" he asks.

"Nothing. My colleagues are asking me to go out, but since they don't know I'm pregnant, I don't want to go and not drink and raise questions. It will be easier once I tell them."

"You're talking to your boss this week, right?"

"Yes, I can't wait any longer. Besides, I'm starting to show, and I only have so many loose shirts I can get away with."

Camden chuckles. "Send me a picture of your belly."

the Right kind of Wrong

I lift my shirt and open my camera on my phone, snapping a picture and sending it to him. "Check your messages," I tell him.

Camden groans. "I want to see you in person."

"Hopefully, soon."

"I know. I hope so, too. Easton's flying over here this weekend. He's going to visit your mom, and he wants to talk. He had told me before I flew back to Richmond that he wanted to talk in person whenever I was in town."

"Oh…" My eyes widen, and stomach contracts with my deep breath. "Have you spoken to him at all?"

"Nope. I have no idea what he's going to say."

"I've spoken to him here and there, mostly through text message when he asks how I'm feeling, but he hasn't brought you up. I figured he was trying to ignore that part of this equation."

"Thanks for the boost of confidence," Camden deadpans.

I giggle. "Sorry! I didn't mean it in a bad way, but he probably didn't want to think about his best friend and little sister shacking up." It's the truth. Easton is protective of me, and it must not be easy to know that Camden and I had sex.

"I'm sure it will be okay. He probably wants to talk about where you stand. He's your best friend, Camden, and Easton wouldn't just turn his back on you because of this. He's loyal to the bone."

"I know that, but I feel like I was the one who wasn't loyal."

"Hey… That's not true. We slept together, and I just so happened to have gotten pregnant. You didn't manipulate me into doing anything I didn't want to."

"Now, this conversation is making me hard thinking about you." His voice grows heavy.

"Then, touch yourself." I surprise myself with my request.

Camden's voice stutters. "Wh-what?" His own surprise is obvious, but I don't let it stop me.

"Touch yourself. Tell me how hard you are," my breathing grows heavier.

"Fuck, Allyson, I never took you for the phone sex kinda girl." He hisses through his teeth, and my guess is that his hand is wrapped around his dick.

"It's a first for me," I confess. "Are you touching yourself?"

"Everything about you makes me hard as steel, no pun intended this time."

I giggle. "I know what you mean. You turn me on, too."

"Oh, yeah? How much? Are you wet?" His questions rush out, and I hear him groan. I close my eyes as I imagine him stroking his dick.

"Soaked," I respond when I sneak a hand into my underwear and feel my slickness. "I wish you were here to take care of me."

"Soon, babe," he growls. "Fuck... I want to be inside you."

"Yeah," I sigh, lazily rubbing circles over my clit, pretending it's his rough hand pleasuring me.

"This feels so good, Kiwi. The way you make me feel. You drive me wild, those big green eyes when you look up at me right before you take me in your mouth."

I moan at his words, thrusting a finger into my pussy. It's not the same as if he were here, but his voice in my ear helps.

"I'm so tight," I tell him.

the Right kind of Wrong

"Finger fuck yourself. I want to hear your moans."

I thrust my finger faster, bringing my thumb down on my clit, both creating hot friction that spikes throughout my body, causing goosebumps. I moan and tense, Camden whispering and growling.

"I'm going to fuck you until sunrise when I see you again." His dirty talk gets to me as I close my eyes and envision him over me, thrusting into me hard and fast. My core begins to contract around my fingers as my orgasm washes over me at the same time that I hear Camden hiss and curse. He groans, and I know he's losing himself in his own pleasure. I move my hand with determination, amplifying my orgasm as my body tenses and jolts, my moans loud and breathing heavy.

"Shit…" Camden draws out. "I can't wait until you're in my arms for real. This helps, but damn it if it doesn't make me want you even more."

"I know what you mean." I stand and make my way to the bathroom to clean up. "Any idea of when you might make it back?" I risk the question I'm afraid of knowing the answer to.

"I'm almost done fixing Jim's problem and have a couple more meetings with clients. I hope to fly out by the end of next week."

"Okay." I sigh in relief, holding on to the hope that I'll see him soon.

Chapter 21

Camden

These past weeks in Richmond have been stressful. As much as I want to prove to Allyson that we could make this work, it's not. There are only so many phone calls and phone sex we can have before one of us snaps and calls it quits before we actually get a chance to see where we could go together.

I've never been one to believe in fate or destiny, but I am starting to believe that there is a reason Allyson landed on my bed that night. Even more so since she got pregnant. If there is some hokey purpose, then surely it means we will find a way to make it work despite living in different countries.

All I know is that I want to be back with her, take care of her. I've become a man possessed, lured by a woman's touch, smile, and eyes. She's all around me.

I twirl my beer bottle on the bar top before taking a pull from it.

"Sorry I'm late."

I spin on my stool when I hear Easton's voice.

"No problem." I nod with pursed lips. He stands awkwardly before taking a seat next to me. Easton's been like a brother to me. Facing him now, both of us unsure of how to act around each other, makes my chest clench.

"How's Everton?" I try to break the awkwardness.

the Right kind of Wrong

"Cold as fuck already."

"I bet. You want a beer?" I lift my bottle.

"A scotch, actually."

"Ouch." I cringe. "Maybe I need to up to liquor, too, if this is going to hurt."

Easton stares ahead, with his hands clasped together on the bar and his jaw ticking. No trace of humor to break the tension.

Once he has his scotch and I swap my beer for a vodka tonic, he turns to look at me with hard eyes.

"I've been trying to figure out what to say since I found out you knocked up my little sister." I flinch at his harsh tone and choice of words. He's right, though. I knocked her up.

"Listen, Easton…" I trail off when he lifts a hand to stop me.

"I know she's an adult, and she's got free will, and all that bullshit Faith told me, but she's still my sister. She'll always be the little girl I'll want to protect—from a wild horse or a guy." He eyes me over the rim of his glass as he takes a drink of the amber liquid.

"I don't know if you realize the severity of this situation. You aren't playing house with a woman and have the choice to walk away when you get bored. If you decide to be in that child's life from the beginning, you better fucking stay 'til you take your last breath. It's not the kid's fault his or her parents conceived him some drunken night."

"Hold up," I interrupt him. "It wasn't exactly a drunken night. Look, it happened. Yes, we had a few drinks, but we were damn well aware of what we were doing. I'd never, for a second, have taken her to my room if I thought she had no idea what she was doing. I wouldn't have taken advantage of her, or any other women, but especially not your sister."

My jaw clenches, and fist tightens around the cool glass. I take a sip in hopes the vodka will calm me.

"Fuck, yeah, I've never exactly been the kinda guy to stick around with the same woman for the long haul, but I'm determined to be the best father to this kid." I hold Easton's stare, not backing down.

"How exactly will that work since you live here and Ally lives in Spain?" When he arches his eyebrow, I want to knock his glass out of his hand. Fucking childish, but if he's going to treat me as such…

"We're working through that. We don't have everything set in stone, and any plan we make will need adjustments once the time comes, but I ain't walking away from this kid." I shake my head.

"And what about my sister?" He drinks his scotch with a smug expression.

"This is all backward. Maybe if things hadn't happened the way they did, I wouldn't have looked her way. Not because she isn't beautiful, but because she is your sister. I respect that, and I respect our friendship despite what you may believe at the moment. But I did look her way. I saw her, I felt what it could be like to be with her, and I never knew such heaven existed. I never realized how good it'd feel to have it all, and now that I've had a taste of it, I'm going to fight 'til my death to live each day in that sort of paradise."

I take a deep breath, stabilizing my racing heart. I refuse to be the first to look away. I'm not playing games with Allyson.

the Right kind of Wrong

Easton nods as he narrows his eyes before finishing off the rest of his scotch. I almost think he's going to get up and walk away, so it surprises me when he reaches his hand out.

My eyebrows lift as I stare at him, and then I shake his hand.

"It'll take me a while to get used to this, and if you ever hurt Allyson, I'll be the last person you see before you take your last breath." His hand grips mine, and I swallow down my complaint.

"We've got miles of land in Everton, where no one will find your body." Then, he has the balls to smirk. Motherfucker.

"Good to know my best friend wants me dead," I deadpan, finishing off my own drink.

"If you hurt her," he lifts a finger as if correcting me.

"Honestly, Easton, where does this leave us?" I feel like a girl asking, but I don't want this to cause a strain on our friendship.

"I'm not sure. I want to believe you'll do right by her, but I've witnessed your *relationships* for too long to question if you're capable of settling down."

That's a low blow, but I can't argue it. "So fifteen years of friendship down the drain?" I shake my head in disbelief.

"No, but she's my blood."

"And all those years of saying I was your brother was bullshit? If the tables were turned, I'd give you the benefit of the doubt despite your past choices. I trust you enough to believe you when you tell me you're sure about something. I guess you don't trust me when it comes to Allyson." I stand and drop two twenties on the bar.

"You may be that child's uncle, but I'm the father." With that, I walk out of the bar, frustrated as hell.

It isn't fair to think I don't have what it takes to be a good father and a partner, especially after putting my vulnerability on display the way I did. Allyson, she's different. Not in a cliché way, but she's different for me. She brings something out in me that no one ever has.

Screw this. I make a few calls and head back to my apartment. I'm going to see my girl. Hell, I'm going to go make her my girl.

I jumped on a late-night flight yesterday and headed straight for Ally's apartment when I landed at the airport. I called my clients after my conversation with Easton and told them I had to travel. If they want to replace me, then I'll give them the names of a couple people I trust to do as good a job as I do. Thankfully, they were all understanding, Jim included. I do most of their work remotely anyway.

A few seconds after I buzz Allyson's apartment, the front door opens. I make my way to the elevator, my eyebrows bunching in confusion. She didn't even ask who it was; she simply let me in.

I knock on Ally's door, excited and anxious to see her. My conversation with Easton left a sour taste in my mouth, and I'm determined to prove I'm worthy of Allyson. I won't lose both my best friend and the girl.

The door opens, and Allyson's eyes widen as her mouth drops open.

the Right kind of Wrong

"Do you just let anyone up here without asking?" I cross my arms over my chest and smirk.

"What are you doing here? I thought it was my lunch order." Her hand comes up to cover her mouth, and her eyes soften as she looks at me.

I'm the one that can't tear my eyes away from her. She could've sent me a million pictures, but nothing would've prepared me for the emotions I'd feel when I actually saw her. She has the perfect round bump and there's no denying she's pregnant.

I drop to my knees and lift her shirt, dropping a kiss on her stomach. When I look up at her, I notice a few stray tears. I kiss her stomach one more time before standing and wiping her tears again.

"I missed you. You look stunning." I grab the back of her neck and slam my mouth against hers in an urgent kiss. Our tongues swipe together, and I kick the door closed. My hands run down her swollen stomach, lifting her shirt and sneaking my hand under it.

"You're freezing." She shivers, wrapping her arms around my body. Pride swims inside of me at the way she holds me, the way she looks at me.

"You look… So damn beautiful. Pictures don't do you justice, Kiwi." I kiss up her neck to her jaw. When I hear her moans, I smile against her skin. Her flowery scent hits me with a feeling of home, and I desperately need to hold on to that.

"Need you now," I say between peppering kisses across her collar bone.

She takes off her shirt without a second thought, and I lean back, staring at her. "I can't believe I missed seeing this grow." I rub her belly and drop a kiss on the swell of her breasts. Nothing is sexier than her in simple cotton underwear that remains true to herself.

"I'm so fucking hard for you."

I hiss when she palms my erection over my joggers.

"Hard as *Steele*," she smiles, using the pun I told her months ago.

"All for you, baby."

"Fuck," she moans, her hand sneaking into my pants. "Room, now." Her throaty, desperate words make my cock even harder. I grip her ass and lift her, her legs coming around my waist.

Seeing her glow, needing me as much as I need her, it makes me a wild man. I become primal, instinct taking over as I lay her on the bed and kiss up her throat until my lips find hers. Ally's hands go to the back of my head, tugging my hair, and arching her body up to mine. She strokes her tongue along mine, her kiss becoming wild and lighting something inside of me I've never felt.

I've been with women in the past, but Allyson's touch and kiss leave me hungrier for more. It's never enough. I don't give a shit what Easton thinks. I'm all in when it comes to Allyson and this baby. *All. Fucking. In.*

Her hands hold my cheeks, and she stares into my eyes, abruptly stopping the kiss. "What's wrong?" Those green orbs burn into me.

"Nothing," I shake my head, shifting on the bed to lie next to her.

"You're a terrible liar," she points out with a smile. "Talk to me."

the Right kind of Wrong

"I'd rather continue what we were doing." The last thing I want is to talk about her brother while I have her half-naked on a bed. I suck her earlobe into my mouth, and she groans.

"Fine, but we talk after." Her hands come to the hem of my shirt, bunching it up until I have no choice but to remove it. Pleased, she smiles as she traces my chest, smoothing a finger down my skin as she trails it toward my abs. My stomach contracts at the sensation, but I let her continue her exploration.

When she reaches the band on my pants, I look at her with a raised eyebrow, waiting for her next move. A wide smile takes over her face, brightening it and making me forget about everything but the two of us in this moment. She doesn't hold back, instead reaching into my pants and stroking my length.

"Shit, Kiwi…" I shift and run a hand down the side of her body.

"That nickname used to annoy me, but don't you ever think about calling me anything else but that." She leans forward, brushing her lips against mine.

I take her bottom lip between my teeth and tug, flipping us, so I'm on top of her. I thrust my hips into her palm before removing her hand and holding both of them above her head. I wink and smirk, kissing down her jaw and chest, using my free hand to unsnap her bra and remove it.

"Gorgeous," I whisper, running my tongue across her nipple and savoring her reaction. Her body tenses beneath mine, but I don't relent. I move to her other nipple, flicking it with the tip of my tongue. Ally's moans are music to my ear.

"Camden…" She calls out when my teeth scrape along her sensitive skin. And when I take her nipple between my lips and suck, she goes buck wild, her legs coming around my waist and holding me to her.

Keeping her hands above her head, I kiss down her body until her legs have no choice but to fall from my waist. I take advantage of her surrender and stare into her eyes. "Keep your hands up there. Hold on to the headboard. Good," I say when she grips the metal railings that make up the headboard.

My fingers hook into her leggings, trailing them down her legs along with her underwear. Her pussy glistens just for me, and my dick begs me to let him play. But first, I need to taste her. It's been too long.

Once she's naked, I swipe my tongue up her core, catching her by surprise if the yelp that leaves those pretty, full lips is telling.

"Hands," I remind her in a warning tone before dipping my tongue back up her pussy, sucking her clit.

Allyson thrashes and pleads for more.

"Is this what you want?" I fuck her with my tongue, giving her all I've got as I get my fill of her.

"Y-yes…" she stutters on a moan, her hip arching toward my mouth and her hands gripping the headboard.

"My greedy girl." I kiss the inside of her thighs as I twist a finger into her, her tight core gripping it.

I look up at her as I thrust my finger inside of her, a stunning view of her naked body tensing as I enter a second finger. When I hook it and find that spot she loves, her face scrunches up.

"Look at me," I demand. My voice is hoarse to my own ears. Watching her like this, surrendering to me, tests my patience and self-control, but I know the result will be sweeter.

the Right kind of Wrong

I flick her clit with the tip of my tongue, and her hands land on my head, pulling me toward her.

"Kiwi, hands," I say against her body.

"Damn it, Camden, let me touch you." Her nails scrape my scalp, and I groan, which must affect her by the way her body jolts. I take her in my mouth again, relentlessly bringing her to the brink and back down until she's begging me to let her fall. And hell if I don't want her to fall straight into my arms and heart.

I take every bit she gives me until her body is limp on the bed, her breathing heavy as her chest rises and falls rapidly.

I kiss my way up her body, settling between her legs. My dick begs to enter her, but I kiss her first, letting her taste herself as I tease her with the tip of my erection.

"This gives just the tip a whole new meaning, Camden."

I chuckle, and my forehead falls onto hers.

"This baby is mine, and so are you. No one else, babe, no one else." I say through clenched jaw as I thrust into her, taking her lips with mine. I claim her, body and soul until she's crying out my name.

After we're both satiated and eating lunch in her living room, I ask her if she knows of any other hotel near the area.

"I need to find a new hotel. The one I'm staying in only had a room available for today."

"You can stay here. I mean…if you want to. No pressure. You probably want your own space, and that was weird of me to ask." She trips over my words adorably.

185

fabiola francisco

Heat rises to her cheeks, turning them red as she keeps talking. "You know, save money since I'm gonna need that money for child support. Oh, my God. That was a terrible joke. I'm only kidding. I don't want your money. It's just…I like to make things more awkward than they already are." She covers her face with her hands, and I bite back a chuckle.

I peel her hands away and stare into those gorgeous eyes, kissing her softly. "Deep breath, Kiwi." I smile, holding back my laughter. "I'd love to stay with you."

"Okay, cool." she nods.

I chuckle and pull her to me. "You're something else."

"Awkward as fuck. I hope this child gets your confidence."

"Whoa…" I stop pulling her to my lap and stare at her with furrowed brows. "You're confident, strong, smart, and funny. I hope this boy is just like you—looks, personality, and heart." I grip the sides of her face, and my eyes pierce into hers. "I'm nothing compared to you."

I tear my gaze away, dropping my head.

"Hey, that's not true. You've always been a great person, and these last few months, I've seen a different side of you. One that I wish I had known earlier. I believe you should show it to the world more often. This child is lucky to have us both." She shifts on my lap and hugs me. My arms curl around her body, keeping her close.

"That's not what your brother thinks." I shake my head, releasing a heavy breath.

"Cam, Easton is coming around. He's afraid you'll hurt me because he knows one side of you, but I've gotten to know *you,* and I trust you…with my baby and my heart."

the Right kind of Wrong

I brush my thumb across her bottom lip, smiling sadly. "Thank you." I grab her chin and bring her lips to mine, kissing her with every ounce of emotion I possess. I won't stop until I make her mine, even if it takes me a million years. I'm so deep with her that I never want to find my way out.

Chapter 22

Allyson

When Camden showed up at my door some weeks ago, I couldn't believe it. I was waiting for him to call me and let me know when he'd be flying back. After extending his trip while he was in Richmond, I wasn't sure if I'd see him anytime soon.

Then, he surprised me, and my doubts about him returning dissipated. When he kissed me, I felt as if all the stars in the universe were aligned.

We've spent as much time together as we can. He's met my friends, we hosted our own Thanksgiving dinner in my apartment, and I've shown him more of the city. Rubén and Vanesa have made it a point to help Camden with his Spanish whenever we get together, which has been more helpful than I thought. The weeks leading up to the holidays always feel a bit lonely since I can't fly home for Thanksgiving, but this fall has felt different.

I rub my stomach and sigh. I'm waiting for Camden to finish up in the shower so we can go to my doctor's appointment.

My boss took the news well, and I told everyone at the office afterward. Now, at twenty weeks pregnant, there's no denying I'm with child.

the Right kind of Wrong

I hear his steps nearing the living room and smile up at him when he leans against the wall with an easy grin on his face. He's been staying with me since he returned, and it's been my own brand of perfection. Laying with him at night, talking about our child, and the articles he's read about pregnancy and parenthood has given us a chance to work through this.

Camden walks toward me on the couch. He leans down and brushes his lips against mine while his hand touches my belly. "Ready to find out if we're having a boy or girl?" His eyes twinkle with excitement.

"I thought you were confident it's a boy."

"I'm positive, but since you doubt my psychic skills, I'll humor you." He winks and reaches for my hand to help me up, lacing his fingers with mine.

Once outside, Camden waves down a cab and opens the door for me to slide in. "I thought we'd ride to the doctor's office."

"Thank you." I scoot over and wait for him to sit before giving the cab driver the address.

Camden's fingers brush my palm in soothing circles. I've been waiting for this day for weeks. My heart hammers against my ribs. I know the baby is healthy, but it's always nerve-wracking going into a check-up. Today, though, I'm excited to find out the gender, so the nerves are caused by an overwhelming sense of joy.

"Are we going to tell our families right away?" Camden interrupts my thoughts.

"We can," I nod. "Maybe we can record a video and send it to them in the group chat."

fabiola francisco

"I like that idea." He leans in and kisses my temple. Then, he runs the tip of his nose down my jaw, inhaling deeply, and his hand runs slow circles over my swollen stomach. A shiver runs up my spine.

"You smell so good." His voice sounds gruff. Heat creeps up my neck. I'm still getting used to being this way with Camden.

Following his lead, I inhale his masculine scent. It's spicy and woodsy and reminds me of Everton for some reason—which is ridiculous since Camden has nothing to do with that part of my life.

As soon as he got back, he opened up about giving a relationship a try. He was ready for every excuse I threw his way. Truthfully, I want nothing more than to see if we could be a family, but there's still the fact that we live in two different countries, and legally, his stay here will end soon. I also worry about what will happen if we break up. If that's the case, I hope we can be adults and still co-parent, so our child has a happy and healthy upbringing.

I turn my head and smile at him. "Thank you. I bet you never thought I'd be your girlfriend," I tease him.

"You're the best surprise I never expected."

My breath hitches as tears fill my eyes. Camden strokes my cheek with his thumb. His lips touch mine, and my heart swells. I reach up and cup his cheek. "Thank you for being here."

"I want to," he assures me with a firm nod.

"I know." I lean into his side, resting my head on his shoulder as we weave through the busy streets.

When we arrive at the doctor's office, Camden holds my hand while we wait for them to call us. Once I'm in the

the Right kind of Wrong

examination room, Camden stands by my side. The technician goes through the explanation I've heard numerous times from my other check-ups, and she goes on to do the sonogram.

After letting us know that everything looks good, she taps the keys on the computer and zooms in. With a wide smile, she congratulates us, telling us it's a boy. Camden whoops so loud, both the technician and I jolt. I cover my mouth as tears stream down my face. Camden grabs ahold of me and kisses me shamelessly.

"A boy," he whispers against my lips. "You owe me a date." He winks.

I nod, still overwhelmed with emotions.

"Pretty sure we already had plenty of dates."

"Nah, this one is special, Kiwi." He kisses me again before staring at the screen again.

The technician smiles at us, and we wait for the sonogram to print before leaving the office.

"I'm so damn happy." Camden's face is lit up as we walk down the sidewalk. "You're not going to work until four, right?"

"Yeah." I took the morning off for the appointment, and it's one day I'm especially grateful for Spain's odd work hours. I stare at the printout in my hand—our baby boy. I can't believe it.

"Let's have lunch." He swings his arm around my shoulder and pulls me toward him. I put the sonogram away in my purse, careful not to wrinkle it, and wrap my arm around his waist.

At times I can't believe this is my life.

"Can we do something before?" I peer up at him with a smile.

"Anything you want."

I bring out my phone and signal Camden to bend down a bit so that his six-foot frame is even with my five-five one. I flip the camera until it's facing us and hit record.

"We just got the best news." I look over at Camden. When I stare back at the camera, I yell, "We're having a boy!"

Camden laughs, confirming our news. I choke up when he tells them that we're using my dad's name as the baby's middle name, and we're so excited to meet our son.

I end the recording, but my tears flow down my face. He kisses my cheeks and dries my tears. A boyish smile takes over his face; it's my favorite smile of his. My heart slams against my ribs as I stare into his face. Everything fades but the man in front of me, looking at me with so many emotions. My entire body freezes when I realize I'm falling in love with him, irrevocably so.

My realization has been on my mind all afternoon, distracting me from work. *Falling in love with Camden.* I chew on the inside of my cheek as I ponder this. He's definitely the kind of guy I'd fall for, but we're still nowhere close to figuring out where the future will lead. I'm afraid I'll end up with a broken heart.

"Tick, tock." Camden taps my forehead. "What's on your mind?"

I turn my head to look at him as the steady subway takes us to our destination. He looks handsome in dark jeans, a baby blue button-down shirt, and a gray coat. His eyes are bright, and the perfect amount of scruff frames his face.

the Right kind of Wrong

I smile and shake my head. "Nothing." I lean my head on his shoulder, comforted by his warmth as he holds me to him. His fingers rub circles on my arm over the coat, and yet his touch causes chills through a wool barrier.

"Are you excited to see your family when we fly home for Christmas?" His deep voice washes over me like refreshing summer rain.

I sit up to look at him. "I can't wait. I think my mom is going to flip when she sees my stomach," I laugh.

"She's going to be so happy. She misses you, but she's so damn proud of you."

I nod as tears fill my eyes. Blinking them away, I smile and kiss Camden's cheek. My mom has been my rock during this pregnancy. She's always sharing her wisdom with me and reassuring me everything has a divine plan, even if I can't see it.

I've flown home for Christmas the past two years I've been living here, but this Christmas will be special. I place my hand on my belly, and Camden's warm touch lands over my hand.

I'm a ball of emotions bouncing all over the place today. I've been thinking about my dad, especially after finding out we're having a boy.

I gasp and snap my head to Camden. "Did you feel that?"

His eyes are wide. "Was that…" His question trails off as I nod.

Both of his hands land on my stomach and his mouth splits into the most beautiful smile I've ever seen. His eyes mist over. "Come on, boy, do that again." We both look down at my stomach, waiting for him to move again.

I've never felt something quite like that. Everyone always says that being pregnant is magical, and I've never really put much thought into it, but I now understand why they say it. I feel him move again and smile. My eyes water, and as much as I try to hold them in since we're riding the subway with strangers, a few tears roll down my cheeks.

Camden tilts his head with a smile before grabbing my face and kissing me, no care in the world that we have an audience. "That was amazing," he says against my lips.

"I know," I whisper, wrapping my arms around him in a hug. I catch the eyes of a mom sitting near us with her young child, and she smiles knowingly.

Soon after, We get off the subway and walk the short distance to the restaurant Camden chose. When I see the stationed railroad car, I look over at Camden with furrowed eyebrows.

"I was told it's a hidden gem." He squeezes my hand and walks us toward the railcar, guiding me up the few steps.

When I walk in, my eyes widen. Square tables are set where the seats would be, all covered in white table cloths that remind me of old, high-class trains I've seen in historical films. Light pink roses in a short vase sit on the center of each table. The lighting is dim and romantic.

"This is beautiful," I smile over at Camden.

"I'm glad you like it."

Once we're seated with menus and sparkling water, Camden raises his glass. "To our healthy baby boy and to the gorgeous woman keeping him safe." The corners of his eyes crinkle with his smile; that one dimple making an appearance.

Before he can tap my glass with his, I add, "And to the selfless man who takes care of us both."

the Right kind of Wrong

The way he looks at me gives me chills. It's as if Camden were staring into my soul, communicating something so deep, it surpasses the human brain and goes straight to the heart. His free hand reaches for mine, linking our fingers as he taps our glasses together and takes a sip of water.

"Thank you," he whispers.

"I mean it. You've been…" I shake my head. "No adjective I use will be enough to express what I'm trying to say, but know that I'm not blind to the sacrifice you're making by being here as much as you can."

"Wouldn't want to be anywhere else." His fingers tighten around mine, and I shiver.

Sitting across from him in a romantic restaurant, staring into his chocolate eyes, I hope that if Camden and I are on this path together, it's because we can make it work. After getting to know him on a more intimate level, I don't think I can go back to just being his best friend's sister.

Chapter 23

Camden

I drive through Everton, Ally's hometown, in the rental we picked up when we landed here. The whole town is white, piles of snow covering everything. It's a beautiful sight. We're spending Christmas here with Easton, Faith, and her family. Charlene flew over as soon as the semester ended at the university, and I know she's anxious to see Allyson.

Ally and I have been stateside for a few days. First, we drove to Virginia Beach to see my parents and sister. Although I live in Richmond after going to college at the University of Virginia, my family remains in our hometown.

I smile to myself as I remember my mom and sister's reaction when they saw Ally. No matter the pictures or videos we had sent them, they got emotional seeing her pregnant belly in person.

"What are you thinking about?" Allyson's sweet voice breaks through my thoughts.

"How beautiful you are," I wink.

She rolls her eyes playfully.

"I was thinking back to when we visited my parents."

"They should've come with us," Ally comments.

I squeeze her hand before lifting it to my lips. "Yeah, but Mom always hosts Christmas dinner for the entire family, and

the Right kind of Wrong

with Grandma being so old, they like to spend as many Christmases as they can with her." My grandma has been saying it's her last holiday season for the past four years, and she's still kicking it, but we all worry it might be her last after a pneumonia scare earlier this year.

"You didn't want to stay with them? We could've." She looks over at me with furrowed eyebrows and pinched lips.

I love that she makes us an *us*.

"You tell me now? When we're on the way to face your brother, who thinks I'm no good for you?" I tease. Easton and I have spoken a few times through text messages, but our friendship isn't where it used to be.

"He's coming around." Ally leans back on her seat, rubbing her stomach.

Watching her evolve throughout this pregnancy has been a beautiful experience. I never imagined what it'd feel like to watch her body change and transform.

"Yeah, I know he is, but we're definitely not the friends we were before this happened." My lips press into a straight line as I take the road that leads to The Farm House, the bed and breakfast we stayed at for Easton's wedding.

"I can't believe we're back here," Ally says with a shake of her head.

"And this time, you won't be running out of my room, Kiwi." I chuckle lowly when she glares at me.

"Can you blame me? I woke up and was like, what the fuck?" She talks with her hands, and the pitch in her voice rises as she finishes off her sentence.

"I know, babe." I kiss the inside of her wrist. "But this time, you're staying in my bed and in my space."

"Yeah," she sighs and leans in to kiss my cheek as I put the car in *Park*. I grip her hip and turn my head to catch her lips in mine.

"Let's go." I give her a final kiss.

"Yeah, before we get caught making out in the car and rumors start to run. I'm pretty sure as soon as they see me pregnant, other types of rumors will be whispered in grocery lines and church pews."

I chuckle and hop out of the truck. By the time I make it to Allyson's side of the vehicle, she's already stepping out.

"It's freezing." She rubs her hands together and blows into them. "Start heading in. I'll grab our bags."

"I can help," she argues.

"I got it." I peck her lips and open the back seat, grabbing our two carry-ons. I watch Allyson take careful steps up to the bed and breakfast.

As I walk into the house, I hear a squeal. "When Faith told me you were pregnant, I couldn't believe it." Averly, the owner of The Farm House and one of Faith's best friends, holds Allyson's hands wide and smiles at her.

"I should add a slogan to this place. The Farm House: Where the magic happens." Her hands spread in front of her as she laughs.

"Yeah, definitely magical," Ally chuckles.

"If that's sarcasm I hear in your voice, I'll have to remind you how magical this place really is." I lift my eyebrows and stare into her eyes, placing the bags on the floor next to my feet.

Averly laughs while shaking her head and walks behind the counter to look at our reservation. "Camden, you'd fit right in if you lived here," she says. "Poppy is also pregnant.

the Right kind of Wrong

I'm not sure if Faith had told you. She's having a girl in March."

"No way! That's awesome," Ally's face lights up with a smile. Poppy is another friend of Faith's. It seems like everyone in this town is connected in some way, but they're all great people and Easton's friends.

"Your room is ready, so you're welcome to go up and get settled in. If you need anything, let me know. I assume I'll see you guys at Clarke's tonight?" Averly smiles.

"We'll be there," I nod. Clarke's is this town's favorite watering hole. I went the first time I visited Everton with Easton and then again when I came for his wedding.

"Awesome. I'm glad you guys are spending Christmas here."

"Thanks, Averly," Allyson smiles and grabs the key from her.

When we make it up to the room, Ally walks to the far wall and stares out the large windows that give us a clear view of the snowed mountains. I hug her from behind and drop a kiss on her neck.

"Do you ever think about moving back here?" I whisper into her ear. She shivers at the contact.

"What? No." Allyson shakes her head and sighs. "I moved when I was a kid, and most of my life happened in Virginia."

"But?" I prompt because I can sense there's something else she's not saying.

"It's weird. I was thirteen when we moved, so I've lived more of my life away from this place than in it, but it will always be home. It's where I was born. Where my family comes from. Now that I've visited more often since Easton moved, I feel like maybe I did miss something by leaving this town."

I tighten my arms around her and feel our boy kick. Ally giggles and I press my palms against her stomach to see if he'll kick again. When he doesn't, I turn Ally around and hold her face, kissing her.

"If you ever want to move back here, we can talk about our options." My thumbs rub her cheeks as she nods. I see no future that doesn't include Allyson. If she eventually wants to move back to her hometown and raise our son here, then I'll pack our bags and move us. All I know is that where she goes, I go. Nothing will stand in our way.

"Maybe one day," she shrugs. She may not be as connected to this place as Easton is, but I see it in her eyes when she talks about it or when she visits. She may not even be aware of it, but she misses this place.

"You let me know." I kiss her deeply and take a step back. "Your family is waiting for us."

"We could lie and say our flight was delayed, and we'll be arriving at their house later." She mischievously waggles her eyebrows.

I chuckle and shake my head. "No can do, Kiwi. They've been following our flight." I tap the tip of her nose. "We'll spend time with them, and we'll come back to rest before heading out to Clarke's tonight."

"Okay." She squeezes my cheeks with her hand until my lips pucker and drops a kiss. "You're cute." She winks and laughs, stepping around me to grab her gloves from her bag.

I stare at her for a moment. I'm so in love with this woman, and she has no idea. Or maybe she does. That woman's intuition could've kicked in.

the Right kind of Wrong

Allyson tilts her head in my direction as she bends over to look in her bag and smiles at me. Loose strands of hair from her messy ponytail fall across her face. The light in her eyes shines brighter than the sun reflecting off the snow. She's stunning, and she's all mine.

I fish my phone out of my pocket and snap a picture of her before she could realize what I'm doing. I want to remember her like this.

"Hey." She stands tall and walks to me. "A little warning would've been nice." She plucks my phone from her hand and inspects the photo. Her nose scrunches up as she looks at me. "Take another one."

I shake my head. "No can do, Kiwi. I wanted you in your natural state, not some fake pose. You're beautiful, and I'm keeping this picture." I shove my phone in my pocket and hug her to me. My hand sneaks over her stomach.

Allyson shoves the strands of hair away from her face as we stare at each other. A moment of silence passes between us, and I brush my lips against hers. Those three little words are on the tip of my tongue, but I swallow them down.

"Ready?" I ask.

"Yeah," Ally whispers with a nod. Her breath catches, and then she smiles. "Let's go see if Easton is going to kick your ass or give you a hug." Her laughter fills the room.

"Not funny," I grumble.

"I'm only kidding." She loops her arm in mine and opens the door, leading us down the stairs and out of the bed and breakfast.

I'm not sure what to think when we walk into Easton's house. Instead of knocking, Allyson just barges in. My sweaty palms are going to be sore from scrubbing them against my jean-clad thighs, but I'm nervous as ever. Sure, Easton has sent messages to me here and there, but we haven't exactly had a real conversation since I saw him in Richmond, and he practically laughed in my face when I told him I was committed to Ally and the baby.

"You're here!" Faith hops from her stool and rushes over with Charlene right behind her. Faith wraps her arms around Allyson before rubbing her belly. Charlene smiles at me warmly, hugging me, before focusing on her daughter. Easton stands a few feet away, hands in his pockets.

"You're gonna say hi to your sis or what?" Ally smiles at him. "You can't be mad at me forever, or I'll have to choose a different godfather for this kid." Her smirk turns teasing as her hand lays on her stomach.

"I'm not mad." Easton walks over to her and hugs his sister, whispering something in her ear. Allyson nods at whatever he says before stepping back and looking at me.

"Hey, man," Easton extends his hand. I shake it and smile.

"What's up?" I nod.

"How was your trip?" He turns to face us both.

"It was good. Pretty smooth ride," Allyson responds.

"I can't get over this belly," Faith says. "Let's take a seat." She guides Allyson and Charlene to the living room.

Before I can follow them, Easton stops me. "Do you want a beer?" He opens the fridge.

"Yeah, sure." I thank him when I take the bottle he offers and take a sip.

"Things are good around here? Work?" I ask.

"Yeah." He nods, taking a pull from his beer.

the Right kind of Wrong

"Listen, I owe you an apology…" Easton starts. I furrow my eyebrows as I eye him. "I shouldn't have doubted you. You're my best friend, and I should've known you'd never do wrong by Ally."

My heart thumps in my chest, and I nod. "Thanks. What made you change your mind?"

"I see the way you look at her. The way you looked at her when you made the video with the gender reveal."

I place the beer bottle on the counter and cross my arms. "And how's that?"

"Like you're in love with her." Easton calmly drinks his beer as if he didn't just say I'm in love with his sister. "You should tell her." He points his longneck toward me.

I nod, grabbing my beer and taking a deep pull. Even though he's right, I would've much rather told Allyson before her brother knew.

He claps my back with a chuckle. "I know you pretty damn well, but I'm sure I didn't have to tell you that for you to be aware of your feelings."

"Nah, you're right. I just didn't think you'd know before her." I chuckle.

"Just keep her safe." He reaches his hand out, and I nod, shaking it.

"I plan on it." I would hate for our friendship to get ruined because of something like this. I'm determined to do right by Ally and our son, and I'm glad that she's on the same page as me.

When I walk into the living room with Easton, Allyson looks my way with a bright smile. The orange hues of the fireplace make her shine like a guiding light. She's my guiding light, showing me what I've been missing my entire life, and I wasn't even looking for it.

Now that I know life with her, I never want to know what it feels like to be without her.

Chapter 24

Allyson

I hadn't realized how much I craved family time until I spent Christmas with them in Everton. Each time I visit my hometown since Easton moved, I feel more and more connected to it. I was caught by surprise when Camden asked me if I'd want to move back there. I had never put much thought into it until he asked. Now, the idea of raising my son where I grew up is becoming more appealing. *Maybe one day.*

"Are you excited to see Noel and Berkeley tonight?" Camden squeezes my hand as he drives us to his apartment in Richmond. My mom doesn't return from Everton until after the new year, so I had to say my goodbyes to her as well when I left Everton since Camden and I leave for Madrid tomorrow evening.

"I am." I smile over at him. "Although I video chat with them all the time, it's so different hanging out in person. I'm long overdue for girl time." I sink into the leather seat of his Audi and rub slow circles over my ever-growing belly. I can't believe how big it's gotten in just a few weeks. I swear, I'm growing by the day.

"You definitely are, and once this baby comes, we're going to be busy adjusting to life with a kid." He lifts our tangled hands and brushes his lips against the top of mine. I shiver when his stubble tickles my skin.

"I know. I can't believe we're three and a half months away from having a baby. How crazy is that?"

Camden chuckles. "Some days, I can't believe it. I've been enjoying you pregnant that I can't imagine you not being pregnant. I may have to knock you up again soon." He winks at me.

Butterflies swarm in my stomach. Does this mean he sees us together for the years to come? Building more than just this small family?

"Slow your horse." I shake my head. "One at a time, sperm boy," I tease because seriously, he must have super sperm.

A deep laugh rumbles through him, and it hits me directly in my core. Everything about him turns me on.

"We have time to grow our family," he agrees. "I love seeing you like this, so I plan on having more babies." He releases my hand and moves his over my stomach. "Sexy as hell," he says hoarsely.

Plans of the future, his words and actions, they make me want to demand that he pull over on the side of the road and have his way with me. People weren't kidding when they say pregnancy hormones make women sex-driven. Or maybe it's just my natural reaction to Camden—pregnant or not.

"At what time is Berkeley picking you up?" He pulls into the garage in his apartment building.

"Six-thirty."

"Good, we've got plenty of time to get dirty before I clean you up in the shower." Camden kills the engine and looks at

the Right kind of Wrong

me with the expression of a starving man faced with his favorite meal.

His hands cradle my face, and his lips land on mine in a demanding kiss. His tongue desperately traces the seam on my lips, begging entry. I open for him, my own lips and tongue moving of their own accord, seeking him and stealing every kiss from him.

"Need you." His hands roam down the sides of my body.

"Take me," I whisper against his lips before fusing our lips together and kissing him deeply.

Camden breaks away and opens his door. "Let's go." It's a simple command that moves a shiver up my spine. I'm out of the car and next to him in record time. My body hums with anticipation.

As soon as we step into the elevator, Camden's mouth is on mine again. I swear, this is the scene from every sexy movie I've ever watched. All we need is for Marvin Gaye to play over the speakers.

A giggle bubbles in the back of my throat, and I try to swallow it down, but Camden notices, and when he leans his head back, I sputter all over him.

"What's so funny?" His eyebrows pinch together.

"Nothing." I lean in to kiss him, but he inches back.

"Tell me."

"It's nothing. I was laughing at my imagination." I shake my head.

"Oh, yeah? And is there something fucking hilarious about what you'd be imagining while I kiss you? I was hoping for moans, not giggles, Kiwi." He lifts his eyebrows as his voice rings with amusement.

"Ugh." I toss my head back against the elevator wall. "I was just thinking that this is right out of a hot movie scene. You know, the elevator make-out, not caring if there are cameras watching because you desperately need the other person."

Camden smirks and steps close until our bodies are as flush as possible. "Kiwi, I'm about to give it so good that every fantasy you've had will pale in comparison."

I thickly swallow as anticipation builds like a slow-coming snowstorm. His hands tangle in my messy hair as his eyes pierce into mine.

One beat.

Two beats.

My heart punches my ribs with each beat as I wait for Camden's next move. His body is pressed against mine, and it's not just his muscles that are hard against me.

"Cam," I whisper, leaning my mouth to his.

"I'm gonna make you forget every fantasy and replace them with my body, my lips, my touch." He's wild when he kisses him, his hands roaming down my back until he grips my butt and presses me into him. I gasp into his mouth when I feel his erection so close to where I want him.

When the elevator pings open, Camden drags me down the hall and hastily unlocks the door. As soon as the door slams, he has me pinned against the wall in the entrance, arms above my head, and teeth nipping my jaw before he kisses trails along my neck. I moan and arch into him, needing some kind of friction.

"Need to taste you." He drops to his knees, and I squeeze my eyes closed. Cool air hits my lower body as he yanks my leggings down my legs and helps me step out of them.

the Right kind of Wrong

Camden blindly flings them over to his side as his sole focus is on me.

I cry out when his thumb moves along my core, teasing my clit.

"Eyes open and on me. I want you to watch me make you feel so fucking good." *His dirty mouth.*

I peer down at him, and when our eyes lock, Camden runs his tongue over my pussy, causing me to jolt. A crooked smile marks his lips before he grabs my leg and swings it over his shoulder. Next thing I know, I'm crying out in pleasure as his mouth devours me.

His gaze flickers between my eyes and my body. His lips close around my clit, and he sucks it into his mouth, thrusting his fingers inside of me. The sensations swirl together, leading me to the brink as my body buzzes with my orgasm. I feel like I'm soaring as my heart drums in my ears and my body tenses. Camden laps up every last bit before standing and kissing me.

"You taste so good. I'll never get enough of you. And when they ask me what I want my last meal to be, my only response will be you."

I groan, and my hands fly to his jeans, messily working on undoing the button and zipper. Camden stops my hands and finishes the job for me. Before I can fist his hard length, he grabs the back of my thighs and lifts me. My legs wrap around his body as he thrusts into me against the wall of his apartment like a man on a mission, every nerve-ending in my body reacting to him as if he were the sole owner and in this moment, no one else owns me the way he does—body, mind, heart, and soul. I'm all his.

"Spill the tea," Noel says as soon as Berkeley and I walk into her apartment. "I've been dying to hear what's going on with you and Camden. Since he's always around, we haven't really been able to get into details during our talks, and I'm dyyyying," she draws out dramatically and finishes off by tossing her head back in exasperation.

"She has been. She keeps asking me if I know anything, and I only know what you've told us," Berkeley says as she sits on the sofa.

"Also, you're the most adorable pregnant woman ever, and I miss you like crazy." Noel hugs me before placing her hands on my belly and bending down. "Hello, beautiful boy. I'm your Aunt Noel. I'll be the one to teach you all about how to sneak in drinks before your twenty-first birthday."

I laugh and sit on the sofa next to Berkeley. "You're crazy." I point at Noel.

"But you love me," she shrugs. "Anyway, I know you can't drink alcohol, so I made a mocktail." She walks over and places a tray with a pitcher full of a bubbly, light pink liquid. "And…" she lifts a bottle of vodka. "I've got this to spike ours," Noel winks at Berkeley.

"I very much approve of this plan. I could use a drink or five." Berkeley fills her glass with the mocktail and then adds a hefty shot of vodka to it, stirring it with her finger. No shame in her cocktail game.

"What's going on?" I turn to look at Berkeley.

"Tough week at work," she shrugs. "We have an older woman staying at the hotel, and she's difficult. I'm just glad

the Right kind of Wrong

I'm off today, so I could see you." Berkeley takes a drink of her cocktail.

She's a receptionist in a hotel here in Richmond, but she's always wanted more out of her career. Although she studied hospitality, she's been stuck in the same position for years.

When I told her about Averly's bed and breakfast in Everton, her eyes lit up. I know Berkeley dreams of having her small hotel one day, and I hope she makes that happen soon. If not, this job is going to suck her passion dry.

"So, tell us what's going on. How are things with Camden?" Berkeley smiles.

"They're good, great actually. We're together, together, and honestly, he's been amazing. I never thought he'd be the kind of boyfriend that he is, but he's blown my expectations way out of the water."

I tell them how caring and thoughtful he's been and how attentive he is with the pregnancy. Noel and Berkeley sigh and smile.

"I'm so glad things are going well. Are you guys going to get married before the baby's born?"

I choke on my drink when I hear Noel's question. "Married?" I squeak. "We're together, and yes, we're having a baby, but I don't want to rush into something just because we're having a baby together before we're sure if things will work out. It isn't the right reason to marry someone."

As much as I want to have a family with Camden, I don't want to make a decision based on what society rules as right or wrong. If we get married, I want it to be because we're both ready for that step, whether our son is one or eighteen. Well, I hope I wouldn't have to wait eighteen years if we're still together.

"I think that's smart," Berkeley comments.

"I bet we'll be hearing wedding bells sooner than you think." Noel tips her half-empty glass in my direction. "Which brings me to my next thing." She stands and grabs a gift bag. Berkeley snorts next to me as she tries to hold back her laughter.

"What's going on?" I move my gaze between them. "We said no gifts."

"I know, I know, but we saw this thing that was *so* perfect. We had to get it."

"But—" I begin to argue, but Berkeley lifts her hand to stop me.

"Open it before you say anything else." She laughs again, and Noel glares at her.

I take the gift bag and pluck the tissue paper from it before grabbing the present wrapped in more tissue. As I peel back the tissue paper, I burst out laughing.

"Oh. My. God. This is…" I gasp for air. "I can't even." I lift the boxer briefs in front of me, staring at a red pair of boxers with the phrase, *This cock belongs to Allyson*, on the crotch, except that instead of the word cock, there's a rooster.

"It goes perfectly with the rooster from your apartment building. Now you really got yourself some cock," Berkeley says on a chuckle.

"How did you get a picture of me?" Next to the crotch is a picture with my face and someone else's body hugging the crotch.

"Instagram, duh," Noel playfully shakes her head in exasperation.

"This is… I don't even know what to say," I shake my head.

the Right kind of Wrong

"Just thank us and record Camden when he first sees it," Noel adds.

"He's going to love this," I say, placing the boxer briefs on my lap. I can't help but laugh again as I stare at it.

"Own it, girl. That cock is yours." Noel laughs. "I wish we would've recorded your face when you saw it." She leans back on the other side of the sofa, next to me.

"This is the best gift I've received in a long time." I place it in the bag, giggling.

We spend the rest of the evening catching up, laughing, and eating pizza. I miss having my friends nearby, but I'm lucky that I get to hop over to this side of the Atlantic and see them. I somber realizing it might not be as easy to do once the baby is born.

"I know you have a boy in your life now and all that, but let's not lose our daily chats." Noel hugs me.

"You ladies should come visit me soon. I miss you more than you know." I give them both a hug when Camden arrives to pick me up.

"We will." Noel nods.

"Yes, as soon as I get some vacation time, we'll make plans to see you. Don't forget to show Camden the gift," Berkeley giggles.

I stare at my best friends for a few minutes before walking away, holding back tears. Living far from the people I love is hard, but the experience of living and working abroad is an amazing opportunity.

By the time I get to Camden's car, he's standing by the passenger door. His hands land on my hips as he leans in for a kiss.

"Did you have fun?"

"Yes, I miss them so much." I smile as I get into the car when he opens the door.

"I'm glad you had fun," Camden adds once he's seated in the driver's side.

"How about you?" I shift to look at him as he pulls onto the road.

"It was good to see Luke, although it hadn't been that long since I'd seen him like it's been for you with the girls." He reaches for my hand as he drives us back to his place.

"Noel and Berkeley got us a gift. Technically it's for you but also for me. I'm not sure." I shake my head and giggle.

"What is it?" He glances at me from the corner of his eye.

"You'll have to wait 'til we get home." I squeeze his hand.

As soon as we arrive at his place, Camden asks to see the gift. His eyes widen, and a loud cackle bursts out of him when he sees the boxer briefs.

"This is hilarious." He holds the boxers out in front of him as he inspects it. "Well, this cock is yours," he winks.

"One day, they called me after I had heard a rooster crowing from my bathroom, and I made the joke that I moved to Spain for the cocks, which, of course, held the double meaning. It's been a joke ever since, so this is perfect."

Camden loops his arm around my waist and pulls me to him, my swollen belly limiting how close we get. "The only cock that's yours is mine. Or am I going to have to make you forget all others before me like I did earlier today?" He arches a brow.

A shiver moves through me, and I swing my arms around his neck. "I'm not thinking about any other but yours," I smirk. "Besides, it's not like there were a ton before you," I add on a whisper.

Camden groans and squeezes my behind, pulling me as close to him as I can get, but there's no mistaking the hardness pressed against me. "You're the only one I want, too."

"I'm going to assume you mean pussy and not cock because this would be really awkward if so." I laugh at my own joke, and Camden growls, slapping my butt.

"Kiwi… You, only you." His lips sneak into the crook of my neck, kissing and sucking until I'm melted goo in his hands.

"Glad we're on the same page," I tease, tugging the back of his hair until he's looking at me. I get on my toes and whisper so close to his lips. "Are you gonna kiss me or what?"

Everyone who came before him, every heartache, every kiss, every touch melts away as Camden's lips fuse with mine, and I get swept into a fairytale that is guaranteed to have a happy ending.

Chapter 25

Camden

Sitting next to Allyson on the flight to Madrid reminds me of the first flight we took together to New York after spending the night together. She was a nervous wreck, babbling and giving me shit. What a difference six months and a pregnancy make. Now, her head is resting on my shoulder as she sleeps, her hand protectively over her stomach.

I love how she's always aware of the baby, protecting it in some way, and already being the best mom possible. I could watch her like this for hours, and it would never be enough. This woman has stolen my heart, and I sure as hell don't want it back.

I lift the window shade and peek out into the sea of clouds. We're almost to Madrid, and I can't wait to sleep for the next fourteen hours. I've never been one to sleep on a flight, let alone one this long. Closing the shade again, so the light doesn't wake Allyson, I lean my head back on the seat. Seven hours on an airplane will drive you stir-crazy after a while. To make matters worse, none of the movies on the entertainment television sound interesting, and I've already seen the TV shows.

I press the screen on the seat in front of me and look at the games. I touch the Solitaire icon and watch as the cards

the Right kind of Wrong

load before I start playing. Halfway through game three, Allyson shifts and lifts her head. I look over at her with a smile.

"Hi." Her voice is raspy.

"Hey, Kiwi. How'd you sleep?"

"Good. Not the best position for my neck, though." She smirks and sits up, stretching her arms out as a wide yawn splits her mouth open. She covers it quickly with wide eyes.

I chuckle and wrap my arm around her shoulder the best way I can and pull her to me, kissing her full lips. Then, I move my hand to her neck and start massaging. Allyson moans near my ear with closed eyes. I watch her face twist and relax as I work out a knot.

"That feels so good," she whispers.

I wish we were in the privacy of her apartment. My boxer briefs feel tight around my crotch—not the red pair with Ally's face on it that her friends gave her. I chuckle to myself.

"What's funny?" She looks up at me through her lashes, and she's a real beauty—all soft and sweet and innocent with a twist of mischief and trouble that I love bringing out in her.

"Just thinking about those boxers."

Allyson giggles, hiding her face against my shoulder. "They're so funny."

"Definitely a unique gift."

"I can't wait to get home, shower, and sleep. I swear my feet are so swollen I have cankles."

I bring my hand around from her neck to her face, splaying my fingers across her cheek as I hold her. "You'll get to sleep on your comfy bed soon." I kiss her forehead and then bend to kiss her stomach.

"How long do we have?" Her voice is soft, and she looks at me with what could only be love. I recognize it in her eyes the same way I feel it in mine.

"Forty minutes, according to the map."

"I can't wait." She rests her head on my shoulder again, her hands holding mine as we wait to land in Madrid. Having her in my arms, even in an uncomfortable airplane seat, is heaven. I'll take crowded seats, snoring strangers, and swollen feet any day if it means having Ally in my arms.

The customs officer begins talking in Spanish instead of stamping my passport and letting me continue on my merry way.

"Sorry, but do you speak English?" I raise my eyebrows. No amount of months I've spent here has prepared me to communicate with a customs officer in Spanish. I'm still limited in my knowledge.

"Sir, you've exceeded the number of days allowed to visit the country. I cannot let you continue beyond this point," he informs with a heavy accent.

"What?" My body shakes. "How is that even possible if I was allowed to buy a plane ticket?"

"The airlines don't monitor the length of stay of each customer. That's the individual's responsibility to know the laws."

"What's going on?" Allyson steps toward me, but the officer stops her.

the Right kind of Wrong

"Ma'am, you cannot return to this point. I need you to continue going." The officer steps out of his box office to guarantee she's listening.

"But he's my boyfriend." Her eyes widen.

"Do you have a visa?" the officer asks her.

"Yes, I work in Madrid."

"Then you must go on." He points in the direction she needs to go, but Allyson stays planted with a frown and wide eyes.

"Go, Ally. I'll sort this out and let you know what's happening." The last thing I need is for her to stress or get into legal trouble for not following the officer's command.

She opens her mouth to argue, and I shake my head. "Go," I mouth.

Allyson hesitates a few seconds and then walks away. I look at the officer and ask, "What do I do now?"

"You have to return to the United States. If you wish to extend your stay in Spain, you'll need to apply for a visa at the consulate. Only then will you be able to return. Your other option is to wait for the days to roll over. There is a maximum of a ninety-day period to visit Spain within a one-hundred-and-eighty day period."

I'm hearing his explanation, but all I'm thinking about is having to wait half a year to return. There's no way I'm going to miss the birth of my son and being there for Ally when she needs me.

"Is there a way to apply for a visa here instead of flying back and returning? As you saw, my girlfriend is pregnant."

"No. You'll have to leave the country and apply from your native country."

"Fuck," I murmur. "So, where do I go?" My shoulders slump, and I shake my head.

The next few hours are a nightmare. Between interviews with customs, booking a flight home, and figuring out how the hell to return as soon as possible, I'm exhausted and frustrated.

Thankfully, I was able to send Ally a message so she wouldn't worry more than necessary, and I promised I'd be back soon. I hope I can keep my promise. All I wanted was to be home with her now, holding her as we slept off the jet lag. Instead, I'm getting ready to climb into another crowded plane as if I were some kind of prisoner or some shit.

It was an honest mistake, and they're treating me as if I'm a criminal. As soon as I land, I'm going to the consulate and applying for a visa. I'd give my life savings away to be back by Allyson's side.

The first thing I do when I land in Richmond is call Easton. I arrived after the consulate closed—of course, they're only open until one in the afternoon.

"Hello?" His voice is drowned by loud music.

"Hey, sorry to bother you, but I have a problem."

"What's wrong? Is Ally okay?" Panic rings in his question as the background noise quiets.

"Yeah, sorry, she's okay. She's in Madrid."

"Wait. Where are you?" His question lingers with confusion.

"I'm back in Richmond. That's why I'm calling. When I got to customs in Madrid, they said I had reached my maximum days to visit required by law, and I need to apply for a visa. Do you have any experience with this?" Besides being my best friend, he's the closest lawyer I know that I can call up during the holidays and not get taken advantage of with high fees.

"Shit," he mumbles. "I'm not familiar with immigration law, but from my limited knowledge, you do need to apply for a visa in order to stay in the country longer than is permitted by law."

"Fuck," I growl, and people standing nearby outside the airport stare at me.

"Go to the consulate office tomorrow morning. It's in DC. I remember Ally having to go a few times when she was preparing for her move. Also, go with patience. It's an exhausting process from what she told me." Easton's advice does little to calm my nerves. There's nothing I want more than to be with Ally right now, not standing in a cold airport, waiting for my Uber, and hoping to God I can be there for the rest of the pregnancy and my son's birth.

"Thanks, Easton." I run a hand through my hair.

"Anytime. And Camden…" Easton pauses, and I wait for him to continue speaking. "Things will work out."

"Yeah," I sigh and end the call.

By the time I get home, I'm exhausted and in need of a shower and uninterrupted sleep. I send Ally a quick goodnight message since she's probably deep in sleep and crash. The frustration from the last two days melts away, and I close my eyes.

My heart races as I listen to the employee in the consulate tell me it could take up to three months to receive either an approval or denial for my long-term visa. This is insane.

"Sir, my girlfriend lives in Madrid with a work visa, and she is pregnant. In three months, she could have my baby, and I'll miss it." I try to remain as calm as possible, keeping my voice even.

"According to your travel dates, you'll be able to return in three months as a tourist again." He looks at my dates and does the calculations, informing me that I will indeed be able to return if my visa is denied. The problem is that I want to be there now, not in three months.

"Is there anything else I can do?" I tug at the roots of my hair and stare at the man.

"You're not married?" I shake my head. "If you were married, then you could live in Spain with your wife since she has a work visa. Spouses are granted permission. Since you aren't, you'll have to follow the same protocol as everyone else."

My shoulders slump. Then, he slides a paper toward me with a nod. I skim the contents and lift my eyebrows. Is he suggesting I marry Ally so I can live with her in Spain?

After I fill out all the paperwork to apply for the visa, I leave the consulate office. Still clutching the paper in my hand, my mind is spinning, and I don't know what will happen if I get denied. Ally and I are good, and I know that eventually, we'll get to marriage, but it doesn't sit right to marry her just so I can move to Spain. I haven't even told her that I'm in love with her.

I grab my phone and call a buddy of mine from college. Maybe he knows of a job in Madrid for a computer engineer. A work visa will guarantee I'm there with her.

Chapter 26

Allyson

I'm going insane. Getting back into a routine since I arrived in Madrid two weeks ago has proven to be difficult. Camden has no idea when he'll hear if he's approved for a long-term visa or not. I'm trying to remain calm, but with each passing day, I question everything going on in my life.

Am I making the right choice by staying here? Will my child be American or Spanish? How will I handle parenthood in a foreign country with very little support? When will I see Camden if his visa gets denied?

A jumbled cloud of thoughts fills my mind with every worst-case scenario and doubt. I look down at the pros and cons list on the paper in front of me. Neither one feels right, though. Sighing, I lean back on the sofa.

In need of a distraction, I grab my phone and open my Instagram app, scrolling through pictures of my friends, liking different ones before moving on to another app. When social media doesn't give me the distraction I crave, I open my e-book and continue reading the book I started weeks ago and haven't had a chance to finish.

I settle on the couch, positioning the pillow behind me so I can lean back on the armrest and bend my knees as much as my pregnant belly will allow.

The buzzing of my phone disrupts my reading, not that I was fully invested, and I groan as I prop myself up to grab it from the coffee table.

"Hey," I say, angling the phone to my face as Noel's smile fills the screen.

"How are you doing?"

"Eh, I'm okay. Torn on a few things but trying to remain positive." I shift on the sofa and sit criss-cross.

"Are you sure you don't want me to fly out there?"

"I'm sure. Thank you, though." Noel has been offering to come spend a few days with me here, but I'd rather be alone. Between my emotions from being pregnant and the harsh reality that Camden and I may not be able to be together right away, I've been a hermit. I go to work and come back home.

"I'm going to fly over anyway. You can't be alone right now. This stress isn't good for you." Noel takes on her caretaker role, turning serious.

"I'm okay. I'm just super emotional from the hormones. When you get pregnant, you'll understand."

"Psshh… Don't even, girl. You know I'm not the pregnant kind. Or having babies. Or a family for that matter."

I shake my head. "Maybe one day, but even if you never do have your own family, you'll always live the life you want." Noel goes for what she wants and gets it. She may want different things out of her life than most, but she's happy. That's what counts.

"Anyway, if I find a decent flight, I'll let you know. It's time for Life with Noel to hit Spain." She lifts her hand, palm facing up, and I laugh. Her blog is called Life with Noel, and I agree that it's time for her to visit Spain since I know she'll

the Right kind of Wrong

love it, but I'm not in the mood for someone to bring me out of my cave.

"You don't have to. Honestly, I'm fine."

Noel arches a brow through the screen. "And you know what 'Fine' means." She rolls her eyes and pinches her lips.

"Fucked up, insecure, neurotic, and emotional," I respond with the acronym she taught me years ago. "And you know what, I *am* fine because I definitely feel some of those things." I clench my jaw.

"Ally, I love you, and that is why I'm going to say this, you can't lock yourself up in your apartment and stop living just because Camden couldn't go back to Madrid with you. You're smart, independent, and strong. You two will figure out how to be together if that's what you want, but putting your life on hold for a man is a no-go in my book and yours."

My shoulders drop, and I exhale deeply, looking at my best friend through a phone screen, wishing she were here in person, that someone was here to help me through this time. Maybe I should let her fly out here. I'm scared. Scared I'll have this child alone in a foreign country without his father's support. Scared that I'll make the wrong decision and end up regretting it down the road.

The choice should be easy to an outsider, but nothing that tears us in two ever really is.

I know Noel is right, but what keeps me holed up is the pressure of deciding what's best for me, this baby, and Camden. Is it fair for him to be the only one to be willing to uproot his life for us to be together? No.

"Earth to Ally. Did you hear my speech? It was fucking powerful and great, so don't tell me you spaced out." Noel's eyes widen.

I chuckle. "I heard it, and you're right, but I'm just... I don't know what I am. I feel weird and sad and powerless. As if things were out of my control when, in reality, they aren't. I have a choice."

"What are you saying?" She leans forward on her chair and rests her chin on her hands, sitting closer to her tablet so I can clearly see the furrow of her eyebrows.

"That I do have choices in the matter, but I'm worried I'll make the wrong one. I could move back to Virginia, ask my boss to put me back in my old position and be with Camden. Or, I can stay here, be somewhat selfish and let Camden be the one to uproot his life, and hope he gets a visa." I swallow thickly and take a deep breath.

"Either way, one of us is making a sacrifice for the other and giving something up."

Noel shakes her head as she speaks. "Ally, you need to change your mindset. This isn't about sacrifice but about gaining something new, bigger than you ever imagined. Change always requires shifting our lives so we can open up to new opportunities and experiences. If we remain in the same routine, the same cycle, we can't expect to live new things. They just don't go hand in hand." She sighs and leans back on her chair.

I give her a small smile, my eyes welling with tears. She's right. Nodding, I unsuccessfully swallow back my emotions, and a few tears roll down my cheeks.

"Don't cry," she whispers.

"I'm not," my voice tightens. "Okay," I laugh between tears. "I am, but not because I'm sad. I already told you I'm emotional. I know you're right. Thank you for helping me put things into perspective."

the Right kind of Wrong

"That's what I'm here for." She smiles widely. "Anyway, I'll let you know if I find a flight that's within my budget, and I'll go visit. Berkeley is swamped at work, so we could make her jealous by sending her a ton of pics of us out and about in Madrid." Noel laughs evilly.

"You're terrible." I shake my head, giggling. That's just like Noel. One minute she's a wisdom guru, and the next, she's plotting how to make her best friend jealous.

"But you love me. Gotta go, babes. We'll talk. Call or message me if you need another pep talk." She winks and blows me a kiss.

"Thank you," I say honestly. I was feeling like the world was crushing me before she called. Thank goodness for great friends.

After we end our call, I lean back on the couch, clutching my phone and grabbing my pros and cons list. Something still doesn't feel right.

As if a light bulb's been turned on, grabbing the pen, I begin scribbling a third option on the list.

A vibration stirs me from sleep. I try to shift, but my stomach won't let me lie on my side as comfortably as I used to, especially on the sofa. I groan when my phone starts vibrating again and sit up, my lower back pulsing in pain. A soft sigh moves past my lips, and I answer the phone.

"Hey," I smile.

"Hey, Kiwi. How are you? Were you sleeping?"

"No," I lie.

Camden chuckles. "You wanna go back to sleep, and we'll talk tomorrow?"

"No." I shake my head even though he can hear me. "Let's talk." I clear my throat and lift my legs to the coffee table in front of me, dropping back into the couch cushions. Hearing his deep voice on the line soothes me and my doubts.

As Camden asks me how I'm feeling and how our son is doing, my heart melts. How can I live without him in my life? It's impossible. Not now, when I've seen what a life with him could be like. Not when we're going to have a child together. When we could be a family.

"I'm hoping I hear back from the consulate soon. It may be wishful thinking, but I'm going to do everything in my power to be by your side as soon as possible."

"Cam…" I sigh.

"I promise, Kiwi," he interrupts me. "I want to hold you, feel our son move, kiss you, make love to you…" he trails off, and my breath catches in the back of my throat. We haven't said those three little words to each other, but I'm so irrevocably in love with him.

"You've given me a different purpose in my life, and I refuse to give that up now." His words are stern and kind at the same time.

I wipe my cheek and smile. "I get what you mean. I feel the same way." My free hand drops to my stomach, rubbing slow circles. I never imagined this to be my life, but I don't want it any other way. I'll take an unplanned pregnancy so long as I have Camden in my life.

"We'll overcome this." The promise in his voice shines a light on the situation I couldn't see as anything other than impossible.

the Right kind of Wrong

"We will," I whisper. Just then, our baby kicks as if confirming that our wishes will come true. *I hope so, baby boy.*

"I know it's late, so let's video chat tomorrow," Camden suggests after talking for a bit.

"Okay." I hate hanging up with him. I hate going to sleep alone after sleeping in his arms.

I think of Noel's advice about changing my mindset. I take a deep breath and focus on the positive and all I'm grateful for, starting with this man. If Camden were a different man, I'd be doing this on my own. I'm lucky to have his support.

"Goodnight, Kiwi." His voice turns soft.

"Goodnight." I end the call and get ready for bed, all the while telling myself that this baby and I will have his daddy in our lives. And until then, I have to continue living my life instead of locking myself up in my apartment. I came here to experience the culture, the people, and the lifestyle. I'm not doing any of that. If I stop truly living and become a hermit like I have been, then living in Spain is pointless, and I might as well move back home.

Home. That's my current challenge. Where exactly is home?

Chapter 2

Camden

Your visa has been denied.

I stare in disbelief at the letter I received in the mail today. My heart halts with each word I re-read as everything crashes down around me. I wasn't expecting to receive a response so soon after I submitted my application, and yet here it is a month after I submitted the form. I expected it to take the full three months they said it could take, and I had high hopes for an approval.

I slump back on my couch and run a hand down my face in exasperation. My other fist clenches around the paper. How am I going to give Ally this news? I've been promising her that we'll be together soon, and now that bubble has burst. I'm here in Virginia, and she's in Spain. A vast ocean interferes with our destiny.

My phone rings again, and I silence the call. Ally's been calling, but I haven't had the heart to answer and tell her what's going on. Instead, I keep sending her to voicemail.

I've already missed a month of watching her grow and transform, a month that I haven't been there to comfort her and hold her. I miss her like hell, and the idea of not seeing her for at least another two months kills me.

the Right kind of Wrong

I grab my phone off the coffee table and stand, stretching my arms over my head. I need to get out of this apartment before I lose my damn mind. I call Luke to see if he's free to have a few beers and head out to a local bar. After the shit letter I received, I need to clear my mind and have a drink. I also need to figure out the best way to tell Ally that I won't be moving to Spain anytime soon, and I wish I could tell her in person. Video calls are great for a while, but they get old fast. I want good old fashioned communication—face to face and skin to skin.

"Hey, man." Luke sits on the empty stool next to me as I sip my beer. I didn't bother waiting for him to arrive.

"Hey." I lift my chin.

"Not a good day?" His eyebrows lift on his forehead.

"Not a good month," I say through clenched teeth.

"What's going on?"

"My visa for Spain got denied. No long-term stay as I had hoped, and I need to break the news to Ally. It's been rough being apart, and I don't want to cause her more stress during the last trimester of her pregnancy." I sigh, leaning back on the stool.

"Ah, fuck. Sorry to hear that. Is there another option?" Luke grabs the beer the waiter places in front of him and takes a drink while I respond.

"I don't know. If we were married, then I'd be granted a visa. That's what I was told."

"Don't you think you'll eventually get to that point? Why not do it now and save yourself the headache and stress of living apart?" Luke eyes me over the rim of his glass, his shaggy blond hair falling over his eyes.

fabiola francisco

"Because that's not romantic. I don't want a shotgun wedding just because she's pregnant or because I need a visa to live in another country." I shake my head.

"Look at you talking about romance." Luke chuckles, waving the waiter down. "You want something to eat?" He looks at me.

"Sure," I shrug, wondering if marriage is the solution to all our problems or the beginning of bigger ones.

Yeah, I want that with Ally, more than I ever thought I would, but I don't want to rush anything or use something like a visa as an excuse to get married. I want to get down on one knee because we love each other and want to spend the rest of our lives together. I want it to be natural and honest, not because of some legal deadline stabbing our sides.

Luke and I order burgers and fries and another round of beers. It's nice to relax and talk to someone, whether it be about my current situation or sports. I'll take any distraction at the moment.

After I get back home with zero clarity, I decide to call Ally back. She's probably worried sick that I haven't answered her calls.

"Hello?" Her sleep-induced voice feeds my guilt.

"Hey, did I wake you?" I grab a water bottle from the fridge and drop on the couch, lifting one leg onto the coffee table.

"No, not really," she lies, and I chuckle.

"Kiwi, you wanna talk tomorrow? You sound exhausted." I smile, imagining her with messy hair and puffy eyes.

"No, talk to me. Are you okay? I called you today, but you never answered."

the Right kind of Wrong

"Yeah, I'm fine," I lie. I don't want her to lose sleep over this, especially with how late it is over there. I didn't take the time change into account when I hit her name on my screen.

"Are you sure?"

"Yeah, just stressed." I'll tell her tomorrow when she's well-rested and has the entire day to process the news.

"I know, me, too. I miss you," her voice is gruff from sleep.

"I miss you, too, Kiwi. Miss holding you and kissing you and watching you experience this pregnancy. I hate that I can't be there." The reality of all I'm missing hits me like a freight train, and I squeeze my eyes shut. I've gotta get to her.

"I know," she whispers after a beat. "This is hard, and I hate that we're essentially living two different lives."

"We'll be together soon," I add before realizing *soon* won't get here fast enough. "Go to sleep. I'll call you when I wake up."

"Promise?" Her voice shakes, and it kills me.

"Promise." I give her every ounce of my heart in that one word. I won't stop fighting for us.

As soon as I hang up the phone, I get ready for bed and lie on my back, staring at the dark ceiling. I need a plan, and I need it quickly.

I make a strong pot of coffee after a sleepless night and grab my phone off the coffee table where I left it last night. I need to talk to Ally today. The more I put it off, the worse it will be when I tell her the truth.

I stare as the coffee drips into the pot, the tapping sound in tune with my heartbeat. As soon as the coffee is done, I'll call her.

With a steaming cup of coffee in hand, I stare at her name on my phone before pressing the icon for video calls. I take deep, even breaths as I wait for her to answer.

Her gorgeous face pops up on my screen after a few rings. Smiling, I take in her soft features. Her hair's tied up on her head, and her face is clear of any makeup. She's stunning.

"Hey." Her eyes light up.

"Hi, babe, how are you feeling?" I lean back on the sofa, allowing the leather to comfort me as I build up the courage to talk to her.

"I'm good. My feet are a little swollen, but it's all part of the journey, right?" She giggles softly and then angles the phone toward her belly.

"Look at you," I comment. "Beautiful."

"Thank you," she says quietly as her face reappears on my screen. "Are you sure you're okay?"

I take a deep breath and shake my head. "No. I got a letter in the mail from the consulate yesterday. My visa application was denied."

I watch as her eyes widen for the briefest second, and her breath falters. "What?"

I nod. "I'm sorry. I could've sworn I'd get approved." I shake my head. "But it was a no from them. I need to double-check exactly what day I can travel over there again, and I'll book a flight. I need to see you."

"Cam… I can't believe they denied your application." Her words are strangled by her emotions, and it feels like a knife straight through my chest.

the Right kind of Wrong

"I know." I bow my head. "I just... I don't know what to do. I should have a solution to this, but I've never felt so helpless before." I rub my eyes in frustration.

"Hey, this isn't your fault. You don't have to have the answers to everything. I sure as hell don't. We'll be together," she adds with confidence.

"Let's talk about something else. How's my boy doing?" Ally smiles widely.

"He's growing each day. I think he's definitely going to be an athlete with how much he moves." I smile as I hear her talk. I can't wait to see her holding our son, watching her be the best mom. My chest tightens as the idea of not being able to witness that firsthand twists my insides.

Ally tells me about work, the disastrous date Rubén went on this week, and about the light snow that fell yesterday. I love talking to her, even if it's about the weather. I love her. Irrevocably so. And I haven't even told her yet.

Talking to Ally melts away my worries for a little while. She's like a soothing balm on a third-degree sunburn—a gentle touch to my wild heart. She brings something to my life I never thought I'd have, never imagined I'd want—safety and calm. Instead of going out each night and finding someone to warm my bed, I wrap up work early so I can talk to her before she goes to bed. I want no one else but this woman, and I'll be damned if one rejection letter will stand in our way.

Chapter 28

Allyson

When Camden told me last week that he didn't get the visa to come to Spain, everything shifted inside of me like a stubborn Rubik's Cube finally clicking together. My list of pros and cons no longer mattered, as there was only one clear list in my mind. The fog had lifted from the uncertainty clouding my brain, and I knew what I wanted more than anything. I put a plan in place with the help of Easton. I just hope Camden is on the same page as me.

These last seven days have been full of planning, organizing, and life-changing decisions.

"Are you ready?" Noel smiles at me. I nod, grabbing my bag, but she takes it from me before I can drag it a few inches. "You're super pregnant, and I will not allow you to do any force." I roll my eyes and cross my arms. I'm right at the cut-off where I can travel, so I've had to act quickly.

"I'm capable of carrying a bag. How do you think I get my groceries home?"

"Psshh… Not if I'm here," she continues to argue. Goodness, I thought Camden was overprotective, but Noel has been a million times more protective.

She flew out here a few days ago as promised and helped me get everything sorted, which I am forever grateful for. She

the Right kind of Wrong

even made some contacts in Madrid for her blog and will be featuring Spain in a future post.

"Are you ready for this?" Her voice turns soft. I nod, swallowing the emotional lump in the back of my throat and look around my apartment one last time. I want this, more than anything, but change can be scary.

Noel hugs me tightly and whispers, "Everything will work out exactly as it should."

I wrap my arms around her and cling on to her for support before taking a step back, a deep breath, and closing the door behind me.

***

I take a deep breath before knocking on the wooden door separating me from my future. I run my sweaty palms down my leggings and then bring them to my stomach. My heart slams in my chest as I wait for the door to open.

Everything will be all right. Everything will be all right. I repeat the chant in my mind, taking deep, steady breaths.

The door swings open, and wide, brown eyes stare at me. "What the… Ally?"

I smile and nod, tears blurring my vision. Camden's arms pull me into a hug and hold me tightly.

"What are you doing here?" His warm breath tickles the shell of my ear.

"I missed you." I bring my arms around his back and step closer with tears in my eyes. I giggle when my stomach stops me from getting as close as I want.

Camden leans his head back to pierce down at me and brushes wayward strands of hair from my face. His lips touch mine in a slow and gentle kiss.

"I missed you, too," he murmurs against my mouth. "Come in." I walk inside, and he grabs my bag and rolls it into his apartment. His unique scent hits me instantly, and I finally feel like I'm home. He's my only home.

I turn around to face Camden, who is staring at me with furrowed brows. I crack a smile and walk toward him, taking his hands and placing them over my stomach. As if knowing his daddy was touching him, our baby boy kicks.

"God, you smell good, like home." He reads my mind and pulls me in again to hold me. His hand runs a soothing trail up and down my back and his lips touching my neck. I shiver at the contact and shift, combing my fingers through the strands of hair at the nape of his neck.

"How long are you here for?" Camden's brown eyes stare into mine, joy and worry shining back at me.

"How long will you have me?" I bite my lip and hold my breath.

"Huh?" He scratches the side of his head. "What does that mean?"

"I'm here for good. I quit my job."

"Like quit, quit? You're not going to work at the Richmond office?" His eyes bug out.

I shake my head. "Let's sit, yeah?" I hold his hand and walk toward his sofa.

"I'm so confused," he runs a hand through his messy hair as he sits next to me.

"How about I explain from the beginning?" One side of my mouth tilts in a smile.

the Right kind of Wrong

"Yeah," he breathes out with a firm nod, his hands back on my belly as he listens to me speak. Peace fills me being this close to him.

"Remember when we were in Everton for Christmas last month, and you asked me if I'd ever want to move back there?" He nods, so I continue talking, his eyes focused on me.

"I had never thought about it. I moved when I was a young teen, and Virginia became my home, but seeing Easton back in Everton, visiting my hometown, it's stirred up emotions and memories. I remember helping my dad around the ranch, learning to ride a horse, preparing for winter… It was such a different lifestyle than I later had in Charlottesville when we moved." I search his face as I speak.

"I loved my life in Virginia, and I always felt like Everton was a distant part of me, but now…" I suck in a deep breath and let it slip from between my lips as I gather my emotions.

"Hey… What's going on?" Camden scoots closer to me when he sees the tears in my eyes. I shake my head, and he pulls me into a hug. He whispers sweet words in my ear as I gather myself.

I lean back and look at him, cupping his face with my hands. His scruffy beard tickles my skin as Camden turns his head to kiss my palm. "Talk to me, Kiwi." His voice is gruff, and I'm afraid of what his reaction would be.

"I want to move back to Everton." I rip it off like a Band-Aid, blinking my eyes rapidly as I wait for his response. Any reaction that will give me some insight into what he's thinking.

Camden leans back, causing my hands to drop to my lap. His eyebrows rise, and my heart pounds as I fear this will be a deal-breaker.

"Is that what you really want?" he asks.

I nod. "Yes," I say softly. "I never thought I did. I thought I was okay never living there again, but…" I shrug. "I miss it." Moving back to Everton was never in the cards for me. We moved away, and I never felt a need to return the way my brother did. Now, I crave the open spaces, reconnecting with my roots, and having a different life for our son and me.

"Wow." Camden runs a hand through his hair. "This is a big decision…" He shakes his head, and I try to swallow past the lump in my throat.

"I know it is, and I can't ask you to uproot your life for me—"

"Kiwi," his stern voice interrupts me. "I was going to uproot, *as you say*, my life and move to Spain. I want to be with you so badly, I was willing to speak my broken Spanish just to be near you and our son. You're my family." He places his hand on my stomach.

"I want you, whether that's in Virginia, Europe, Everton, or the fucking moon. You're my world, babe. Get that?"

Tears trail slowly down my cheeks and off my chin.

"Don't cry," he whispers, brushing my cheeks.

"It's a lot to ask. Spain was different because I was working there, already living there, but moving to Everton came from left field." I weave our hands together and look into his brown eyes. I wonder if our son will have his eyes or my green ones. Maybe hazel—the perfect blend of his mommy and daddy.

"You're allowed to think about it." I squeeze his fingers.

"What will you do? Work in HR?" Camden tilts his head.

the Right kind of Wrong

"I spoke to Easton. He'll need help in the firm since it's just him right now. Faith helps him when she can, but he'll need someone there all the time, more administrative work."

After the only lawyer in Everton retired, my brother took over the firm, not only working with the mayor at Town Hall but also becoming Everton's go-to person for any and all legal issues.

"You've really thought this through."

"Yes, that's why I'm telling you to take your time to think about it. I've had a chance to catch up with this idea, but I just threw it on you. If this isn't what you want, we'll create a plan together." I smile, scooting close to him and placing my head on his shoulder.

Camden's arm comes around my shoulder, his fingers combing through my ponytail. "I love you," he whispers.

My breath catches, and my heart halts. I sit up and turn to look at him. His eyebrows are slightly scrunched, and his eyes mirror love and fear as he stares at me.

A slow smile tilts my lips as I regain my composure. "I love you, too." I tilt my head, more tears spilling over. Goodness, my emotions are out of control.

"You do?"

My shoulders drop, and I lean forward, my lips a hair's breadth from his. "Of course I do. Did you think I couldn't?"

"I hoped you did," his honesty rings around us.

"I love you," I repeat for emphasis. "I may have never thought I'd be in this situation with you, but I'm so happy that we are. You've been the best kind of surprise."

I touch my lips to his in a gentle kiss, and Camden's hand comes around my neck, keeping me close to him as he growls and deepens the kiss. His tongue pierces through my lips, demanding my full attention.

Everything feels right in my world as I kiss him back with as much passion. My hands come around his neck, tangling in his hair as my tongue strokes along his. A shiver travels down my spine, and with Camden's help, I move over his lap, straddling him.

Camden chuckles, breaking the kiss and looking down at my bump. "Our boy's growing, huh?" He rubs my belly, which keeps us from getting too close.

"He sure is." My hand lands over his.

"You're gorgeous," he says. "If you wanted to live in a run-down shack, I'd say yes just to wake up to this smile every day and kiss these lips each night." His other hand cups my cheek, his thumb brushing my lips.

"Everton may be a rural town, but we'll have a real home." I lean into his touch.

"Does this mean I'll finally get to ride a horse?" Camden's eyes light up in mischief.

"Uh, yeah, no." I shake my head. "Easton told me you've been wanting to ride, but you'll need lessons first."

"With a hot teacher?" His eyebrows waggle, and my head drops back in laughter.

"We'll see about that. I'm not sure this teacher will be up for riding lessons anytime soon." I point to my belly.

"I'll give you a different kind of riding lesson," Camden counters. I can't help the laugh that moves through me as his eyebrows dance on his forehead.

"I may be up for those types of lessons," I wink.

"Kiss me," Camden demands, so I do. I kiss him all night long as we make love and talk about the future.

Chapter 29

Camden

I lie awake as the sun begins to paint the sky in light shades of orange and watch Ally sleep beside me. I hold back my temptation to brush away the messy strands of hair covering part of her face, so I don't wake her up. I can't believe she's here. She gave it all up for me, for us to be together, and a hint of guilt gnaws in the pit of my stomach.

I don't want her to wake up one morning and resent me for moving back to the States if she had the opportunity to create a life abroad.

And now, Everton. I never saw myself as a small-town guy, but I meant what I told her last night. I'd move to the moon if it meant having her by my side and in my bed, making a life together while we raise our son and make more babies.

Fortunately, I can work from anywhere, and I do see the appeal of raising our boy in a small town surrounded by nature and hardworking people.

No longer able to hold back, I bring my arm around Ally's stomach, planting my palm over it and pulling her back to me. The curve of her ass presses into my lower body, and I bite back a groan. She gets to me every time, whether she's made up in full glam or in sweats at home with messy hair.

"Hmmm…" Her hoarse voice sounds softly around my room as she wiggles her ass against me.

"Kiwi," I groan, pressing my hand firmly against her to keep her still. Her giggles are quiet as she stretches, untangling our legs, and turning over to look at me.

"Good morning." Her hand moves to my face, palming my cheek. When she leans forward to kiss me, I suck in all her sweetness like a greedy bastard stealing all the honey from the Queen Bee. My hand moves down her back to cup her ass, and I grab a handful, pulling her to me.

"I realized something in the middle of the night when I got up to go to the bathroom."

"What?" I sneak my hand into her underwear, feeling her round ass in my palm.

"Stop doing that, or I won't be able to speak." She shivers as she peeks up at me through her lashes.

"I'll behave," I promise with a wink, which rewards me with a throaty laugh from her.

"Liar," she points out and then continues talking. "Anyway, I just assumed we are gonna live together, but we never really discussed that. Spain was one thing, but I can move in with my mom until I get things sorted, or I can find a place in Everton, and then we play it by ear." She rambles on and on, her cheeks flushing pink, making me smile.

"Kiwi…" I wait for her to look at me. "What else do I have to do to make you see that I want this." I bring my hand over to her belly. "I want where this relationship is headed—a home to share with you, a kid to raise, hell I might even put a ring on your finger." My smile widens as her eyebrows lift. Yeah, I've got plans to marry this woman.

the Right kind of Wrong

"I want a home with you. It's why I wanted to move to Madrid. To be with you, not necessarily to perfect my Spanish. Where you go, I go. I was thinking about it early this morning. Everton sounds perfect. Easton is there, we know some of the people, and our son will be raised in a nurturing and strong environment. Let's do it."

"Just like that?"

I nod, smirking. "Yeah, just like that. It suits us if you think about it. We fell into bed one crazy night because it felt right at the moment, and now this feels right. Besides, it'll be kinda fun to rub our relationship in Easton's face." I wink.

Ally shoves my chest playfully. "You're terrible. You say that now that you guys are okay, but you wouldn't have been saying that a few months ago."

"You're right. I didn't want to lose my best friend and the woman I love. If he told you to leave me alone, you might've."

Her face grows serious, a slight pinch to her eyebrows. "Cam," she cups my face. Shaking her head, she says, "Easton could've told me to drop you off in a burning building, and I would've made a U-turn and kept you safe. It's not just about me. It's about our son now, and I want him to know his dad. Even if this wouldn't have happened between us." She moves her free hand between us, motioning to our relationship.

"You sure?" I can't help the question from escaping me.

"Positive." She leans forward and brushes her lips with mine. "Oh."

"What happened?" I'm on high alert.

"Your soccer player kid just kicked my bladder. Be back." I let out a belly laugh as she ungracefully jumps off the bed and waddles to the bathroom, sighing as she makes it right on time.

I sit up and lean back against the headboard, rubbing my face. Life is changing fast, and I'm excited and scared at the same time. I question if I'll be a good father, know how to support Ally when she needs it. One look at her, though, and I want to give three-thousand percent of my effort to be everything she needs.

I watch Allyson as she walks to my side of the bed in one of my t-shirts and her cotton underwear. I scoot over when she sits on the side.

"I want to visit my mom today."

"I'll take you."

"Are you sure? Don't you have work to do?"

"Nah," I shake my head. "I can catch up later. I don't have anything pressing, and it can all be done from home when we get back. Does she know you're here?" I wonder what Charlene's reaction would be to seeing her daughter Stateside.

Ally shakes her head. "Only Easton and Noel knew. Berkeley's going to be pissed." She giggles before adding, "Noel had flown to Spain and helped me pack and fly over."

"I could've done that," I offer quickly. "Well, technically, I could've for like three days as I wait for the rest of my days to open up with this rollover bullshit."

"I'm here now, though." Her warm hands hold my cheeks.

"Yes, you are." I kiss her softly. "Go shower so we can see your mom. Will she be at home or in class?"

"Um, it's Saturday…" Her words trail off as her eyebrows dip. Ally chuckles as it dawns on me that it's the weekend. With talk about work and her surprise visit, I've lost track of the days of the week.

the Right kind of Wrong

"You know what then? Screw work, it can wait 'til Monday. I've got my girl here for good, and we're going to celebrate."

"Yeah? How?" She arches a brow.

"First, we shower together." I jump off the bed and grab her, lifting her, so her legs wrap around me. Ally squeals as she holds my shoulders.

"Giddy up," I gallop. "My first lesson." I wink.

Ally laughs, tossing her head back. "I'm pretty sure I'm riding you."

"Kiwi," I growl, rubbing myself against her core. This gets me a loud moan from her full lips as I set her feet on the floor. I throw the shirt she's wearing on the floor and hook my fingers into her underwear, tearing them down her legs.

I take a step back to admire the beauty in front of me. Ally's curves lure me in like a moth to a flame. This pregnancy has only made her more beautiful, accentuating her body in ways that drive me crazy.

Her hands are on me, lifting my shirt off my body and then sneaking into my pajama bottoms. I hiss when her palm wraps around my dick, and my legs almost give out when she begins to stroke my length. I'll never tire of her touch, her gorgeous eyes, or her infectious laugh. I want her in my life for the rest of forever.

My hands gently caress her skin, palming her breasts and reaching for her pussy. Ally whimpers when I rub her clit, her lips fusing to mine in a desperate kiss.

"Shower," I murmur against her mouth, but I bring my hand to the nape of her neck, holding her to me as we remain where we are.

"Fuck, Kiwi..." I draw out as she continues to stroke my length with determination. I grip the sink behind me to keep myself steady. "I'm going to come in my PJs like a fourteen-year-old boy if you don't stop."

"Come for me," is all she says as her lips find mine again, and take control of the kiss.

Damn, and I do. I come for her in my pants as if I have no self-control. When it comes to her, I don't. I'm wild and desperate for anything she'll give me.

"Now we really need to shower," Ally giggles as she removes her hand from my pajama bottoms and nudges me out of the way to wash her hands. I stand behind her, encasing her with my arms. Our gaze locks in the mirror—darkened by desire.

With one hand, I get rid of my pants. Staring at Ally in the mirror, I rub my hips against her so she can feel me. I may have just released myself, but seeing her naked in front of me only fuels my desire. It's been too many weeks without her.

"Babe..." she moans quietly.

"I love you," I whisper, bringing my hands around her stomach and pressing her back to my front. My lips move down her jaw to her neck, and I suck her sweet taste as if it were my last meal.

"I love you, too." Ally turns around in my arms. She tilts her head to give me better access as her arms come around my neck. My hands roam her body wildly, like a man lost at sea in desperate search of a guiding light.

I lift Ally and carefully set her on the vanity. I take her lips in mine, my body lighting up like fireworks. She moans when my fingers tug her nipples, and my dick is ready to claim her. I'm taking my time, though. As I steady my breathing, I kiss a

the Right kind of Wrong

trail down her neck and chest, sucking a nipple between my lips.

"Cam," she calls out, her fingers tangled in my hair. "So sensitive."

"Hmmm…" I murmur, not stopping my task.

"So good." Her words get mixed with her moans.

I kiss across to her other breast, giving it the same attention before I move further down, dropping kisses on her belly. When I kneel before her, Ally gasps. I wink and smirk, bringing one of her legs over my shoulder.

"Fuck, I can't wait to taste you."

My mouth and hands move of their own accord, trailing kisses up and down her inner thighs before licking the length of her pussy. Ally tenses above me, her nails piercing my scalp.

My lips suck her clit, and Ally cries out. I continue to fuck her with my mouth, tasting every last drop she gives me as she encourages me to continue. My dick is begging for its release, but my focus is all on her. Her body, her reactions, her moans, and the way she tastes.

"Oh, my goodness…" Ally's words come out in a strangled cry as her body tenses and then relaxes. Her eyes pierce down at me, and a lazy smile takes over her lips. "That was…" She shakes her head. "Stand up," she demands, and I follow her orders.

Standing between her legs, she locks her ankles around me, and her hands frame my face. "I want you inside me. Now."

"Your wish is my command," I wink and stroke my cock a few times, angling my body to hers. Ally loosens her legs from around my body to give me space to move, and I tug her gently to the edge of the bathroom counter.

fabiola francisco

Staring into her eyes, I make silent promises as I enter her slowly, reveling in the way she makes me feel. My heart pounds and fills with love for this woman—a feeling totally foreign to me and one I never cared to chase. That's the funny thing about life. We don't need to chase what's for us; it will always find a way.

Tangled up in each other, I make love to the woman I plan to spend the rest of my life with.

Chapter 30

Camden

I hold Ally's hand as we drive into Charlottesville to visit Charlene. Her mom will be so happy to have her here, and I wonder how she'll feel about us moving to Everton in the near future. Ally has been all smiles, her hand placed on her belly. I still can't believe she's here. I'm processing the news she dropped on me last night, and I want to make sure she isn't a figment of my imagination.

"Do you think my mom will be happy that we're going to move to Everton? I've been away for a few years, and I feel guilty moving somewhere else that isn't Virginia where she is." Ally traps her lower lip between her teeth as she looks at me with wide, doubtful eyes.

"I think she'll be happy that you're following your heart." I squeeze her hand and turn to look at her when we stop at a red light. "I mean that, too. It's not just a cheesy line to calm your nerves. She's always wanted what's best for you."

"I know that, but I feel like I should be close to her in case she needs me."

I shake my head. "Your mom would never let you give up the life you want because of her. She's selfless like that, and she knows it's time for both you and Easton to do what you want and need for your own families. Besides, maybe she'll retire soon and move to Everton, too."

Ally laughs, shaking her head. "I don't know if she would, but that would be great. Thanks, Cam." She tilts her head.

When the car behind us honks, I focus on the road again and pull into Charlene's apartment building.

Watching Charlene's face light up as she opens the door and sees Ally makes me smile. I've been a part of this family for years, as a friend, an outsider in a sense, but now I have a different role in the Locke family, and it fills me with pride.

"Did you know she was coming?" Charlene smiles at me before pulling me into a hug.

"I had no idea. I was as surprised as you."

"Come in." She moves out of the way, letting us enter her apartment. Then, her hands are on Ally's stomach, whispering to her grandson. Ally and I lock eyes, and I wink at her.

"Let's sit. Do you want coffee, tea? Had I known you were coming, I would've made breakfast." Charlene begins moving around the apartment.

"Mom, calm down. I didn't want you to stress. Besides, I wanted to surprise you." Ally hugs her mom. "Let's talk."

They sit on the sofa, and I take the armchair next to them. I give them their time to talk, offering to make coffee and tea.

"I have decaf. Would you prefer that over tea?" Charlene looks at Ally.

"Yes, please." She smiles up at me.

"Coming right up." I clap my hands and give them their space to reconnect. I know how much Ally missed her mom, and I want to make sure she can talk without interruptions or feeling the need to include me.

the Right kind of Wrong

"Do you need help?" Charlene appears in the kitchen as I'm placing the mugs, steaming milk, and coffee on a tray.

"I've got it. Go back in there." I motion to the living room.

Instead, she crosses her arms and stares at me. "Everton, huh?"

"I think it's a great place to raise our son." I nod. "Besides, I can work from anywhere, fortunately."

"I want to make sure you've thought about this. Everton is very different than the pace and lifestyle you're used to. Ally will adjust. It's in her blood to live in a place like that, even if she can happily live in a big city."

"I know. It took me a bit to wrap my head around it, but I like the town, and I want to be where she is." I open up to Charlene.

She smiles, placing her hand on my arm.

"I want to marry her," I confess. All I've thought about since last night is buying a ring and getting down on one knee.

"I wouldn't expect anything less."

"Not because she's pregnant, but because I love her," I explain, wanting it to be understood that when I marry Ally, it will be out of love and not convenience.

"Like I said, I wouldn't expect anything less. That day you came to see me after Easton's wedding, I saw you looking at the photos I have, specifically the one of Ally. I figured something was brewing."

I crack a smile and chuckle. "Nothing gets past you," I joke.

"She's my daughter, and you're like a son. I've known you for many years, Camden. Be good to her."

"I will. So, do I have your blessing?" I lift my eyebrows and give her my best smile.

"You do, and I'm positive you have James's as well." Her eyes mist over, and I hug her. I also wish he were here to watch his kids get married and build their families.

"Mom? Are you okay?" Charlene and I step back to look at Ally by the kitchen entrance.

"Of course." Charlene wipes under her eyes. "We were just talking about your father and how much I wish he were here to meet your baby boy."

"Mom…" Ally says quietly, walking toward her mother. "I wish he were here, too, but he's watching over us." Her words choke up as she hugs her mom.

"I'll set the coffee in the living room," I say before carrying the tray out of the kitchen.

Once I set the tray on the coffee table, I walk to the family photos and grab one with James.

"Sir, I'd like to marry your daughter. Charlene gave me her blessing, but I'd like yours, too." Goosebumps fill my skin as I stare at the most hardworking man I knew, and one of the best people I've come across in my life. When I hear Ally and Charlene walking into the living room, I place the frame where it was and sit on the chair.

Charlene smiles at me, knowing something no one else does and asks us about our plans for the future.

"Thank you for coming with me today," Ally says as we drive back to Richmond. Her eyes close as her breathing becomes steady.

the Right kind of Wrong

"You don't need to thank me." I lift her hand and kiss the top of it.

"I'm so ready for a nap." She pats her stomach and smiles. "Wanna nap with me?" She turns her head slightly, opening one eye. I turn my attention back to the road and nod.

Quiet peace enters me as Ally holds my hand with both of hers, her thumb stroking my skin. This moment is perfect, and I plan to make it permanent soon. I begin to formulate a plan, think of ways to propose, and what type of ring suits Ally. We've got a future to plan that includes her taking my last name.

When we get home, Ally goes straight to my room, getting under the covers as promised. I watch her for a moment before joining her and wrapping my arms around her body.

"Now that we know it's a boy, should we choose our son's name?" Her breath fans across my chin.

"I've got a few ideas, including those I mentioned a while ago. You?" I brush her hair away from her face, so I've got a clear view of those green eyes.

She nods, and her smile grows.

"We know his middle name will be James."

Ally nods, tucking her lips into her mouth. "Thank you for that," she whispers.

"No need to thank me, babe." I kiss her.

"Tell me your ideas." She perks up and cuddles into me.

"I already mentioned Jasper, Isaac, and Liam. I also like Ryker, Andrew, and Reilly," I say.

Her expression is pensive. "I thought of Walker or Colton. I like Ryker, too."

fabiola francisco

"And I like Walker. So, Walker or Ryker?" I ask, and she yawns in response. Chuckling, I kiss her forehead. "How about we sleep on it and see our favorites after a nap?"

"Yes," she nods, her eyes already closing.

"Sleep, Kiwi. I've got you."

Before long, my eyes are also closing, and I dream of a brown-haired boy with green eyes calling me Daddy.

Chapter 31

Allyson

The past couple of weeks have been interesting. Camden and I have gotten used to living together since I bombarded his life and moved to Richmond without any real plan but to be with him.

Faith has been helping us find a house in Everton, sending me links or pictures of any places she comes across that she thinks would be great for our family. God bless my sister-in-law for all her help. It hasn't been easy between my pregnancy, Camden's work and preparing his clients for our move, and my stress that the baby will be here in just ten weeks.

The last thing I want is to be mid-move when our baby boy decides to make his entrance earth-side. I place my hand on my growing stomach and sigh, leaning back into the sofa. I look around the living room, and my heart begins to race as my anxiety peaks.

I haven't unpacked all of my things since we'll be moving at some point, but it's made it difficult to find everything I need. Camden has made space in his closet and dresser for me, but it's still all a pile of mess.

Taking a deep breath, I stand from the couch and continue sorting some of my belongings into one of my suitcases as I look for a clean pair of leggings. Groaning as I bend to grab the leggings, my hand flies to my stomach mid-reach when I feel a cramp press into me.

I cry out in pain, and my other hand slams against the wall, holding myself up. Then, I feel a warm liquid trail down my legs. My heart races as panic sets in, and tears burn my eyes. I whip around on autopilot, looking for my phone, and call an ambulance. I grab my purse, so I have my ID on me and scream out when another cramp takes over, my purse landing on the floor.

Please be okay, baby boy.

Crippling fear holds me in place as my arms cradle my belly as if I were holding my son. Tears soak my face as I try to catch my breath. I sigh when the door swings open. Camden halts when he sees me, his eyes widening.

"What's wrong?" His words rush out, and he's by my side immediately.

"The baby," I choke out. "Called 911." My face twists again, the pain coming stronger.

"He's early." Camden combs a hand through his hair. "Too fucking early." He starts making his way around the apartment, grabbing my purse off the floor and other things that I can't see. I don't care about clean clothes, only that my baby is okay.

It's all a blur when I hear Camden guide the paramedics into the apartment. I faintly hear what they say above the gushing sound in my ears. Thankfully, Camden is by my side the entire time, holding my hand and promising me a future together with our son. I hope to God he's right.

In the ambulance, I explain what happened and how I felt like my water broke in between asking how the baby is doing and if we'll be okay. Once we arrive at the hospital, I'm wheeled into the emergency room with Camden walking beside me, his face marred with worry and fear. I reach for his hand with my IV-clad one and squeeze his fingers.

I've never been so scared in my life.

Everything happens so fast. Checking my vitals, the baby's vitals, questions thrown at Camden and me. The next thing I know, I'm in labor, and our son will be born prematurely.

Throughout it all, my heart slams in my chest as nausea threatens to rear its ugly head. I'm terrified of what this all means, even if the doctor has assured me that women have premature babies often.

I look over at Camden, talking to the doctor, and my eyes mist over. I want this family with him. My eyes squeeze shut when my stomach contracts again in a painful cramp. Camden is by my side in a rush, and the doctor is checking on me, doing whatever her responsibility is, which I count includes keeping my baby and me alive and well.

"I'm scared, Cam," I whisper as his hand brushes my hair away from my forehead, and his lips smooth over my skin there. I was supposed to have more time. My baby boy is supposed to have more time to get stronger.

"I'm with you, Kiwi. I won't let anything happen to you."

A sob rips through me, and Camden holds me in his arms. He can't keep promises that are out of his control.

Camden

I've never, in my fucking life, felt so terrified, angry, and useless. There's nothing I can do but hold Ally and keep empty promises that hold no weight. If I were God, I'd promise her the world, but right now, I'm questioning where the fuck God even is.

The doctor told me that a baby born at thirty weeks has a ninety-five percent chance of surviving if there are no complications. The fact that I don't have a one-hundred percent statistic makes me anxious and stressed.

"I'll be right back," I whisper in Ally's hair when she gets her emotions under control. She nods silently, but I see the fear in her eyes.

I step out of the hospital room and run a hand down my face. I'm trying to be strong for her, so she doesn't see my cracks, but I'm only human. I'm scared like she is—that I'll lose our son and the woman I love. I need a moment to compose myself and continue being strong for her.

If I hadn't gone to a meeting today, if I would've stayed home like I wanted, I could've been there for her. I would've kept an eye on her, making sure nothing was off, and we wouldn't be here now. I could've prevented it.

I drop to my knees in the stark hallway and clasp my hands.

God, I know I haven't been the best example of a Christian life, and I have no right to ask you this, but keep Ally and our son safe. Fuck, I'm even too selfish to offer my life for hers because I'm not done living by her side. I'm not done making a life with her. Please, God.

the Right kind of Wrong

Tears fall down my face, and I don't give a shit what I look like. The love of my life is fighting for her life, and there's nothing I can do but hold her hand.

Don't let her die.

"Dad?" I look up to see one of Ally's nurses standing above me. "It's time."

I nod, sniffing, and scrub my eyes so Ally won't see any trace of my turmoil. My heart pounds as I follow her into the room and see Ally crying out. "Cam?" She asks through her clenched jaw.

"I'm here, Kiwi." Those greens eyes peek up at me, an array of emotions reflecting back at me. She nods, swallowing a lump when her throat bobs and grips my hand.

I'm not sure what happens after. There's coaching from the doctor, Ally squeezing my hand as she pushes, a nurse guiding her to breathe. It all happens in fast forward and all at once. I don't know where to focus or what to do besides keep my hand in Ally's and whisper loving words.

Before long, we hear a wailing sound, and I watch the doctor lift our son. He's tiny in her hands, and I can't help but choke up. I look at Ally, who is crying as well, and bend to kiss her swollen lips.

"I love you," I murmur.

The doctor asks me if I want to cut the umbilical cord after they've allowed some time for what the doctor explained was umbilical cord milking. Something about keeping the blood flow from the mom to the baby a couple minutes after birth, so the baby receives all the nutrients it can.

I stare at my son as I clamp the umbilical cord, his small body staring at me. I wipe my eyes and smile.

"He's going to be okay if I can help it," the doctor promises.

I nod and thank her, going back to Ally as the medical team cares for our son in the room. They announce he weighs three pounds and is fourteen inches long, not too far from a full-term baby in that respect. I'm more concerned about his organs working properly.

"How do you feel?" I ask Ally.

"I'm still scared, but I'm relieved he was born okay."

When the doctor explains that our son will be transferred to the neonatal intensive care unit, Ally and I both jump at her with questions. She assures us we'll be able to visit him as soon as Ally recovers from giving birth.

"Walker James," I whisper once Ally and I are alone in the room.

"What?" Her brows scrunch together as her head tips back to look at me. We were torn between Ryker and Walker, but after seeing him, Walker is perfect.

"Walker James, that's his name."

The smile that greets me is priceless. "Really?"

"Yes, babe." I kiss her.

"Tell me about him. What does he look like?" I wish we were able to hold him, but I know he needs to be with the doctor and nurses right now.

"He's small but strong. He's beautiful." Ally scoots over on the bed for me to join her as I continue telling her the little I was able to see and how damn proud I am of her. I've never witnessed anyone fight the way she did today, and I'm in awe.

When her breathing evens out, and her eyes close, I hold her to my chest and keep her safe. My promise to her and

the Right kind of Wrong

Walker, from this day forward, is to always keep them safe. It's an honor to take on that role.

I look at the door when it opens and wave Charlene in. Careful not to wake Ally, I scoot off the bed and talk to her. Charlene's eyes are marred with worry lines. I called her as soon as we arrived at the hospital, but she was in the middle of a class and drove over as soon as she finished.

"They're okay," I assure her. When her arms wrap around me, and she begins to cry, my heart breaks.

"Will they make it?" Her broken words punch me in the gut.

"Yes," I promise her.

"I've been so worried. I came as soon as I could." Charlene steps back to look at me. "How are you?"

"Scared. We have a long journey ahead of us. The baby will stay in the NICU for seven weeks to be monitored. If they feel he's strong enough and ready to be discharged after those seven weeks, we can take him home with us."

"He will be," she assures me with a squeeze of my hand. "I see Ally's sleeping."

"Yeah, she fell asleep a few minutes ago." I run a hand through my hair.

"Get some rest, too. I'll bring you both something to eat in a bit."

"You don't have to—"

Charlene shakes her head. "I want to. My first grandchild was born today, under tense circumstances, and I'm going to take care of my family."

I nod, giving her that much, and get back on the bed with Ally.

Chapter 32

Allyson

I never knew how much my life would change after having a child. More so, having a premature baby. The last few weeks have been more stressful than I could've imagined. From the time my water broke until today, it's all been a daze and a flurry of emotions.

Walker was tiny compared to what I imagined he'd look like, but he is getting stronger each day. I've been dealing with guilt—feeling at fault for his early birth. A psychologist in the hospital has been crucial in my healing. She's assured me time and again that nothing that happened is my fault, but I should've been able to protect him from this.

Clearing my mind of those negative thoughts, I gently stroke the back of Walker's head as he lies on my chest. We've been doing skin-to-skin contact starting a few days after he was born to help with our bonding. Both Camden and I have had the opportunity to hold him, and the feeling is inexplicable.

This isn't how I imagined spending the first few weeks with my newborn, but I'm grateful that his health is okay, and so is mine. Every worst-case-scenario raced through my mind, but we're doing well now and on the road to recovery.

the Right kind of Wrong

My family and friends have visited, all of them offering support, for which I'll forever be grateful. They've bought preemie clothes and diapers that we were unprepared for. Berkeley and Noel even bought Walker a small onesie that says, Small but Mighty.

"Hey." I turn to when I hear Faith whisper. She and Easton flew down to support us and help us get Camden's apartment ready for a newborn. Until Walker is one-hundred-and-ten percent healthy, we won't be moving to Everton.

"Hi," I whisper back, keeping my arms around my son.

"How is he?" She smiles kindly, lowering her head to see his sleeping face.

"He's better. Day by day, right?" I give her a closed-lip smile.

"Yeah, Ally. Things will only get better." Faith rubs my back in encouragement.

"Thanks. Did Camden come with you?"

"Yeah, he's outside talking to a nurse. He'll be right in." I nod and look at Walker. I still don't know who he looks like, but I don't even care. I'm just glad he's breathing with minimal support.

He's been incubated for three weeks, with another four weeks to go. However, the doctor told us that if he continues to improve at the rate he has, we may be able to leave earlier, especially if he can begin breastfeeding this week.

Faith strokes Walker's back. "I'm so glad he's okay. How are you?" Her eyes meet mine as the weight of her question settles between us.

I shrug, swallowing back my emotions, but that doesn't stop the tears from welling my eyes. "I'm okay. I have my moments, but I'm pushing through them for him." I gaze down at my baby boy, innocent and perfect. I won't let him down.

"You've gone through a lot of changes—hormonal, physical, and emotional—it's only normal. Add in the scare of premature birth. You look good, though." My sister-in-law smiles.

"Thanks." Changing subjects, I ask, "Any new houses in Everton pop up?" I lift my eyebrows.

"I may have found a few," she winks. "I'll show you tonight."

The one thing I hate is leaving Walker here at night and going home without him. Camden usually finds me crying in the bathroom, and he tries his best to support and hold me, and I love him even more for that.

Faith leaves us in the NICU when Camden walks in so he can have his bonding time with Walker. We sit quietly for a bit once Walker is in the incubator again. Our thighs graze, and his hand searches for mine. I lean my head on his shoulder and my other hand sneaks into the opening in the incubator so I can touch Walker.

"I love you." Camden pushes my hair aside and kisses the top of my head.

"Love you, too." I lift my head to look him in the eye. "So much. Thank you for being my rock during this time. I don't think you know how much it means to me." I inch closer to kiss him.

"More like you've been my rock." His hand cups my cheek. "I don't know what I'd do without you." He swallows thickly, his throat clogging with emotions. "The thought that I could've lost you, both of you." His eyes move to our son.

the Right kind of Wrong

"I couldn't have handled it." His rough thumb brushes my cheek. I turn my head and drop a kiss on his palm.

"We're here with you."

"I know," he murmurs, dropping his forehead against mine.

"I'm glad this happened when I was here and not alone in Madrid," I confess. The thought of going through this alone is a million times scarier than it already was.

"Me, too. I'd never forgive myself for not being there for you."

I look at him, my eyebrows pulling together. "None of this was your fault, nor would it have been."

"I just wish—"

"No," I interrupt him. "This isn't your fault," I repeat sternly. "Don't think that for one second."

"You either," he counters. I nod, bringing his face to mine and kissing him.

We get updates as the nurse does her check-up on Walker as he gets fed, and I get to hold him a little longer before saying goodnight to our son and heading home.

Exhausted, I hold Camden's hand as we head up to his apartment. I stop in my tracks when I see a dresser and changing table set up in the bedroom and a small bassinet next to the bed that were not there this morning. My eyes fill with tears as I look around.

"Thank you," I tell Easton when I see him in the living room. My brother wraps me in a comforting hug, running a soothing hand down my back.

"You're welcome, Ally. We're here for you."

I nod against his chest, squeezing my eyes shut to trap the tears. I'm tired of crying.

"How about we order pizza and hang?" He looks down at me with a small smile.

"Yeah," I nod. Faith and Camden are talking in the kitchen area, discussing which pizza topping is the best.

Having Easton and Faith here for the past week has made me more excited and confident that moving to Everton is the right choice. It's also brought Easton and Camden closer together again after the tension between them when Easton found out about Camden and my relationship.

"Ally, tell her pineapple is a pizza topping." Camden looks at me for support.

I giggle and shake my head. "You're on your own on this one. You know I don't like pineapples on pizza."

"You ate it last time we had pizza." He crosses his arms and arches a brow.

"Pregnancy cravings make me eat weird shit." I shrug.

Faith laughs and high-fives me. "No pineapples."

"Sellout," Camden says playfully.

"I still love you." I lean in for a kiss, which causes Easton to groan. "Get over it." I look at my brother over my shoulder.

For the first time in weeks, I feel like myself, and I want to hold on to this feeling for as long as I can.

"Love you, too, Kiwi." Camden winks conspiratorially and trails his hand to my ass.

"Seriously, bro?" Easton grumbles, turning around and sitting on the couch. Faith, Camden, and I laugh before giving my brother a break and ordering pizza. I'll never be able to repay my family for the amount of love they've given me.

"Where's Mom?" Easton asks as he scrolls through the channels.

"She went to dinner with friends. I told her to go, although she felt guilty leaving. She needs a break and to enjoy herself." My mom has given up teaching a few classes to be by my side, but I want her to continue her routine and not worry more than she has, which I know is a lot to ask for now that I'm a mother myself.

"We should watch the new Ronan Connolly movie," Faith suggests once we settle on the couch and wait for the pizza to arrive."

"A chick flick?" Camden lifts his eyebrows.

"It has some action," I defend.

"You only want to watch it because of Ronan," Easton counters.

It's true. Ronan Connolly is a Hollywood hunk, and his Irish accent adds to his hotness.

"Fine," Camden appeases. His arms wrap around me, holding me close as his warmth and love surround me. I close my eyes for a bit, basking in the way he makes me feel cherished and protected.

I could stay like this with him forever, and soon we'll be creating special moments like this with our son.

Chapter 33

Camden

I take in Ally's tired face and the dark circles under her eyes. I want to reach out and hold her, but our son is finally breastfeeding, so I'll have to wait to have her in my arms. Despite the exhaustion she carries, Ally's been a warrior. I've never met anyone as strong as her, and I have no doubt in my mind that she's the best mother that exists. I'm a lucky bastard that I get to witness her day in and day out.

Our life has been turned upside down the last six weeks. Ally and I have been dealing with what we experienced in different ways. She cries when she's alone, and I swallow my guilt. Rationally, I know that neither of us is at fault—it's just something that happened as it does to many other parents.

I'm focusing on the positive—we have our son alive and healthy. Other parents can't say the same. I've met some of the others who have their babies here in the NICU, and Ally and I are truly blessed. A lot of these parents don't know if their child will make it through the night.

On the other hand, Walker will be going home with us soon, especially now that he's breastfeeding.

We're also lucky our families have been here to help us. My parents and sister came to Richmond for a few days to meet Walker and help us in any way they could. Sammy bought him a onesie that says, *Auntie's New Homie*. I chuckled when I saw it—typical Sammy.

I smile when I hear a small sound come from him. He already looks so different than when he was born, a lot more alert to our voices. When he finishes eating, Ally keeps him on her chest so she can continue to bond with him.

I stand behind her and tip her chin back. When our eyes meet, all the love I feel for this woman crashes down on me, wonderfully overwhelming. I kiss her lips and place my hand on Walker's back as he begins sleeping. The medical team has finally removed the breathing tubes, and his lungs are pumping on their own. That was a huge relief for us.

Each day since that dreadful one where I found Ally in pain has been stressful but followed by good news. Once Walker was born, and we knew he would survive, I dropped to my knees again and thanked God. If He wanted to make me more of a believer, mission accomplished.

"Do you want to hold him?" Ally whispers.

I shake my head. "You keep him there. He's already sleeping. I'll grab him next time." I sit next to her again, gently stroking his back. We're going to be all right.

A little later, a nurse comes in to check on Walker. I smile when she talks to him as if he were a big kid and not a tiny infant that has been fighting for his life.

"Mom and Dad." The nurse smiles. "Walker is doing great. The doctor will be by this afternoon to check on him herself, and I'm sure she's going to have positive things to say. He's a fighter." She gives us a few updates on Walker and moves on to another baby.

"A fighter like his momma," I say.

Ally shakes his head. "I'm convinced it was my dad helping him fight." Her eyes mist over, and I pull her into my arms.

"Kiwi…" I kiss the top of her head. "You're right. It was him watching over our son and you. He wouldn't let anything happen to the two of you."

My lips brush over her forehead before finding her lips. I inhale all that is Ally, grateful that she's here with me right now. I wouldn't survive losing her.

"Thank you," she mumbles against my chest.

"What for?" I lift her chin so I can look at those stunning eyes. Emotional and tired, Ally's still the most beautiful woman.

"For staying when you could've left. I know this isn't easy to deal with, but you're here."

My eyebrows pinch together as I stare at her. "Why would I leave? Babe, I love you and our son more than you'll ever know. I'm not going anywhere. A premature birth isn't enough to scare me away. I'm here for the long haul."

She's insane if she thinks I would leave her alone to deal with this. My mind wanders to the ring I bought before this all went down. Waiting for the perfect time to propose, I hadn't done it yet. I'm changing that. No way am I going to let her think I'm not all in.

With Walker sleeping in the incubator, I grab Ally's hand and say, "Come on. Let's go down and get some coffee."

She gives Walker a longing look, and I squeeze her hand. "He'll be okay," I promise her, finally feeling like I have a foundation to keep my promises.

"Okay, I'll tell the nurse to call us if anything happens." Of course, I'll give her that. I'd want that as well.

the Right kind of Wrong

As we sit in the hospital cafeteria with shitty coffee, Ally and I discuss our plans for the future. Moving to Everton is still on, and Faith sent us a few house options to look at. Sitting side by side, Ally shows me the different houses and we narrow them down to our two favorites.

We want to give Walker time to mature before we make such a big move, but I'll feel better when we have a house to move to, even if it takes us a month or more to get to the point where we actually move.

The doctor told us that once he's discharged, we can live our lives normally, but Ally and I both want to stay here for a bit so he won't be as young when we make that move. I've got all the time in the world to live out my life with my family.

"I really love this one." Ally sighs as she stares at a one-story ranch house with wood siding and large windows.

"It's beautiful. And realistically, having one floor is safer than a two-story home."

"It's in our price range." She smiles over at me with wide eyes.

"How can I say no to that?" I swing my arm around her shoulder and pull her to me, keeping her safe in the crook of my body.

She sighs softly, placing her head on my shoulder. "It's going to be amazing." Her voice is soft, almost dreamlike when she speaks.

"Yeah, and I'm going to hold you to those horse riding lessons," I tease.

Ally giggles next to me, her body shaking lightly. When her arms wrap around my body, I want to pull her to my lap and keep her there.

fabiola francisco

We go back to the NICU where Walker is, and I hold him against my skin. When the doctor makes her way over to us, she informs us that Walker will be ready to go home in a few days, which gives me a sense of happiness and relief I've never known. I look down at him and smile.

"You're coming home with us soon, buddy. I can't wait to teach you everything I know and learn from you. You've already taught me so much." I place a soft kiss on the top of his head.

I look over at Ally when she sniffs and see tears in her eyes. I lace my fingers with hers and wink, keeping my other arm on Walker. Nothing has felt more right in my life. Only one thing is missing, and I'm going to change that really soon.

Chapter 34

Allyson

My body is tense and tired when we get to the apartment, but my heart is so full of joy knowing Walker will be home soon. What a whirlwind of emotions.

Camden runs a hand through his hair and hesitates before opening the apartment door.

"What's wrong?" I ask around a yawn.

"Nothing." He unlocks the door and steps in, holding it open for me.

My eyes pop open, and my heart stops beating for a second as I take in the transformation in the living room. Blush pink peonies with baby's breath sit in a vase, and candles flicker in the dim room. My head snaps over to Camden, and I see him down on one knee. I bring a trembling hand to my mouth as tears stream down my face.

"Allyson Kiwi Locke." Camden winks. "You are everything I never knew I wanted—my whole world. You've made me a better man, shown me what love feels like and how to love someone besides myself. You've made this selfish man selfless, all because of a one-night-stand." A laugh bubbles up in my throat.

"I love you more than words and flowers can show. You've given me a son that I never knew I wanted and the opportunity to experience unconditional love. I promise I will always take care of you and Walker. You two will always be my priorities and owners of my heart. Marry me."

I swallow thickly and nod, my words caught in my throat. "Yes," I croak through tears.

The smile that covers Camden's face is unlike any I've seen before. His eyes light up, and the small wrinkles around his eyes deepen. He stands and wraps his arms around me, swinging me around. I laugh and hold on tight, searching for his lips and melding mine to his in a deep and passionate kiss.

Camden places me on my feet and slides a princess cut ring down my finger. "I can't wait to continue spending the rest of my life with you, Mrs. Steele." He grabs my face and kisses me hard.

"I guess this cock really belongs to Ally now." I wink and cup his crotch.

We both freeze when we hear giggles and whispering from nearby. "What the…" Camden says, turning around.

He looks behind the couch and crosses his arms, lifting an eyebrow at whoever is there. "What are you doing here?"

Noel and Berkeley stand up, and I snort a laugh. "What *are* you doing here?" I lift my brows.

"Camden asked us for help organizing this, but we wanted to make sure you had pictures and a recording of the proposal." Noel shrugs, holding up her phone.

"Yeah, you would hate it if you had no evidence of this day," Berkeley adds.

"Evidence," Camden huffs. "As if this were a crime."

"Not a crime, but thank goodness you didn't get naked and get your freak on with us in the same room." Noel wipes her forehead in jest.

the Right kind of Wrong

"Thank you for your help, but I'd like time alone with my fiancée." Camden tilts his head.

"Sure thing. We'll make sure to edit out the cock owner comment," Noel winks.

Camden groans, rubbing a hand down his face. "Please do."

I can't help but laugh. It's just like my best friends to place themselves in a situation like this. Berkeley smiles and gives me a thumb's up before grabbing my hand and staring at my ring, Noel following behind her.

"Good job, Camden," Noel praises. When she looks at me, her eyes water, but she blinks them away. Wrapping her arms around my body, she whispers, "Congrats, babe. You deserve this so damn much." I hug her back and thank her. Accepting Berkeley's hug next.

Camden sighs when they finally leave. "I didn't think they'd stay."

"Clearly, you don't know them well enough." I chuckle and walk toward him. "This was amazing and so unexpected." I loop my arms around his neck.

"I've had the ring for weeks. I was planning on proposing before Walker was born, but our plans changed." His head tips down.

"This is perfect." I place a finger under his chin and lift his head. "You're perfect. Thank you."

My mouth finds his, our tongues tangling. We get lost in each other, savoring the moment and tattooing this memory to our personal storybook, making love and promising forever.

fabiola francisco

"Welcome home, buddy," Camden says as he opens the door to our apartment, holding Walker in the carrier. It's been a few days since Camden proposed, and we're finally home as a family of three.

"I'm pretty sure he's asleep," I joke.

"Let me have this moment. I've been thinking about saying that since the doctor told me we could bring him home today." A beautiful smile paints his face in shades of happiness.

"We are finally home." I nod, carrying in the bag from the hospital.

Walker is completely healthy, as healthy as a full-term baby. Now, it's time for us to be parents, and I'm so excited to experience this with Camden.

The offer we put on the ranch house in Everton was accepted, and we'll be closing that sale soon. Our life is finally back on track, and I wouldn't want it any other way. What we lived through was scary, but it's only made Camden and my relationship stronger. I'll never be able to give enough thanks for the man that stands by my side.

We settle in and sit on the couch with Walker in my arms and Camden's arms around me. I smile as I begin to relax for the first time in almost two months. It's been a long journey, but we're here now, safe and sound.

Later, my mom comes over to visit, and we let her cuddle Walker all she wants. Her very first grandson and she feared she wouldn't have the chance to watch him grow. She didn't

the Right kind of Wrong

need to tell me that for me to read it on her fear-stricken face when I was in the hospital.

I show her pictures and videos that Faith took of the house in Everton when she went to see it in person and tell her our plans to move once the doctor gives us the okay to travel with Walker. I can't wait to raise him in my hometown and watch him run around our yard. Hell, I'll even teach Camden how to ride a horse just to watch him ride with our son.

Camden winks at me from across the living room, and I know deep in the pit of my stomach that we can overcome anything that comes our way.

Once we're alone, we get into a routine, changing diapers, feeding Walker, and holding him until he's sleeping soundly. When I crawl into bed with Camden, I make sure that Walker's bassinet is next to me so I can hear any cry while I'm sleeping. I won't be able to overprotect him forever, but on this first night at home with him, I plan to keep a watchful eye.

Curling into Camden's arms, we talk about our wedding, the move, and raising Walker. As nice as a big wedding like Easton and Faith had was, I'm a simpler person.

"I was thinking something small, maybe in a barn with our family and close friends. Nothing flashy, but a ceremony and a nice dinner."

"Whatever you want."

I shake my head and smile. "No, you have to tell me what you want, too. It's *our* wedding, not just mine." My hand skims up his chest and around his shoulder as I shift closer to him.

"Not with the baby in the room." Camden teases me with a crooked smirk, his hand landing on my hip. I giggle.

"I just want you to hold me," I whisper against his lips before kissing him softly.

"Mhmm…" He deepens the kiss.

I laugh when he groans and moves back. "This is probably stupid, but I can't do it with Walker in the room." My laugh grows louder, and Camden shushes me. Gripping my stomach, I let it all out.

"You're insane, and I love it." He pins me on the bed, his body over mine. "I'm going to marry you, make love to you for the rest of our lives, and when we're ready, make another baby."

My laughter catches in my throat as heat consumes my body. I quietly moan when I feel his hardness against my core.

"Challenge accepted." I tease.

Camden shakes his head. "Being with you is no challenge, Kiwi." He kisses me again. In the quiet of our room, Camden forgets about the awkwardness and strips me before making sweet love to me.

Chapter 35

Allyson

Two months later...

"It's fucking freezing out there." Camden walks into our house, wiping his feet on the rug and removing his gloves.

I laugh and shrug. "Welcome to spring in Everton." Truth is, I forgot how cold it got here.

"I can't imagine what the dead of winter is like." He steps into the kitchen, where I'm bouncing Walker in my Boba wrap. "You're warm," Camden adds when he pecks my lips.

"I know." I wink teasingly.

The move to Everton was smoother than I imagined, thanks to Camden hiring movers to do all the dirty work for us. We decided to take our bedroom furniture, Walker's furniture, and the sofa Camden had in his apartment. We'll buy the rest of the furniture here.

Camden washes his hands and grabs Walker from my wrap, lifting him a bit and kissing his stomach. His wedding band shines under the kitchen light, and I smile widely.

My sexy husband. He gives me butterflies every day. We got married as soon as we moved to Everton, our families surprising us with the exact ceremony we wanted. Intimate, whimsical, and joyous. Faith and her best friends helped transform the barn at her house into a magical setting where I married the love of my life.

I couldn't ask for a better homecoming. The people in town have been so welcoming as well, sharing their excitement to have me living back in Everton and asking if my mom will be the next to move.

Although she says she's happy in Virginia, I think she'll be making her way over here, especially when Easton and Faith tell her that they're having a baby. A well-kept secret on my end for now because I noticed Faith's pale face one day and the mention of nausea.

I'm ready for Walker to have a cousin to play and bond with, to create memories the way Easton and I did growing up. I'm confident my dad is looking down at us with a huge smile. We've come full circle, honoring his memory and our roots. Honoring him with Walker's name as well. Our little and strong Walker James, a fighter like his grandad, charming like his father, and green eyes like his mother. He's perfect and he's mine.

I never knew this kind of love existed, and it's so special that no amount of words can describe it. I want to give our son the world and protect him from it at the same time. Then, I look at Camden and can't imagine having a better father for my child. The irony of life—my brother's best friend and the ultimate womanizer is the man I couldn't live without. Who knew when I met him as a teenager that I'd be standing in our house, watching him talk to our son, and be madly in love with him?

"You're staring," Camden teases.

"I can't help it. Do you know how hot you look holding him?" I wink.

Camden's arms flex under his Henley shirt as he shifts Walker, and his usual scruff has turned into a five-day beard,

the Right kind of Wrong

making him look more mature and a lot sexier. I told him he couldn't shave ever again, and when I moaned at the feel of his beard between my legs, he agreed.

"I think it's Walker's nap time," he winks and looks down at Walker. "What do you say? You're really sleepy, right, buddy?"

"We have dinner at Easton's tonight." I remind him of our plans. Easton and Faith are having their friends over to hang out.

Life has changed from late nights at bars to early evenings at someone's house. Most of them have children, focusing on family life instead of wild nights out.

They've welcomed us with open arms, making us a part of their circle, for which I'm grateful. It was easy for Easton since he had Faith, and he knew these people growing up. Being younger, I didn't know them well enough, but they've been nothing short of amazing since we arrived, offering any help we need.

"We have a few hours before then," Camden interrupts my thoughts.

"Hmmm…" I lift my brows and tuck in my lips to keep from smiling.

"Yeah. Besides, Walker will need to nap, or he'll be cranky at your brother's house." He weaves his way toward me, his words perfectly chosen to convince me.

"I guess you're right." I shrug indifferently, even though I want nothing more than to lie in his arms and make love to him.

Camden bounces Walker until his eyes close, and he places him in his crib with a kiss on his forehead. His bedroom is painted in light gray and powder blue with a modern crib on one end and his changing table dresser on another. I love sitting in here with him in the evenings and rocking him, just my little guy and me spending time together.

"Come on." Camden's arms wrap around me, and I turn to face him.

"I love you. Thank you for this. Thank you for agreeing to move here and being further away from your family."

"You and Walker are my family. I go where you go. We're not kids who depend on our parents any longer. Now, it's our turn to show up for our child the way our parents did for us. You are my family since the day I knocked you up 'til the day I die."

I laugh at his choice of words and kiss his chin. "You knocked me up pretty good."

"Best thing that could've happened to me." His lips fuse to mine in a heat-filled kiss, melting away everything around us until it's just Camden and me, promising our hearts to one another.

I may have had a one-night-stand with my brother's best friend, but I can't imagine it happening any other way for us. Lord knows if it weren't for my desperation to have a little fun between the sheets, we might not be standing here today. I can't picture a life without him now. Like Camden said, it was the best thing that could've happened to us.

Can't wait for the next Fabiola Francisco book?

Follow her on her website:
www.authorfabiolafrancisco.com

Books by
Fabiola Francisco

Standalones
The Right Kind of Wrong
Perfectly Imperfect
Red Lights, Black Hearts
Twisted in You
Memories of Us
All My Truths & One Lie
Promise You

Love in Everton Series
Write You a Love Song
Roping Your Heart
Pretend You're Mine
Make You Mine
You Make It Easy
Then I Met You
My Way to You

Rebel Desire Series
Lovin' on You
Love You Through It
All of You
Rebel Desire Box Set

fabiola francisco

Restoring Series
Restoring Us
Resisting You (Aiden and Stacy Novella)

Sweet on You Series
Sweet on Wilde
Whiskey Nights

Acknowledgments

Thank you to you, the reader, for taking a chance and reading this book. Without your support, I wouldn't be able where I am today in my publishing journey. I'm grateful and humbled.

So many people are necessary to publish a book, and I've got an amazing team I can count on. Thank you to Amy from Q Designs for the gorgeous cover, Brittany from The Blurb Whisperer for always proving feedback, Bex from The Polished Author for taking your time to make this story perfect, Cary for perfecting the interior design, and Claire and Wendy from Bare Naked Words for helping me put this story out in the world.

Ally, you keep me sane through all the chaos. Thank you for that! You helped inspire this story and fell in love with it as much as I did. Thanks for introducing me to the cock boxers. lol

Joy, thank you for your friendship. Our conversations seeped into this story and helped create a strong bond of friendship between the characters.

Veronica, you are always cheering me on. Word can't express how much that means to me.

Christy and Rachel, I'm so grateful for your friendship. It's priceless to know that I can count on you and turn to you despite distances, time zones, and life chaos. #SoapyThighs

Brit and Cary, thank you ladies for always being there to listen to me ramble and for providing feedback when I need to put things into perspective.

Savannah, thank you for believing in m work and helping me get my stories out in the world. Having an agent that believes in me is priceless.

Fabiola's Fab Reads, you're the best group a girl could ask for. Thank you for being a part of my writing career and sharing everything from your fave reads to your life updates.

A huge thanks to my review team and master list for stepping up each time I have book news to share, reading and reviewing my work, and being there for me. It means the world to me that you love to share my work.

To all the reviewers, bloggers, authors, and bookstagrammers that have shared my work and supported me, thank you. I couldn't do this without you. It takes a tribe, and you're part of mine.

About the Author

Fabiola Francisco loves the simplicity—and kick—of scotch on the rocks. She follows Hemingway's philosophy—write drunk, edit sober. She writes women's fiction and contemporary romance, dipping her pen into new adult and young adult. Her moods guide her writing, taking her anywhere from sassy and sexy romances to dark and emotion-filled love stories.

Writing has always been a part of her life, penning her own life struggles as a form of therapy through poetry. She still stays true to her first love, poems, while weaving longer stories with strong heroines and honest heroes. She aims to get readers thinking about life and love while experiencing her characters 'journeys.

She is continuously creating stories as she daydreams. Her other loves are country music, exploring the outdoors, and reading.

Made in the USA
Las Vegas, NV
12 September 2021